The View from a Hang Glider

As Jimmy drifted in the hang glider over the ocean, above the seagulls, he gained a new insight into the way things are.

This was something new, something that he wanted to share with Helen. Everything depends on the way you look at it, he thought, *even dying.*

Dying would be just like going off the cliff, he would tell her. A moment of panic and then the thrill of a brand new adventure, like flying toward the sun on his own wings, and even past the sun. . . . He wouldn't like leaving, and he would be a little scared at the first step, but that was what dying would be like—just like flying.

PINNACLE BOOKS NEW YORK

Poem by Hester Storm used by permission of the poet.

This is a work of fiction. All the characters and events portrayed in this book are fictional, and any resemblance to real people or incidents is purely coincidental.

LOVE LISTENS

An original Pinnacle Books edition, published for the first time anywhere.

First printing, March 1981

ISBN: 0-523-41034-4

Cover illustration by John Solie

Printed in the United States of America

PINNACLE BOOKS, INC.
1430 Broadway
New York, New York 10018

To Cele, who has taught so many
the joy of love

a great fox tawny as gold
carried me away
over the jewelled hills of spring
to his hole on the edge of day

he was agile and beautiful as wind
but tears ran down my face
I am not ready yet I said
to come to this lonely place

and then the shining fox was gone
and the presence smiled in the luminous
air
and I too smiled at the setting sun
and the night came on, and the night
was fair

—Hester Storm

Love Listens

CHAPTER ONE

The familiar white car arrived and the woman got out. Jimmy watched her through his binoculars as she tucked her book under her left arm as she always did. Then she picked up the little straw mat she always sat on, locked the car, and started down the slope toward the beach.

He checked his watch and made a notation of the time in his notebook. *Thursday, October 12, 11:06 a.m.*

As she reached the bottom of the slope where she might be able to see his hiding place under the porch of the beach house, he lowered the binoculars and put them carefully back into their case. Then he flattened his stomach to the damp sand and watched as she spread the mat and sat down with her book on her knees, her back against the rock. He began timing to see how long it would be before she took off her sweater. Though the October sky was slightly overcast the sun was still warm for a person like her. For him it was different. When they talked she might say something about his sweat jersey, and she might wonder why he wore his hat down over his ears. He would think of an answer. Turning over several possible replies, he settled on telling her, "I just like this hat." He nodded once, decisively, then pondered it again. What would her reaction be if he said, "This is the way my dad wears his hat"? No. She might see his dad sometime.

The woman looked up from her book as though she were thinking about what it said and turned her face in his direction. He made himself blend right in with the sand, perfectly still and flat. Since he was in the shadow under the porch the white hat wouldn't give him away, he felt sure.

She would have blue eyes. He had never risked using the binoculars when she was looking in his direction, so he hadn't seen her face close enough to tell the color of her eyes. But she had very white skin and blond hair that was so clean and soft-looking she must have blue eyes to go with all that. He had decided that the one he would pick should be about thirty-five to forty years old, but not much more than forty. He had worked it out to that because he wanted her to be a little older than Virginia, but not too old.

Jessica had caught him spying on the woman one day last week and had asked him a lot of questions. He told her he'd been watching the woman for a couple of weeks, then showed her the notes on the days and times she'd come to the beach. He also showed Jessica notes on other people who came and went, and when the sea-gulls fed and when the tides went out and came in, and what boats went by. Since it was mixed in with the other notes like that, Jessica had missed the significance of it and had just laughed. He had planned it that way. If Jessica had looked closer she would have seen that the notes about the woman came first, several days before he put in those other things.

It would be a secret, just between the two of them for a while. And it wouldn't have to be for long, maybe not even until Christmas. And he wouldn't tell her about the Thing. She would have to find out some day, but he could keep it from her for weeks, maybe months.

When the time was right he would just walk up and start talking, and she would like him right away. She was a very kind person, he could tell. Her mouth wasn't stiff like Virginia's, with thin lips that looked tense all the time. Her lips looked soft and sometimes she smiled even when she read her book. Other times, through the binoculars, he had been able to see a very peaceful look come over her face as she walked along the water's edge, obviously thinking about things. He liked the way she walked, too, with long strides of her thin legs. She seemed very tall for a woman and strong. And he liked the way she let her pants legs get wet when the surf caught up with her, and the way she laughed at the ocean as if it were a playful animal that had just surprised her. Other times she had a look on her face that was very serious, as though there were people she cared about or wanted to help or something. He felt sure that nothing would scare her, not really. No matter what it was, she was a person who would always do what was right and what was best. Not like Virginia.

The day would come soon now when he would go right up to her. There would be a day that would be right for it. She concentrated so much on the book he'd have to stand right in front of her. She was reading so hard, he could probably creep around behind her and over to those rocks on the other side and near her without even getting caught. From there he might be able to find a hole between the rocks and if she looked that way he could see her eyes. They should be blue, like his own. He began crawling across the sand on his hands and knees, working his way around behind her.

If she should happen to see him and they should begin to talk he wouldn't tell her too much. You have to be careful with adults, he thought. You have to protect them.

CHAPTER TWO

The boy annoyed her with his sneaking about and spying. No doubt it was a harmless enough game, but where did he come from? And why did he have to pick on her? There he was, crawling on his stomach and elbows now, commando-style. He was off to her left, apparently trying to circle around behind her without being seen. He didn't frighten her; he looked to be no more than ten or eleven, judging by his size. But he irritated her. He was succeeding in completely destroying a beautiful afternoon of delicious solitude.

He was behind her now, out of sight. She fully expected him to come charging over the rocks at any moment leveling an imaginary machine-gun and yelling "Ack-ack-ack!" or whatever youngsters yelled these days, and then she would politely tell him to leave her alone and go play war games somewhere else. She would say he was disturbing her study time. She would call it "study time" though Helen knew it was far more than that to her; it was *her* time. It was time to think of something other than Arthur and the house they had lived in together for twenty years. Time to balance things out, to digest the many new impressions and ideas that going back to school at forty had brought her. It was time to search for herself, to probe around among the too-familiar memories of a quiet life and see where she had gotten to. She had managed to lose touch with herself, even to the point where she had been surprised to find she could still read a college textbook and take notes at a lecture. New things were happening in her life and she needed this time alone. The little cove on the beach had become her haven, but now it was being invaded.

She glanced behind her. The boy was out of sight now, possibly hiding behind the rocks that separated her cove from the public beach to the north. She opened her book against her knees and tried again to concentrate on her reading. It was no use; it was as if the boy had perched upon the stone she used for a backrest and was peering over her shoulder.

Katie O'Donnell, she thought, would probably find the situation comical. Helen had confided in her friend, telling her how important the quiet hours on the beach were becoming, and Katie had said, "I'm not surprised. You're just finding out you're alive."

It was Katie who had talked her into going back to school now that Helen's daughter, Sharon, had left home for college. Katie was always going to school or classes or groups of some kind. She talked constantly of being "a free woman" and "really living" as she plunged into everything she could join. A convert by temperament, ripe for enlistment in any cause that would keep her out of the house and give her something to tease her husband with, Katie's real cause was always Jim O'Donnell. Helen suspected that even Katie's sense of freedom came from the joy of battling Jim.

Arthur Long, Helen's husband, was Jim's direct opposite; he was no fighter. Their relationship threw off very few sparks and never had. It was just sort of there, unexciting, perhaps, but fixed and permanent. Arthur was a bit shaken by Helen's current "restlessness," as he called it. He just couldn't comprehend her wanting to go back to school in any terms but in reference to Katie. "You're just doing it because Katie's doing it," was his sole comment.

What on earth was that boy doing now? Helen turned her head in his direction and no longer bothered to hide her annoyance as she searched the rocks to her right and the sand behind her. Not seeing him there, she turned and looked down the beach toward the row of private beach houses. His white tennis hat and gray sweatshirt were nowhere in sight. She began to relax, thinking that now she could finally get to her book. She was just opening it, pressing its spine back against her knee and holding down a page that rustled in the wind, when a movement to her right caught her attention. The top of his white tennis hat could be seen snaking along behind a row of large rocks. The image of the boy crawling along on his stomach made her grin in spite of her annoyance. For at least fifteen minutes this strange child who had appeared seemingly from nowhere had made her the focal point of a great deal of effort. There was something pathetically cute about it. There was the hat again, a white thing sliding along behind the top of a large rock close to the surf. He couldn't creep much further in that direction, Helen observed, without getting soaked. He wasn't dressed for swimming. She had removed her own sweater after just a few minutes in the piercing October sun, but the boy was wearing a sweatshirt. Why isn't he in school? she wondered. The day was Thursday, and a child of that age ought to be in school.

With a sigh of resignation Helen closed the book and stared in his direction. Perhaps if she caught his eye she could wave and let him know he'd been seen and get this whole thing over with. But suddenly she was surprised to see him leap to his feet, looking upward and waving both arms at something in the sky. She glanced quickly upward and saw the source of his excitement, a colorful hang glider descending from one of the high cliffs of the beach-bordering palisades. It was gliding on a banking turn toward shore from out over the water, and the direction of its flight was toward their part of the beach. Helen watched its shadow reach the sand and snake toward the rocks and the boy. The shadow passed over him, traveled toward her, and seemed to melt into and out of her in a breath, for a moment darkly linking the boy and herself.

Such contemplations were shattered instantly as the boy began yelling and running down the beach in hot pursuit, quite forgetting all about Helen and whether she had seen him or not. There was another game in town.

It was hard to tell if the glider passenger was male or female, animate or inanimate as it dangled from the bar of metal that was its perch in the sky. The passenger might have been the victim of some giant orange and green bird, the way it lay inertly sprawled beneath those huge wings. Only when two very identifiable legs were lowered for landing gear was the illusion of a piece of carrion being borne aloft shattered. The landing was clumsy and the driver was sent sprawling into the sand, to the delight of the boy.

As the child ran toward the glider, Helen noticed that he was awkward and uncoordinated. He held onto his funny tennis hat with one hand, that elbow flopping, while all his other limbs seemed inclined to go their own way, only to be brought into line by incredible effort. He ran all over, giving Helen the impression of a boy who has been too sheltered.

She had barely begun to realize that with the boy gone she had regained her precious solitude when a second glider cast its shadow on the sand near the water's edge and winged toward the first. The arrival of this one set the odd boy whooping again and dashing back toward her spot as the glider touched down less than fifty feet away. A shapely girl dressed in a white bikini, tall and tanned with flowing golden hair, had alighted on the beach, gracefully stepping out from under the glider like a goddess from some heaven-sent chariot. It gently settled back on its side as she strode across the sand to greet the man who had landed first. Both of them turned and looked up at the cliff and began signaling to others Helen could see on its crest. They were obviously intent on turning her stretch of beach into a landing strip. And since the man was now waving a champagne bottle he had produced from somewhere, there was evidently going to be a party.

Helen stood, dusted the sand from her slacks, rolled up her mat, tucked her book under her arm and trudged through the sand back to her car. "What is this?" she snorted as she opened the door. "Bug Helen Long Day?"

She threw the car into reverse and backed out onto Pacific Coast Highway. She sped along faster and faster until she found herself passing too many cars and made herself slow down. She was angry, unreasonably so, and began trying to analyze it. Why was she reacting this way? Why did the little cove on the beach mean so much to her? Did she need her privacy and freedom that much? Yes, by God, she did. And the boy had spoiled it with his creeping about and spying on her. The image of his oddly disjointed, ungainly dash after the gliders came back to her. He had looked like a wounded seagull.

Well, she was not going to surrender her pleasure to a wounded seagull or to those gliders that had come down on her privacy like birds of prey either. At least not after one brief skirmish. Tomorrow is Friday, she thought. It will surely be quieter there on Friday. She knew she wasn't making sense, of course. Why should Friday be any different? Well, she concluded, they were not going to drive her from her spot on that beach, not if she could help it.

Her spirits picked up at home during the afternoon as she attacked the job of preparing dinner for four. The O'Donnells arrived early, as usual, and in the kitchen Katie regarded the carrot curls and radish flowers, the homemade guacamole dip and other evidences of Helen's manual labor with a scowl.

"What are you trying to prove? Jim gives me a hard enough time about your cooking compared to mine as it is. He sees these things and that roast and those brownies you're whipping up and he starts calling me the Swanson kid again."

"Not brownies. Chocolate mousse."

"Egad."

"I just felt like cooking," Helen laughed.

Katie munched a carrot curl. "Why is it when you feel good you do something for your man rather than for yourself?"

"What's wrong with that?"

"You sound just like Arthur."

"What do you mean I sound like Arthur?" Helen was aware of a familiar reaction, defending her husband no matter how slight the implication of offense.

"Haven't you noticed? I'm not criticizing, it's just that Arthur has the habit of always saying 'What's wrong with that?' when you mention anything he does."

"Arthur does that?"

"When he brought the drinks in a few minutes ago, Jim kidded him about drinking bourbon instead of scotch, no big thing, just conversation. Arthur comes back, 'What's wrong with that?' like a kid who's caught doing something wrong. Jim and I call it his morality fixation."

"Katie—never mind." She had started to say something in return about Katie and Jim's own fixation, their fascination with everything new that deviated from traditional morality, while all the time they were as square as—well, Helen and Arthur.

Katie shrugged off the aborted but nevertheless implied criticism and opened the oven door to poke Helen's roast with a fork.

"You just listen. Any time any kind of statement suggests Arthur might be doing something a little off the center line, that's his reaction."

"Katie, you are on such a kick . . ." That time it almost came out. Helen bent over the arrangement of hors d'oeuvres, biting her tongue.

"Oh, I know, Helen. But I'm living, kiddo. Never again will I let my brain go dumb or my bod go numb. Jim's very happy with me now, whatever he says."

Jim again, Helen noted. She handed Katie the tray of hors d'oeuvres and followed her out to the patio to join the men. Katie went promptly to Jim's side, laid the tray on the patio table in front of him, and with an exaggerated grind of her hips bumped his shoulder. Arthur noticed and grinned, enviously perhaps, but Jim scowled, "Hey, you almost made me spill my drink. Buzz off."

Poor Katie, Helen thought. All the big talk and the flamboyant manner and it all comes down to trying to get the attention of an indifferent husband.

"Hey, we did it!" Katie announced as Helen joined the group under the umbrella, feeling perhaps a little too smug about how good the new paint job looked on the old wrought iron table and chair set, her paint job, white Rustoleum selected by Arthur but applied by her and with a brush, too. And the napkins and glasses that matched the new umbrella and chair covers. Maybe it was silly of her to have devoted so much attention to her house over the years, but that was her habit, and it did give a certain satisfaction in spite of being "domestic." What was Katie saying?

"We decided to stop talking about it and take the 'plunge,' so to speak." Katie waited for the group to react.

"She means we ordered one of those redwood tubs. You always make such a big deal of everything, Kate." Jim lifted his two-hundred-pound frame and pushed his chair back.

Helen saw Arthur check to see if the arms of the chair had withstood the pressure and if the new waterproof carpeting had been scratched.

"A redwood tub, huh?" Arthur got up, winked at Jim and went with him to fix a second drink, saying, "We might have to try one of those things, Helen. What would be wrong with that?"

Katie glanced at Helen.

"I heard," Helen replied. "Funny, I never noticed."

Her opinion about Arthur justified, Katie launched into a description of some book she had gotten into that "really taught me how to look at people." Helen let her mind drift off, as she often did when Katie talked, and found herself thinking about the boy on the beach, then about the beach itself, the patient, constant beat of the surf and the vast sweep of the sky. There was something in all that space and sunlight and natural serenity that was beautiful to her, something that called to her spirit and sought to lure her away. For twenty years her life had been measured out to her by Arthur's needs and Sharon's, by friends and acquaintances demanding so many regular doses of empty chatter and her home requiring so many duties of dish-tending and meal-minding, so many expectations about such meaningless stuff as what dress to wear to a party and which car to drive. Even her personality, her essential self, had been given to her, written out for her like a script. "Helen Thorwald, you will grow up and play Helen Long, wife of one husband, mother of one child, resident of Santa Monica, California, a woman noted for her quiet moderation in dress and manner, temperate in all things—including happiness." Moderate happiness. A moderate amount of pleasure in life had been her almost conscious goal. She tried to remember the last time she had felt outrageously, unspeakably happy. Her mind gave up on the task when she got back to age six. She returned her attention to Katie with a kind of frantic grasp for the present. Moderate happiness, who has more?

"And when the four of us got into that hot water together, I mean that was sexy. No touching or anything, either, just feeling that gushy sort of togetherness and sort of just being on the fringe of getting something going. Know what I mean?"

"No, Katie, I don't. I think I'd better get dinner going. The men are hanging about in the kitchen, a sure sign."

"You're an incurable haus frau," Katie commented, following her.

During dinner Jim and Arthur good-naturedly teased each other about real estate deals. For a long time after they'd first met, Jim and Arthur just tagged along while Katie and Helen got to be closer and closer friends. That was ten years ago. Then the two men discovered a common interest in land investments. Jim, a dentist, was always on the lookout for short-term tax savings and long-term profits. Arthur, usually so conservative about everything else, was more of a speculator, looking for fast turnover based on smaller initial investment. Helen had begun to perceive Arthur's occasional gamble in real estate as his one really spontaneous indulgence and had begun to encourage him, much to Katie and Jim's chagrin. Jim, who had far more money to play with, since dentists usually make more than electronics engineers, assumed the role of advisor, while Arthur played the part of a puckish kid who never took the advice. Arthur was always reveling in some small triumph and Jim was usually acting smug over some neat tax manuever. Neither one ever mentioned the deals that backfired.

Taking advantage of a lull in the conversation, Katie placed both elbows on the table and leaned toward Helen.

"What's up with you tonight?" she asked.

"What do you mean?"

"Oh, come on, after ten years don't you think I know when you've got something on your mind? Is it Sharon again?"

"I don't know what you think you see, Katie. I'm fine, and so's Sharon as far as I know. She's doing well in school."

"You've been quieter than usual," Arthur commented. He showed his concern for her with a long look. "Feeling okay?"

"It is not physical," Katie announced solemnly with her best astrology-oriented, bio-rhythm, health-food-specialist squint of close inspection turned on Helen's face. "It's something else. You are hiding something! Look, you're blushing!"

"Well, something did happen today," Helen explained, "and I'm not blushing—much."

Katie bored in, "Now let me see—don't tell me you slipped away from school with that cute psych professor, Doctor Mays!"

"I went to the beach—alone—as I usually do."

Arthur looked up quickly, suddenly attentive. "You went to the beach?"

Jim laughed coarsely. "You never know where they are these days, buddy boy. Welcome to the club."

"You met someone there—a man!" Katie was triumphant.

"A boy, and I didn't meet him. He crept up on me."

"A mugger?" Katie looked delighted.

"Now just a second, Helen," Jim said. "How old was this kid, twenty, thirty, maybe?" He grinned knowingly at Arthur.

"What do you do at the beach?" Arthur's look suddenly scolded her for never telling him about it.

"I go there to study and think after school, just to be by myself for a while."

"That's news to me."

"Oh, Arthur, be quiet. You two can settle that later. This boy—he did something weird?"

"No, Katie. He was just pretending to sneak up on me. Then he got distracted by something else and went away."

"That's it?" Katie asked. "You've been thinking about that?"

"Sorry to let you down, Katie. The boy distracted me while I was trying to study."

Later, as they cleaned up in the kitchen, Katie wouldn't leave it alone. She kept probing. "That's all there was to it? You're sure?"

To satisfy Katie's prurient interest as well as to shut her up Helen finally said, "What happens on the beach is my own affair."

Even though Katie went all tightlipped and offended-looking, Helen could see her deep satisfaction with the thought that Helen might be doing something scandalous down there at the seashore. She hadn't realized until that moment how that side of Katie put her off.

Arthur said nothing more about it until they were in bed and he kissed her goodnight. Then he turned over on his side away from her and gently suggested, "Be careful when you go to the beach alone like that. A lot of creeps hang out there."

CHAPTER THREE

Her eyes were blue. He had seen them yesterday when she looked over toward the rocks. Letting her catch sight of the top of his hat above the rock had been a good idea. Jimmy took his time putting on his sneakers, thinking over the next step in his plans very carefully. As he pulled his hat on and tiptoed from the house he could hear Jessica already stirring in the kitchen, making breakfast. Why did she get up with the sun just because he always did? He closed the screen door and stepped out on the porch of the beach house and inhaled deeply of the early morning's gift of moist, cool air.

Heading directly to the tidepools that lay down the beach to the south of the house, he began exploring. He had no desire to capture any of the sea things any more. A crab he had taken to care for had died within a day. Now all he wished for was a quiet survey of the tide-pool residents each morning. He felt like a farmer checking his livestock. Only what farmer ever had a herd like his? It gave him a special pleasure to see the new shells and minnows deposited by the tide during the night. Even the bits of metal or pieces of wood said something to him about things hidden in the sea, things that were there out of sight in the depths, then almost magically brought to the pools as if they were samples displayed for his approval. He didn't even mind finding pieces of plastic drinking cups and other signs of the human use of the sea. It is all one somehow, he thought, as he examined a shiny metal tab from a pull-top can that was being pushed about in a pool by a small crayfish. The sun, the regular pulse of the surf and the even pattern of the tides, the rhythm of birth and life and death, all one. Sea and sand, animals and people, light and dark, earth and the stars. It had begun to come to him one day just after he had persuaded his father to let him live at the beach house with Jessica. It was the first morning, way back in August, when he'd sat on the porch for a while, long before Jessica got up, with some time to think about things. Now he felt that there are no opposites; things that look opposite really went together into some other kind of pattern. He'd tried to share some of his thoughts with Jessica and she'd just stared at him and turned away. He would be able to talk about things like that with her, with the woman. He wondered what her name was.

Later, after breakfast with Jessica, he sat on the porch and worked with his shell collection for a while, checking his watch from time to time. By ten o'clock he had tired of the shells. Seeing him staring at the place on the hill where the woman always parked her car, Jessica said, "Jimmy, why don't you find something else to do?"

"No. I've got something to do."

Jessica knew he was waiting for the woman; he could tell she knew because she glanced up to the spot he was watching. A funny look came over her face and she said, "I thought you might want to go shopping with me this morning. We could take in a movie."

"I've got something to do." Jimmy got up quickly and walked away from her, suddenly angry at the look he'd seen in her eyes. He didn't need that this morning. This was going to be a special day. He started to walk down the steps toward the beach when a movement at the top of the hill made him turn and look. The car! She was coming.

He ran in the opposite direction, back down toward the tidepools, away from her rock, far enough away that she would not be aware of him. And to add to his feeling that this would be a special day, he came upon a starfish in the very center of a pool that looked like a mirror, it was so clean and bright.

CHAPTER FOUR

Helen's small worry about being disturbed vanished as she made her way down to the sand. The morning was so lovely and warm now, and her own spirits were so light she almost felt like inviting someone to share them. Arthur had been unusually cheerful at breakfast. He didn't bring up the matter of her going to the beach as she expected. Instead he'd wished her a good day and kissed her goodbye when he left for the plant. That hadn't happened in a while.

She settled down by the rock with her book, thinking that she didn't particularly want to read about psychology on such a morning. She dutifully opened the book anyway, nudged by a slight sense of guilt. Studying was her excuse for all this indulgence, after all.

She had been reading idly, skimming through a dull chapter on the mechanics of sight for ten minutes or so, when a shadow fell across the page. She glanced up quickly and turned to look over her left shoulder. Her eye fell upon a mess of wet, copper-colored seaweed through which she caught a glimpse of the knees of bluejeans. Raising her glance she found herself staring at a pair of blue eyes hidden behind dangling locks of rubbery looking kelp. From inside came a laugh.

"Well, who are you? Or is it what are you?" Helen asked.

He began to peel off the strands of kelp. "I just

wanted to get your attention." His smile was edged with a tight little line of uncertainty so beguiling that Helen felt an immediate impulse to touch his cheek and erase it. It was the boy she had seen yesterday.

She laid her book aside and tried her best to relax him with a smile. "You have my attention."

It was all the invitation he seemed to need. He plopped down on his knees in the sand beside her. "What are you reading?"

"A school book."

"You go to school?"

"Yes."

"How old are you anyway?"

"Too old to be in school, that's what you mean, right? Well, we should never stop learning, should we?"

"Where do you live?"

"In Santa Monica. How about you?"

"Do you have any children?"

"A daughter. She's going to school too. College."

"Is that all? Just a grownup daughter?"

"Yes. Do you have any brothers or sisters?" Turnabout's fair play, she thought. So many questions!

"No. You must be about forty years old. Right? If you have a daughter in college."

"You worked that out very fast. Are you good in math?"

"Pretty good."

She felt he wasn't eager to talk about himself. "Why aren't you in school?" she asked. "I think I saw you yesterday. Wasn't that you?"

There was a glimmer of wariness in his eyes as he replied, "When? Oh, when the gliders came over. I was digging for sand crabs over there behind the rocks."

For some reason he didn't want her to know he'd been spying on her. He wrinkled his nose as he squinted into the sunlight toward his house for a moment, then turned his gaze down the beach. He looked back speculatively. "Hey, how would you like to see something really super in the tidepools?" He jumped to his feet, beckoning with his hands for her to get up. "It's something I just saw this morning. You don't have to read all the time you're here, do you?"

Beguiled away from her little cove by the child's winsome manner and obvious need for companionship, Helen accompanied him on a rambling tour of the tidepools. He showed her the starfish first, then used her interest in that to lead her on for another hour of clambering over the rocks to see his "livestock." While he showed an amazing knowledge of the various life-forms in the pools and talked at length about the feeding habits of sea anemones and the life cycle of starfish and the various seasons when one could or could not eat the local clams, Helen found herself studying the boy. His personality fascinated her. His face showed every emotion he felt. His smiles could be broad and totally unselfconscious when he was enthusing about something he was interested in, or they could be doubtful, tentative little smiles that masked something seemingly dark and dreadful within him. His mood remained steadily buoyant throughout all these changes, but sometimes he seemed to be struggling. The struggle was not just the obvious one of wanting to keep her attention riveted on him, either. There was something else going on in there.

After an hour had passed she caught a look of anxiety on his face as he glanced toward the beach house nearest where she sat and read. A woman had come out on the porch and now stood watching them. The woman was small and shapely and black. She wore a light dress with a flower print. She waved one hand toward them as the boy looked up, then disappeared into the house.

"Who's that?" Helen asked.

"That's Jessica. She just wanted me to know she's back. She wanted me to go to the store with her, but I waited for you."

"You knew I was coming?"

"Sure." He poked under a rock with a stick and

changed the subject abruptly. "That's my house. My dad bought it for me because I said I wanted to live at the beach. My dad's rich. He sells panty hose to stores. He used to sell cars, but he says it's better to sell something people wreck in a week."

She smiled at that and was greeted with his wide grin. There it was, that smile that looked like a cloud lifting to let out the sun. It dazzled her. She had never seen such a radiant child. The smile made her want to throw her arms around him and soothe all those shadows away.

Their tour of the tidepools had produced four prize shells without the slightest trace of chips or blemishes, which the boy wanted to add to his collection. Helen had thought several others were interesting and beautiful enough to be kept but he studied every offering with a critical eye and rejected each one with anything to mar its pristine perfection.

Helen was beginning to tire of the game. She held the four shells in her hand as he searched yet another pool. She began to miss her cozy spot beside the rock and glanced toward it. He immediately sensed her distraction and came to her side.

"I think we should do something else, don't you?" he said.

"I've really enjoyed this," she reassured him. "But I do have to think about going home soon."

A look of near panic came over his fine features. He took the shells from her hands, cupping them in his slim fingers. "Let's take these to the house. Jessica probably has lunch ready. You could eat with us."

"No—thank you. I really must go."

"Please come with me. I think Jessica will want to meet you."

There was desperation in that voice, a pleading that was totally incongruous with what she could see of the boy's situation. She decided it was time to try to find out something about him. She began walking with him toward the house, amused to see him stretch his stride to try to keep up with hers. "What's your name?" she asked.

"Jimmy Banning," he grinned. He seemed relieved that she had opened the way to getting acquainted. "What's yours?"

"Helen. Helen Long."

"That's a wonderful name. Like Helen of Troy."

"You know about that?"

"I read a lot. Dad gets me anything I want to read. You sure you can't stay for lunch?"

They reached the bottom of the stairway that led up to the porch of the beach house. Helen stopped automatically and Jimmy took three steps upward and turned around. They were almost on eye level. She caught her breath as he stared into her eyes with a penetrating look that rose from some incredible chasm of need and said, "You've just got to come back tomorrow if you leave now."

The voice of Jessica broke the spell, bringing Helen suddenly back as from the edge of a precipice, reeling as she looked upward to the top of the stairs. "Jimmy, you have to come in now."

Jimmy turned angrily. "You're not my mother. Don't boss me around." He could be tyrannical, Helen sensed. He turned back to face her and the hunger she had seen in him had changed to something very close to rage. "I don't see why you have to go now. You always stay at least two hours."

She looked to Jessica, avoiding his eyes, and the woman smiled knowingly. "He's been charting your movements. He's a great observer and recorder of everything that happens around here. He can tell you how many ships go by, what time the gulls feed—all kinds of things." She came down three steps and extended her hand past Jimmy. "I'm Jessica Carver."

"Hello, I'm Helen Long."

The black woman had a lovely, warm smile. Helen guessed her age at somewhere around thirty-five.

Jimmy now seemed more resigned to her leaving. He

sat down on the steps and pretended to be occupied with his new shells.

"I really have to go now, Jimmy. Some other day maybe we can talk again. I really enjoyed it."

He looked up quickly, pleading, "Come back tomorrow! I know you don't usually come on Saturdays, but couldn't you? I'll show you my whole shell collection. The gliders come back on Saturdays, too. We can go up on the cliff and watch them!"

Helen glanced up at Jessica as he pleaded and saw a shadow of profound sadness cross the black woman's lovely face. Her lustrous eyes glazed over with sudden tears, and she looked away toward the cliffs. Helen had a feeling she looked there not because Jimmy was talking about the gliders, but as a way of avoiding Helen's eyes, in order to hide that sadness.

"Jimmy," Helen put it very carefully, "I have things to do tomorrow. I really can't come."

Quietly, staring at a fragile pink shell in his hand, he said, "I had fun today, and I thought you did, too."

Helen found herself almost praying that he would not look up at that moment. She stared at the top of his white tennis hat and saw his fist clench tight over the shell it held. Jessica had quietly slipped away, leaving her to face it alone. Helen knew she might easily walk away herself, but felt if she did she would be turning her back on whatever it was that troubled him. With a deep breath, instinctively feeling she would need strength for what lay beyond the decision, she said, "Maybe I could come back tomorrow for just an hour or so."

His answering smile was pure sunshine.

CHAPTER FIVE

"We were going to spend the day working in the yard," Arthur reminded her.

"I'll only be gone for an hour. We can do it when I get back."

"It gets too hot in the afternoon. Besides, I want to watch the USC-Stanford game. What is it about this kid anyway?" Arthur made a studied attempt to keep his voice level and not betray any of the other feelings he had about this surprise change in his Saturday plans, especially the queasy sense of suspicion that had been growing since he'd first heard about this beach thing.

Helen pulled the strings of her sneaker, tying a quick, decisive bow and glancing up at him as he leaned against the frame of the open door to the bedroom. "He had a problem of some kind," she said as she passed him, strode into the bathroom and paused in front of the mirror to touch up her lipstick, scrutinizing herself, Arthur thought, a bit more closely than usual.

"What kind of problem?" he asked.

"I don't know." She finished the self-examination in the mirror with a little nod of approval and passed him again, seeming to be in a determined rush to get out of the house.

"What's the rush? And if the boy's got a problem, how is it you're so fired up about it and don't even know what the heck it is?"

Her eyes snapped back at him with a quiet show of anger that was not characteristic of the Helen he thought he had known for twenty-two years.

"I'm not fired up. I'm—I don't know, Arthur. There's just something about him."

What the hell was that supposed to mean? Arthur followed her to the dining room, feeling compromised somehow by having to fall in line behind her. In the kitchen she stopped and searched around for her purse.

"You left it in the bathroom, on the countertop."

"Why didn't you remind me?" she snapped, and hurried away to get it.

He tried to explain that he hadn't been thinking about the purse during the time she was in front of the mirror, but she did not turn back or comment. Arthur remained in the kitchen. He turned to stare out the window over the sink toward the driveway and the row of small pepper trees that grew along the redwood fence. They had been planning to trench around the trees and do some deep watering today, do it together and chat and laugh about their nice yard and how well the property looked, as they always did, and have a good quiet time together, and maybe that night make love and feel refreshed by a day outdoors together. That's the way it was supposed to be, time together, with a good football game thrown in to boot just to make the weekend complete. And now this.

"What the hell is going on with you, Helen?" It came out the moment she came into view.

She stared at Arthur for a moment and abruptly sat down beside the small table in the breakfast nook, dropped her purse on the table with a thud and said, "Okay, Arthur, let's get it all said."

"This is all pretty dramatic, isn't it? I mean here you are all worked up about some little boy you found on the beach, and it's like nothing around here means anything to you all of a sudden."

"Just because I'm going to spend an hour with him and not here, is that it?"

Where was it all coming from? Arthur wondered. Where was the easy-going woman he'd been married to for twenty years, who'd been so emotionless and cooperative and predictable for so long he used to wonder about her? He answered carefully, not wanting to make more of it than he was truthfully feeling. "You don't usually just slam out of here without some kind of explanation, that's all. I had some plans for today—nothing big, but a nice quiet day at home—together."

"Have you ever considered that I might have some plans, Arthur?"

"What?"

"Look how shocked you are! Well—it's my own fault, I suppose."

"What's that supposed to mean?"

She appeared thoughtful for a moment. She settled back in the chair and toyed with her car keys, holding the little leather thong in her fingers and drawing circles by dragging the rattling keys across the surface of the table. Then she tossed them and caught them in the palm of her hand and held them out toward him.

"Do you know what it means for me to have a car?"

"I know you like the car, Helen, that's why I bought it for you."

"The car takes me to college. I meet people there. I listen to lectures and study the minds and thoughts of all kinds of people, with all kinds of wonderful new points of view about things. The car takes me to the beach, where I spend all kinds of time just looking back on my life, and thinking. And where I met Jimmy. It's very dangerous for me to have a car, Arthur. You want it back?" She kept holding the keys out to him, challenging him with her eyes and with the clenched fist that held the keys.

"No, I don't want the car back." What she was really saying to him was, "Give me room." He'd heard that before. He said, "I'm not trying to crowd you, Helen, if that's what you think. I know you need a life for yourself, now that Sharon's gone."

"But you would like to be able to predict it, to control me a little, wouldn't you? I know you, Arthur. You are worried to death that I'm going to change."

"What's wrong with that?" It came out before he could stop himself. He was not surprised when she grinned. She relaxed and put the car keys into her purse.

"There's nothing wrong with that. I like being cared for and protected—a little. And it isn't just that Sharon's gone. I haven't really felt confined by Sharon since she finished high school. It's me, Arthur. I have to take some time now to see where I am, and where I want to be in another ten or twenty years—and if you say I sound just like Katie . . ."

"I won't say that." He felt more relaxed himself, and slid into the chair across from her. "The only thing about it I don't understand is this boy, where he fits in."

She sighed and smiled softly to herself, then raised her eyes to his. "I don't understand it myself, Arthur. The first moment I saw him something clicked. Then, as we talked I had the feeling that he has a problem or a big need of some kind. I can't explain it. It's just a feeling, almost as if I knew this boy once a long time ago. Katie would probably say, in some pre-existence."

"Katie." Arthur couldn't keep the mockery out of his tone.

"I know. But whatever, I have to see him, Arthur. He begged me to come back, just begged me. And a woman there, a black girl, there was something in her eyes."

"What about his parents?"

"I have no idea. I get the feeling his father is around, somewhere. It might be that his father and mother are divorced or separated. Maybe his mother is dead. I just don't know. You'll have to trust me."

She slid the chair back and stood up.

"I trust you," Arthur said as he stood to walk with her to the door.

She opened it and turned back to face him. She kissed his cheek and said, "Sometimes I wonder what you would have done if I'd ever given you a reason not to trust me."

It sent a shiver through his spine, not just her saying it, but the look on her face, and the fact that she was leaving to go to that "boy" on the beach. He tried to shove down a feeling of apprehension by joking about it. "That's why I trust you now. Let's keep it that way."

She waved a hand as she entered the garage to get into her car, but she didn't look back. He felt like a little kid being left on the doorstep by his mother. Rather than give into it, he shut the door and walked back into the kitchen so he wouldn't be forced to wave again as she backed down the driveway.

Arthur glanced at the kitchen clock. Ten-thirty. He moved to the automatic coffeemaker and poured himself a cup, thinking. She said something clicked, something mysterious. Now that she was gone he could entertain the thought she had predicted he'd have—that it sounded like Katie. Maybe he would have said that, but Arthur felt, considering the situation, that she wasn't like Katie at all. Katie wouldn't be turned on by a ten-year-old kid. Maybe Helen missed Sharon so much she was looking for another child to mother. She had wanted to have a second child but he had talked her out of it, not feeling financially secure enough. When they finally felt secure, it was too late, according to the doctor. But Helen hadn't seemed too upset about it; at least she didn't say anything. That was the irritating thing about what they were going through now—Helen no longer had that deep quiet sort of contentment she used to have. When a woman wants to start changing things, it means she isn't contented. To Arthur that meant she was dissatisfied sexually. He brought that idea up to the surface, rinsed out his empty coffee cup and strolled outside into the yard.

Something was energizing him now as he walked around behind the garage to the little metal shed where he kept his garden tools. Jim O'Donnell had once told him that one of Katie's fem-lib magazines had an article in it to the effect that when a woman is unsatisfied sexually she has an inherent instinct to seek for it anywhere she can. "They think of it as a goddamn right!" Jim had exploded.

Arthur plunged his spade into the dry, sandy dirt at the base of the first pepper tree. He had no illusions about himself and his sexual prowess. His sex drive was about where it should be for a man in his early forties, but he had never been a tiger, not by any stretch of the imagination. In his teen years he had been shy with girls. If it hadn't been for an equally shy and inexperienced little girl in college who didn't mind his fumbling first attempts, he would have been a virgin when he'd married Helen. And Helen had been a virgin, he was sure of that. Aggressive women turned Arthur off. He drove the spade deeper with a plunge of his booted right foot. There was one escapade he'd never told Helen about. It was five years ago at an electronics engineers convention in Chicago. The "friend" had it all set up for him by the time the three of them went to dinner that night. She was small and round and lovely, but too bold. She sat beside him and ran her hand up and down his leg while they were eating. Later his friend dropped them at the hotel and said he would drive around the block while they got together in Arthur's room. On the way up to the room in the elevator they did a lot of stroking and kissing, and by the time they got into the room, Arthur was ready. But then something happened. As he watched her take off her clothes, his desire vanished. It was as if he were being put through a test of his manhood. There was his friend out there driving around, giving him a time limit, and here was the girl stripping off her clothes as if she were getting ready to run a race, and he couldn't bring himself even to take off his shorts. She stretched out on the bed and held out her arms, and he sat down and started talking. He didn't even remember now what he'd talked about, because what had really been in his mind was a clanging sense of alarm that his penis wouldn't cooperate. And the longer that kept happening the angrier he felt at himself and the sorrier he felt for the girl. It was humiliating. After the girl was gone Arthur stood looking down at the streets of Chicago twenty stories below and had contemplated suicide.

For a long time Arthur had carried around a sense of failure and guilt that even made his relationship with his wife difficult. Finally, after about six months, he confided in one of the men from work, over a couple of drinks at lunch. The guy leaned back in his chair and punched Arthur on the shoulder. "Son of a gun," he'd said. "And I thought that sort of thing only happened to me. I always find myself feeling sorry for the girl."

They'd had a good laugh and then the guy had finally said, soberly, "Women have the wrong idea about men. They expect them all to act like stallions. They think a man's cock is automatic, that if a woman takes off her clothes, it comes up. A man's not supposed to have any tender feelings for women. No way. They all want to be raped."

Arthur wasn't sure about the rape part, but he thought his friend was right about the rest. He knew he had to love a woman and feel loved himself before he could get it up. Maybe he was twisted and old-fashioned, but that's the way it was. With Helen everything had always worked like a charm. All she had to do was give him that look, or walk around the bedroom with or without anything on, just exuding that something special he'd always felt from her. He loved her, damn it. And she was changing, and feeling dissatisfied!

He sweated under the late morning sun and stayed with the job until every pepper tree was trenched and watered. The labor lasted well into the afternoon and drained him of most of his anxiety about Helen. She had been gone far longer than the one hour she had promised.

CHAPTER SIX

Jessica lifted Jimmy's pajamas from the dresser drawer and carefully folded them into the little tan suitcase. Though there was need for haste she found herself thinking about the woman Jimmy had apparently decided on. She had come back to the beach house on Saturday, planning to stay one hour with Jimmy, and had stayed the whole afternoon.

Jessica had given Jimmy's actions a lot of thought and had come to the conclusion that the boy might be right. Though he'd never put it into words, Jessica knew what he was leading up to with this woman, and had begun to feel she might be the perfect choice.

The woman had strength and good common sense. During lunch on Saturday Jimmy had started his campaign to get her back on Sunday, and he was at his best. He tried coaxing for a while and when that didn't work he went to charm and flattery.

"I really had a wonderful time today. It was really fun. I don't know when I've had so much fun." Jessica had caught the woman's eye about then and could see her weighing all that and thinking—hey, this has got to stop somewhere. Then Jimmy gave up on that strategy and started pouting, "It's okay, you don't have to play with me. You've got a lot of other things to do. I'll just sit around and not do anything tomorrow."

The woman had good sense, and knew a snowjob when she heard it. She'd said, "How you spend Sunday is up to you, Jimmy. You can make it as good or bad as you choose, can't you?"

He had flown into a rage then. And he almost gave it

all away by yelling, "You don't know anything! You don't know what I can do and what I can't do! You don't even know what you're talking about. And I don't care . . ." He had stopped himself short then and apologized hastily. "I'm sorry, Helen. I didn't mean that." And when she heard Jimmy apologize, Jessica had realized just how much Helen meant to him. He could explode at Jessica and say everything in the world there was in him to say, but not to her, not to this woman he had chosen.

She had strength. Helen had taken the whole thing with surprising calmness, and when he apologized had said, "Thank you, Jimmy. I know you didn't mean it. But I'm going to ask you to respect me and our friendship and never say anything like that to me again. Or I won't come back ever."

Jimmy had turned to Jessica at that point and actually grinned from ear to ear with a look in his eye that said, "See! See what she's like?"

And now Jessica finished packing the familiar little overnight case. The cycle was beginning again. She would take Jimmy to the hospital. She would call his father, if she could reach him, and she would tell Charles Banning about the nosebleed.

The woman was letting herself in for a long, hard ride. Maybe if the boy's father was different things would be better, but the woman would have to deal with that, too. Charles Banning blamed himself for everything. For Virginia, for Jimmy. Unable to face it, the man stayed on the road nearly all the time. Instead of giving the boy steady love and care, he made big gestures like buying Jimmy the beach house and hiring Jessica. When there was an emergency he would come through heroically, of course. But the man had no sticking power for the tough day-to-day ordeal of it all. The woman would see that fast enough with her steady blue eyes. At least Jessica hoped she would.

The woman was going to have a lot to learn and a lot to face. Maybe she would be strong enough, maybe not.

Jessica would leave a note for her when she came on Monday, as Helen had finally promised she would when Jimmy gave up begging about Sunday.

Maybe Jimmy had felt it coming on. Maybe Jimmy knew that things were changing even though the tests said he was doing pretty well. Maybe that's why he'd been so insistent and desperate at lunch on Saturday. He'd felt it coming on. And now it was Sunday afternoon and his nose was bleeding.

Jessica finished packing the small tan suitcase and hurried toward the car. Jimmy was sitting in the little blue Volkswagen as calm as could be, holding the compress to his face and staring straight out the windshield, waiting for her.

The hospital was only a mile away. They would make it in time. Then the ordeal would begin again.

CHAPTER SEVEN

Professor Mays was a young man, Helen thought, to be a full professor at a university. She was in two minds about his beard, which she supposed he wore to give him a more mature look. It seemed a bit too full and fuzzy for the way he dressed, and she imagined a more dashing cut would organize him a bit. It was also a rather shocking color of red, in contrast to his sandy hair. He seemed to please the younger females, though. After class they grouped around him like so many cheerleaders, praising his lecture, while they bounded up and down on their toes in their eagerness to see him and be seen. He seemed to remain quite composed through all of it, however, and as Helen gathered up her books to depart he caught her eye and smiled.

Thinking about her visit to Jimmy in the next hour she climbed the levels of the lecture hall toward the exit door and was surprised to feel a hand on her elbow and to hear the young professor's voice saying, "How about a cup of coffee?"

It was an awkward moment. She was halfway out the door, turning to react to him. When her elbow had jerked away instinctively from the touch of a strange hand the movement had loosened a book which slid away and had to be caught in flight by her free hand. To complicate matters the whole flock of his ardent admirers was surging up the stairs behind him, each one with a look of total absorption in the deeper meanings of his lecture, and each pretty little pink mouth framing a question.

"Some other time, maybe," she managed to blurt out. "You seem to be pretty busy right now."

He looked disappointed.

While she drove out of the campus parking lot Helen found herself reflecting on that look of disappointment, and feeling better about herself the more she thought about it. He had actually looked wounded for a moment. Maybe he had some kind of psychological thing for older women. She caught herself. She wasn't that much older, come to think about it. But why would he invite her to have coffee with him? Was it something about her school work?

She had hoped that a course in psychology might make her more knowledgeable about herself, more able to understand and organize her own feelings. Not that she was a terribly moody person. Just the opposite, really. She felt almost devoid of feeling sometimes. "Steady" was her father's word for her. "Helen's the steady one," he always said when comparing her to her sister. She didn't feel so steady at the moment, with her thoughts still racing about the young professor.

She arrived at the beach several minutes earlier than she had intended. She was aware of having driven in a rather distracted manner, going through imaginary coffee conversations with Professor Mays. Looking down toward her reading place on the beach brought her back to the present. On Saturday Jimmy had been waiting out by her rock with his whole shell collection spread out on a blanket. Now he was nowhere in sight. Was he getting a little tired of her company already?

She was aware of a vague stir of resentment, and she pounced on the feeling as she made her way down the embankment to the sand. Something was wrong with her, and it was reflected in that quick feeling of almost anger that the boy might be bored with her. She was always expecting people to be bored with her. That's really why she had rejected the professor's invitation to coffee. She was afraid she would bore him. She even thought she might bore the boy, the way she was afraid for years that she might bore Arthur, the way she felt she actually had bored him for most of the years of their marriage.

There, she had said it. Being able to find that feeling and identify it and face it made her feel a little better. Okay, she thought, if that's true about me, then I'll do something about it. It's not that I'm bored, as Katie says. It's that I feel boring to other people.

The beach was deserted. She stood by her rock for a while, waiting for him. There seemed to be no life on the beach at all. Close inspection of the porch of the beach house brought the same results. Where was Jimmy? She decided to stroll along the water's edge and let herself be seen in case he was waiting inside the house. She walked slowly, glancing toward the house from time to time. It's strange, she thought, how the boy had come to mean so much to her. A few days ago she would have thanked her lucky stars for a beach so empty, for such unbroken solitude. She had talked about the boy, a little with Arthur, and he suggested that she was missing Sharon, that she needed to feel like a mother again. She and Arthur seldom talked about their feelings with each other any more.

Helen walked to the rocks where Jimmy had shown

her his "herd" and the lovely starfish he had found on that day they first became acquainted. Was it possible it was only four days ago? She turned to walk past the house again, sensing her feeling of irritation returning. Jimmy had insisted that she come on Monday, and now he seemed indifferent. Her irritation made her look toward the porch of the beach house again. She stopped walking suddenly as she caught sight of a flutter of white at the foot of the stairs. There was something there, a piece of paper tacked to the rail of the stairway. Could they have gone off somewhere and left her a note?

Approaching the house, she saw that her guess was confirmed. It was a note, and it was addressed to her, apparently written by Jessica. It said, "Helen, I have taken Jimmy to the hospital. Don't worry. I or Mr. Banning will be back at noon. Please stay as we would like to talk to you. Jessica."

The hospital! Helen stood staring up the stairs toward the closed door and the empty porch. The hospital. There must have been an accident. The note said not to worry. Why didn't Jessica say what had happened? How could a person not worry when she didn't know what happened? Noon, the note said. She glanced quickly at her watch. Eleven. An hour to wait, perhaps even longer. With a determined effort, Helen made herself turn away from the house and walk back to the car for her book.

An hour and a half later she was still trying to tear her mind away from its obsessive desire to create hospital scenarios involving Jimmy in all kinds of emergencies, when a figure emerged from the front door of the beach house. It was a man.

He quickly caught sight of her and made his way down the stairs and across the sand. Helen found herself standing in anticipation of the news. The man wore a light blue casual suit in the latest style, with an off-white sportshirt open at the collar. His hair was dark and slightly gray at the temples. Very tanned and healthy looking, she observed, though he seemed older than she had thought Jimmy's father might be. He approached her with a wide smile that showed large, perfect teeth. She was aware of flashes of jewelry from a gleaming ring on the little finger of his left hand, a bright watch that caught the sun as he tramped through the sand, and upon close inspection, a gold chain at his throat.

"I'm Jimmy's father, Charles Banning. And you must be Helen Long, because I've been told this is your rock. Hello."

He seemed cheerful enough. Helen immediately relaxed. "Nice to meet you, Mr. Banning. Is Jimmy all right?"

The smile shaded off into something else that reminded her of Jimmy's sudden changes.

"Fine. Under the circumstances, fine. His nose started to bleed."

"Oh, my goodness. I imagined all kinds of things." A nosebleed! She felt so relieved she laughed. "A nosebleed can't be all that bad. I hope he's not in any pain."

He did not reply. He turned away from her for a moment and stared out toward the open sea. His profile was fine, the nose straight like his son's, though his cheeks and chin showed a little fullness. She guessed him to be in his early forties. When he turned to face her again he was clenching his jaws as if fighting for control.

"I would like to talk to you about Jimmy, if you have some time. And in the house. I need a drink."

"Of course. I planned to stay a while anyway."

In the house Charles Banning managed to create a great deal of suspense as he fumbled about in the refrigerator finding her a Coke and then fixing himself a drink. He apologized for the lack of an adequate bar. "The house was Jimmy's idea," he said. "He picked it out for the view and because it was right on the sand. He loves the ocean."

She took the soft drink from his hand. The stone in

his ring was enormous. The ice in his glass tinkled as he made his way to a chair near hers and settled into it.

"I love the ocean, too. To look at. Just to be near it does something for me," Helen said, trying to make conversation.

"Jimmy told me quite a bit about you, Mrs. Long. How you love the ocean just like he does. How you two get along. I think it's great. Jessica does too." He took a long drink from the glass and seemed to look right through her, his mind on something else.

Helen felt compelled to help him get to the point. "Jimmy," she said. "You're sure he's all right? I mean is it just a nosebleed or is there something else?"

"Mrs. Long, Jimmy is dying of leukemia."

Leukemia. Cancer. Helen felt the room change around her. Suddenly its smells awoke. Subtle hints of medication now shouted at her. She felt nauseated by it. The room seemed to tilt off center, the whole house to alter its aspect from a place of joy to a place of menace, a house of pain.

"So that's it," she found herself saying. "I sensed something—something sad and heavy. I felt it in him sometimes, and in Jessica. Something in her eyes."

"Jimmy didn't want you to know, not right away. I'm sure you don't realize how important you are to him."

"He seems to need someone to talk to. I'm sure he gets bored here."

"Yes. I know." He drank from his glass and sat staring at it. In the silence Helen was aware of the surf steadily pounding the beach, measuring the length and the depth of the moment that stretched between them. Leukemia. It was only a word, one Helen was not even sure she understood completely, but a horrible word. His father had said he was dying! Instinctively she reached for hope.

"I don't know much about—leukemia. But I've heard there are drugs now, aren't there? Ways they have of keeping children alive for years, even ways of curing it?"

"There is no cure. That's a long way off. The drugs—yes, they work sometimes. At the very best they can do, fifty percent die within five years."

"Fifty percent live, then! For five years or more. That's something." He continued to stare into his glass, seeing it half empty, while she insisted it was half full. She dismissed the analogy, it seemed so trite. "Surely, you haven't given up on him." She felt she had to say it.

He sighed and tossed her what seemed a tolerant smile, then crossed to the little kitchen and began making himself another drink. Perhaps she was too hasty. He had lived with the reality of it. But to give up!

"To look at him," she finally said, "you would think he was perfectly healthy. He's a little thin, perhaps, but the energy! He certainly keeps me moving when we're together."

He turned toward her and set the drink glass aside. "Jimmy needs you, Mrs. Long. He asked if you would come to see him in the hospital."

"Of course I will."

"He's got something he wants to say to you, and to tell you the truth . . ." He stopped talking, turned abruptly and picked up the drink. He downed it all at once and set it firmly on the sideboard of the sink as if settling something in his mind once and for all. He came back into the room and sat down, saying, "This isn't easy to do, but I'm going to tell you what Jimmy has gotten into his head about you."

Helen couldn't imagine what could be so difficult. Again she found herself helping him to get it out.

"I can't imagine what the problem is, Mr. Banning. If Jimmy wants something, I'll do anything I can to see he gets it. You must know that."

"What Jimmy wants is a mother. He wants you."

Before she could reply, he continued rapidly, "Jimmy has decided that you were sent here by God to be his new mother. He watched you out there on the beach by your rock for a couple of weeks or more—for as long as you've been coming here, I guess. Jessica says he even watched you through the binoculars. Then he found a way to make contact. Don't ask me how he comes up with these things. He has a very active mind, and when he wants something . . . Anyway, he's decided. You're it. Now don't ask me what that means, or how you're supposed to do it, because that exists only in Jimmy's mind. I just thought you ought to be forewarned. If you go to that hospital to see him, just be prepared. I know it may sound crazy, Mrs. Long, and I wouldn't blame you if you just walked away from it. Believe me, I wouldn't blame you. I feel responsible—in so many ways. I think I'd actually feel better about it if you said no, forget it, it's not my problem. It's like I'm laying this in your lap—oh, the hell with it." He waved his hand as if he could somehow wave it all away and fell silent, staring out the front windows toward the sea. Then he rose quickly and walked away from her, out to the porch, leaving her alone with it.

Helen felt there was just too much to be dealt with all at once. She got up quickly and walked out on the porch.

"Tell me something, Mr. Banning, about Jimmy's real mother. Where is she? I think I have a right to know, if I'm to be involved like this."

"She left six months ago, when she found out he had cancer."

CHAPTER EIGHT

As Helen dialed the number for Arthur's office she tried to remember when she had last bothered him at work. Bothered him. That was her feeling. Distracted, she dialed improperly and reached something that sounded like "Seymour's Plumbing." She hurriedly hung up and dialed again.

"Hello, dear, how was school this morning?" Arthur sounded different at the office, stronger and more in charge than he did at home.

"It was all right, but I'm calling about something else, Arthur, about the boy at the beach, Jimmy."

"Sure. What about him, any problem?"

"It's just that, oh Arthur!" She found her voice breaking. "Arthur, he's sick—so terribly sick."

"Helen? What is it? Do you want me to come out there? Where are you?"

"No, it's not that. I'm sorry to be doing this. It's just very sad news, that's all. I just found out a few minutes ago that he has leukemia."

There was silence for a moment, then Arthur's voice, sounding very close and reassuring. "I'll be right back on the line, dear. I'm in an outer office. Just hold on till I get to my own phone. Hold on now."

She felt herself relaxing, sensing at the same moment how much she depended on Arthur's quiet strength when any kind of emergency arose. He had always been like that.

His voice returned, warm and near. "Helen, I know this must be a shock to you."

"Maybe it's silly of me to be so upset, but you know how I feel about him. And there's more to tell you, something very strange that his father told me. I just felt I had to talk to you."

"Do you want to tell me the rest of it?"

"Not now, not from this pay phone with the trucks and the noise. I'm going over to the UCLA Medical Center. That's where he is."

"Take your time, dear. Do whatever you have to do and don't worry about me. Okay?"

"Thank you. I love you, Arthur."

"Well, I guess you should call me more often."

"You know, we forget sometimes. I do, anyway."

"Forget what?"

"How much I need you, I guess. How good it is, what we have together."

"Are you sure you don't want me to meet you over there? I could make it during lunch hour."

"No, really. I'll be fine now. I'll give you a report at dinner."

Driving up on the vast UCLA campus, Helen felt the immensity of it like a weight. An entrance guard gave her directions and a map, and she still became lost. She could find no pattern to the way the campus had been laid out. Parking lots seemed to move around and hide between buildings, all the signs threatened dire punishment to anyone who happened to park improperly, and spikes projected from the pavement indicating that most of the parking lot entrances she tried were suddenly exits. Throughout the fruitless search she was aware of Jimmy lying helpless in that maze of buildings, one small familiar cell of precious life somewhere within those unfeeling brick walls.

After a half hour of frustration she decided to park off campus, and managed to find an exit road and an empty spot at the curb that miraculously appeared not far from where the map said the hospital should be.

Within the medical center the mood changed. People were friendly and helpful, and a reassuring air of competence prevailed. When Charles Banning told her Jimmy was at UCLA, he had said it was one of the five or six best centers for cancer therapy in the United States. She was struck by the cosmopolitan nature of it; nurses and doctors moved sedately past her, many talking in foreign-sounding accents all seemingly intent on their business. The sense of being immersed in a worldwide enterprise of healing was deeply reassuring.

Her feeling of confidence was shattered upon entering the children's ward. No crisp white efficiency, no polite smiles or hushed tones could dull or prevent the sense of anguish and revulsion that swept over her at the sight of all those children. Her heart melted and her knees began to tremble. She quickly turned into a small waiting room just off the corridor that the head nurse had said would lead to Jimmy's room. A bearded young black man was the only other occupant of the waiting room. He sat reading a magazine through thin gold-rimmed glasses, and he looked up and smiled at her as she tottered to a vinyl-covered couch.

She could feel his eyes on her as she tried to recover. Then he rose quickly and left the room. Helen leaned back, suddenly overcome with nausea and dizziness. She closed her eyes and wished she had asked Arthur to join her. What had she been thinking? Did she expect this to be a pleasant afternoon outing?

"Here. You look like you could use this."

She looked up to see a flash of white teeth and gold spectacles as the black man offered her a cup of water.

"It shows that much?" she asked weakly.

"Umhum. Your first time?"

"Yes. Thank you." She emptied the small paper cup and he took it from her hand, crumpled it and dropped it into a small wastebasket by the end of the couch. He returned to his seat across the small room and smiled broadly.

"Would it help to say you'll get used to it? Because you will, you know. I've been coming here with my son off and on for four years. Leukemia. You have someone here?"

That staid old English sense of privacy she had gotten from her mother instinctively rebelled, and she had to fight it down for a moment. "A boy—an acquaintance. He came in this morning."

"Would that be Jimmy Banning by any chance?"

"How did you . . . ?"

"Jimmy and my boy are old friends. Well, not old, maybe. Jimmy's only been coming for about a year."

"Oh, yes, of course." This stranger knew more about Jimmy than she did. The effect of it was to make Helen wonder what she was doing there. She felt like an intruder, an outsider, as the man went on talking.

"Well, Jimmy looks pretty good. I saw him a couple

of hours ago. They'll get some platelets into him, do a routine bone marrow test, maybe give him a shot or two. He could be out of here in no time."

"What—what's no time?" Bone marrow tests, shots, platelets—her mind was reeling.

"A week, maybe two. Have you seen his dad? He was around here for a while. I think he's down in the lab donating a little blood. I could go down and tell him you're here, if you like."

"Please—no. I just want to drop in for a moment." Oh, Lord, she thought, I didn't even stop for flowers or a toy or anything. What's the matter with me? And she found herself suddenly talking. "I have only known Jimmy for a few days. We met on the beach—they have a beach house—and his father told me just a little while ago that he was here—and what's wrong with him. I'm still in shock, you see. I don't know anything about—leukemia. It's just that Jimmy and I—well, he—he sort of attached himself to me. He seemed lonely and, I don't know, hungry for someone to talk to. It was only four days ago. Four days, and here I am coming in on a part of his life that seems so remote from anything I've ever experienced. I'm sort of off balance."

She stopped suddenly, aware of how much she was sharing with the man, and wondering why.

The smile was as broad as ever. "That's quite a story. But don't let the leukemia bit scare you. My boy is making it. He's making it." He said it with finality, leaning forward and bringing his clenched fist down on the arm of the small couch right beside her. "They have drugs now that give kids remissions that can last up to five or ten years. A lot of kids are beating it. Don't give up hope."

He seemed almost to be begging her, as if they had to battle for that hope together, as if all the kids were one kid, and hope for all was somehow necessary to hoping for his own.

"I want to ask you something," Helen said. "About

that—about hope. Are there some cases where a child could be up and about, I mean running and playing and seeming very strong and active—and there not be any hope at all? What I mean is, Jimmy hardly looks ill at all, and they say he's dying." She didn't stress the word "they," not wanting him to feel it was the family. It was said generally so he would think she meant the doctors or someone a bit more remote from the family. She was sorry the moment it came out.

"I wish I could answer that. There are different kinds of leukemia. And I'm not a doctor. People feel that way, maybe at first. But I sure wouldn't ever want my boy to hear it. They need hope more than they need blood, more than anything. Don't ever let Jimmy hear you say that, no matter how you might feel."

There, Helen felt, there it is. Her instinct had been right, and now she was able to deal with this thing. That was what she had needed to hear. She looked up quickly and discovered that he had slipped out of the room. Silently she thanked him, took a deep breath and walked through the door into the corridor. A question that had haunted her from the moment Charles Banning talked to her that morning now stood out clearly in her mind.

Why have they given up on Jimmy?

CHAPTER NINE

She had learned about the Thing. Jimmy could see it in her face when she walked through the door. Now she would see how ugly he was with most of his hair gone and the darn nose pack all over his face. He wondered how much they had told her.

Helen came to the side of the bed and smiled at him, and she didn't really look at any of the stuff around the bed at all. She just looked at him.

"Hello, Jimmy," she said, and her voice sounded different somehow, like she had made up her mind about something, or was it because he looked bad?

"Do I look ugly?" he asked, and watched her face for the slightest sign that she might lie to him.

"No. To tell you the truth you look a little silly with that thing on. Tell me what it is." She pulled a chair up beside the bed, sat right down on it and took hold of his hand. She didn't move it much because it was the arm that had the needle in it, and she was very careful not to disturb anything.

"It's a nose pack. Makes my voice sound terrible, doesn't it? Like I have a cold."

"What's it for?" She seemed to want a lot of information.

"To stop the blood. Don't you know about that?"

"I know you have leukemia. But you're going to have to teach me about it. Does it make you bleed a lot?"

"There's something called platelets. It's in everybody's blood and it helps it to clot. The leukemia does something to the platelets. See that bottle up there? That's what they're giving me now. You should go down to the lab sometime and see the machine they've got. It takes the platelets out and then people can have the rest of their blood back."

"That's marvelous, isn't it! This is quite a wonderful place."

Jimmy thought she didn't seem to mind about his bald head. Now he wouldn't have to wear that hat all the time. Maybe, he thought, it's a good thing it happened right at the start like this. His dad or Jessica must have told her. Did she know the rest of it? What would she do if he just came right out and asked her now? She was just sitting there quietly holding his hand. Her eyes looked soft and calm, and she didn't seem to be crying or anything. Maybe this would be a good time. But what if she said no?

"Jimmy," she said, "I had a long talk with your father about you. He told me quite a bit about your sickness. You know, it was quite a surprise to me. I thought you were so strong and active. It was quite a shock."

"I am strong, most of the time. I can do about anything I want to do. It's just that I know I'm not going to live very long, that's all."

"Jimmy, please don't say that. You mustn't say that." He felt her squeezing his hand, and he could see her get sort of stiff in the back and in her neck and jaw, like she was going to fight him or something. Why was she so excited?

"It's okay, Helen. Don't get upset about it, okay? It's just something I know."

"Where did you get such an idea? Who told you that?" There was a real fierce look in her eyes now.

"Nobody told me. I just know." Why did she keep talking about it? He'd known right from the start. He'd had the same kind of fight with Jessica and his dad, and he'd seen the same look in them. What's the matter with grownups? he wondered. And yet he felt good about her. She wanted him to live, and that was all right, too.

He felt Helen was trying to understand as she said, "Please don't ever let me hear you say that again. There's hope, all kinds of hope. I was just talking to a man whose son has what you have, and he's getting better. He's making it. And we're going to make it, too, Jimmy. If I'm going to be your new mom, I want it understood that we're not going to give up. Do you understand that?"

She said it! She said "if I'm going to be your new Mom", and she went right on! But she had said it! Jimmy felt something let go inside of him like a rubber band that had been wound up inside a model plane. It went brrrr, and he didn't feel the needle in his arm any more, or the pain from the shot the nurse had just given him, or anything but a soft kind of wave that rolled through him, all warm and peaceful. He looked at her eyes again and saw them looking right into his, and she was talking about something he didn't hear at all. Then her eyes went soft again as if she suddenly realized too, what she had just said, and what it meant to him. Jimmy felt her hand gripping his, and then he seemed very, very tired and happy and he realized, with a feeling of surprise, that he was going to sleep.

CHAPTER TEN

Arthur came home early that Monday evening and ordered her to dress for dinner out. The firm treatment was necessary because he had found her surrounded by stacks of pamphlets from the local office of the American Cancer Society, staring wordlessly at him as he came through the front door.

Arthur was extremely attentive, insisted that she choose the restaurant, and accepted her choice without question. Restaurants were a thing with Arthur. He was very cautious about trying anything new, but when he did find one to his satisfaction, that was it for at least a year. The current favorite was a seafood house set in a small cove on the ocean forty miles above Malibu. Tonight, Helen had said she didn't want to see the ocean. She also hadn't wanted to eat at one of the quaint bistros in Westwood, another of Arthur's tried and true spots, because it was too close to the hospital. She had finally settled on a rather large and busy french restaurant on Wilshire Boulevard.

"Why did you want to come here? It seems pretty noisy for tonight, or is that what you wanted?"

"I heard the food was very good. It will have to be. I have no appetite."

She had already told Arthur the events of the afternoon. At home and in the car they had discussed it thoroughly, with Helen sharing the plan that had begun forming after leaving the hospital.

Arthur's reception of all of it had been ideal, except for one moment when he wanted to know a little more about Charles Banning, and Helen had detected a note of jealousy.

The salads arrived and she picked at hers without tasting it, while Arthur glanced up after every hearty bite until he had finished. "This is the first time we've been out alone, without the O'Donnells, in six and one-half weeks," he said.

"Six and one-half weeks?"

"Since your birthday."

"I thought you liked Katie and Jim." She felt a bit sensitive on that score, having always felt she had dragged him into that friendship with Katie. What would Katie think of all this?

"They're a little too trendy or life-style conscious. Check with Katie. She'll know the latest term for it."

"She does try a bit too hard sometimes, but we've had some good times, haven't we? I'd hate to think . . ."

"No problem. It's just nice to be with you." He lifted his wine glass to her. Then his face clouded a little as he said, "You know what worries me about this thing with the boy?"

"That I'll get too involved and be hurt." She knew that.

"Yes—but that's not all of it. It's the direction you're taking right at the start." He paused and Helen could not guess what he was going to say. "I think if you go into it, you'd better be prepared to lose him. And I don't think you are."

Surprisingly, she found herself prepared to answer that. Somehow the booklets from the Cancer Society had helped to crystallize a lot of feelings. She'd had time to read and to think. Sometimes Helen felt if every event in life would just give her time to sit with it and think a while there wasn't anything she couldn't face.

"I have spent most of the afternoon thinking about that very possibility, Arthur. I can't say how I'd handle it, or how much I'd be hurt. But I can think about it. I can imagine it and not feel devastated by it. What more of a guarantee do we ever have about anything? One of us could be hit by a truck, too, but we go on."

"It's not the same thing. I just want you to take a long look at it, that's all."

"From what I've read I would say the hardest part might be the day to day. If I can be with him for a few hours every day, with all that's going to mean—maybe I can face that if it comes. But it doesn't have to come to that, Arthur. It just doesn't. The worst thing in the world is to give up on a leukemia patient. The books all say that."

"From what you told me, it seems like he's given up on himself."

"But that could be a natural child's reaction. They didn't have to go along with it! Do you know his father bought him that beach house and put him there with that nurse to die? That's what he did!"

"That's what you think he did. You only met the man this morning."

"And I didn't like him. He's—flashy. You won't have to worry about me with him, Arthur. Oh now, don't look so innocent and wide-eyed. I saw your face when I told you about Charles Banning."

Arthur looked sheepish and he actually ducked. The waiter laid his dinner in front of him and he looked up with a grin. "Okay. I admit it. The idea of you hanging around that beach house all hours with a salesman type lurking around, that did occur to me."

"All hours will not be it. I told you, when Jimmy's out of the hospital I will go down to the house and fix his breakfast in the morning on my way to my classes. Then I'll stay with him for a while in the afternoons and be home when you get in from work. His father is on the road most of the time, anyway."

"Super," Arthur said, and dug into his filet of sole meuniere. It didn't sound super to Helen. It sounded as fishy as the dinner. Much as she loved Arthur and as sure as she was of his love and concern for her, she knew what lay ahead for both of them could be difficult.

"I'm going to need your help, a lot," she assured him.

He replied, "I'm right here, love," but he looked away.

Tuesday morning began a period of balancing time between her college classes, daily visits to the hospital, and pellmell dashes through the supermarkets on her way home to Arthur. In spite of Katie's warnings, voiced over the phone on Tuesday night, that Helen would find her time crowded to the point that her "centers of serenity" would be disturbed, Helen found the increased pace invigorating.

When Katie had called again two days later, Helen heard a few more exotic phrases. "The center is the seat of the cosmic consciousness, my dear. When we lose our focus and allow ourselves to be distracted into mundane considerations, we detatch ourselves from the universal one."

Helen had finally said, "Katie, what the hell does that mean, that you've found another guru?" Katie got tense and defensive as usual. Then she explained that there was a master of some oriental philosophy in town, lecturing in the colleges, and that several very prominent movie stars were in attendance. Katie went on for several minutes quoting his speeches as if she'd taken notes. Helen had finally said she was too tired to listen any further and had excused herself and hung up. By the middle of the next week Helen had tried to call Katie again and was relieved to find her not answering the phone.

Jimmy's condition seemed to reach a plateau and stop there. She learned from Jessica that he had been in "fairly good remission" until the nosebleed, and the doctors were trying some new drugs. Now it was Thursday afternoon of his second week, and she and Jessica were having coffee together in the first floor cafeteria. The coffee was even flatter than usual.

"Remission," Jessica explained quietly, "is when the disease backs off, when the drugs have managed to kill enough of the cancerous cells that the bone marrow can produce some healthy ones. In good remission a patient comes right back and it's like a miracle. They can do anything a normal child can do."

"I've read about it," Helen replied, "but it's so different from a normal disease, if there is such a thing. They're never really well, then? They're just in remission?"

"With some cases they find just the right drug or just the right combination, and they can hold a child in remission for years and years. But the doctors don't talk about cures, because for one thing they haven't devised a test yet that can tell for sure if all the bad cells are gone."

"Jessica, I want to ask you something, and you don't have to answer if you don't want to." Helen approached it carefully, knowing the nurse might feel touchy about it. Jessica waited with her almond eyes riveted tight to Helen's gaze.

"Go ahead, ask."

"Have you given up hope for Jimmy?"

"Mr. Banning told you he was going to die, didn't he?" Her smile was genuinely warm and sympathetic.

"As if the whole thing was over and done with."

"Helen, I'm not going to try to explain Mr. Banning. You've got to figure that one out for yourself. I'm just going to say the truth as I know it. Jimmy has a bad case. His family let it go too long, and when they did take him to a doctor they wouldn't believe the diagnosis. A lot of people do that, and I'm not blaming them.

But they wasted time. They got involved with a faith healer of some kind Mrs. Banning found somewhere, and that took more time. Jimmy's first hospitalization lasted far longer than it should have because they let it go so long. They were fighting for his life right from the start."

"I wish I knew more."

"Honey, don't rush it." Jessica's soft voice went on, "If I were you, maybe I'd think twice about this whole thing. I've been watching you. Every time you walk into that ward it's a battle for you. If you're going to help Jimmy, you've got to develop some callouses on your soul, and if you can't . . ."

"You haven't really answered my question yet, Jessica. Have you given up?"

"I have my degree in nursing and ten years of professional experience, Helen. But underneath, I'll tell you the truth, I've got a family heritage of old time religion. Maybe I don't practice it like my dear old mama would like, but there's one thing I still hang on to, and that's this—living and dying, they're in the hands of the Lord. And until He gives the word, my job is just to go on doing my job."

Helen entered Jimmy's room a few minutes later to find him vomiting into a bedpan held by a new and very young nurse. He finished and lay back and frowned when he saw Helen watching. "That looks so ugly," he said. "I wish you'd tell them not to give me that drug, Mom. It makes me so sick."

It was the first time he had called her Mom. She walked to the side of the bed and the young nurse moved between them. "Just a moment, please. I have to give him a shot." Helen backed a step away, saw the nurse hastily flip the sheet aside, caught a glimpse of his thin white flank, and saw him jump as the needle entered. He groaned as if in pain, and Helen's temper flared. Why did she have to be so rough with him? If she wasn't in such an all-fired hurry to get it over with! Helen was about to say something about it when the young nurse turned to face her. There were tears in the girl's eyes.

The nurse could easily see Helen's angry reaction, and she very quietly said, "You've just got one, Mrs. Banning. I've got a whole floor of them."

She was gone before Helen could apologize.

Jimmy had heard the nurse's remark and he was grinning from ear to ear. "She called you Mrs. Banning! She thinks you're my real mom!"

CHAPTER ELEVEN

Jimmy was brought home from the hospital on the ninth of November. The predicted two weeks were extended until the doctors could be sure he was ready for care at home. Though Jimmy had reacted against the new drug with vomiting and headaches for several days, he now seemed to be accepting it, and was looking better than she had ever seen him. His hair was even starting to grow again.

After nearly a month, Helen was beginning to encounter a number of puzzling feelings about her new role. As she began to become intimately involved in life at the beach house, it was as if the boy went through a bit of a reaction about her presence there. Sometimes it seemed to Helen that he had picked her out of the sand in order to make a target of her. When he screamed about the food, he accused her of spoiling it. When he had a bad night after a week at home, it was because of something she had said before she left him in the early evening. That one had so upset her that she had gone out on the porch where Jimmy couldn't see her and had herself a good cry. Jessica had found her there, had brought her a cup of coffee and tried to calm her down by telling her, "You ought to see him the moment you leave here for school in the mornings. He can't wait for you to get back. He's been through an awful lot in the last few weeks, Helen. I think he just wants you to share some of that. Maybe he's testing you a little."

This morning brought a new test, if that's what it was. He was very cheerful at breakfast, ate very heartily for the first time since he'd been home, and wanted to go out to his tidepools with Helen before she went to her class. They'd had a lovely time for the twenty minutes or so Helen was able to spend with him. But when she said it was time to go, he'd gotten angry.

"Why do you have to run off to that dumb school all the time? What's the matter with you, anyway, that you still have to go to school like a kid? You must be pretty dumb, Helen. That's a dumb thing to do when you're old!" And then he had run to the house and locked himself in his room.

When her morning psych class was over, Helen joined the girls around Professor Mays's desk. He noticed her immediately and smiled. "I've been wondering when you were going to say something. You've been late to class for the last three mornings." He managed somehow to scatter the flock around him and get to her side.

"Would you have a minute to talk?" she asked.

"Only if you let me buy you a cup of coffee."

They balanced their styrofoam cups and crossed the student union cafeteria toward what she hoped would be a quiet table in the farthest corner from the serving line. The morning sunlight streaked through a high window beside the table and he moved his chair around to get his back to it. He pulled a plastic chair out for her, then sat across the corner of the little square table, his elbow propped and coffee cup raised in mock tribute. "Here's to blue eyes."

His steady, amused stare knocked Helen off balance and she fumbled for a response. "I—thank you. My father thanks you and my mother, who gave me the eyes, thanks you."

He grinned and sipped his coffee. She had the feeling he had tried to shock her, as if he was testing her for some reason. This had started out to be a teacher-student conference, hadn't it? Was he getting personal, or was she overreacting?

"Thank your mother for me. So you finally decided to accept my offer."

She was caught staring and speechless again.

"The coffee," he explained. "I asked you several weeks ago, remember?" He looked away toward a group of young girls who were giggling loudly on the other side of the room. He turned back to her and shrugged. "I've been teaching here for eight years. It's nice to meet a mature woman once in a while."

Helen found herself tensing under his gaze. One of the things she was very aware of about herself was her inexperience with men. She had carefully avoided private and personal conversations with them for as long as she could remember. Other than her doctor and an occasional plumber or electrician she hadn't been alone with a strange man for years. She caught a gleam in his eye that suggested he sensed her discomfort and was enjoying it.

"This is not exactly the kind of conversation I had in mind," she confessed, "when I stopped at your desk."

"Ah, well, life is full of surprises, isn't it? Or it should be. Tell me about yourself. Are you married?"

"Yes, for twenty years."

"Why did you add on the number of years? Are you proud of it, or tired of it?"

Helen had the feeling that the conversation was moving much too fast. His hand was lying near hers on the table. She removed it and folded both of her hands in her lap. "I know you're a psychologist," she said. "I hope you aren't analyzing me."

"Why not? It might be fun."

"I'm not that interesting."

He sobered quickly and cocked his head, then he very deliberately glanced downward and ran his eyes over her body, or what he could see of it above the table. "You are right, Helen Long. No analyzing, not because you aren't interesting, but because you are a genuine person and very worthy of attention, and just don't know it." He sighed and leaned back in his chair. "Does it frighten you that I might want to get to know you better?"

"I—I'm not sure. I guess it does to some extent." She found her hands sweating.

"Don't believe everything you hear about college psych professors. We don't score nearly as often as the stories say." He cocked an eyebrow and waited for her response, but she had no idea what he was talking about. He explained, "There was a survey published recently. It claimed that some thirty percent of college females studying psychology had gotten involved sexually with their male professors. I just wanted you to know I'm not doing nearly that well."

It made her feel dumb. It was probably something the campus had buzzed with for weeks, but here she was having it explained.

"I'm sorry," he apologized. "I'm making you very uncomfortable and I should know better. I'm not trying to make out with you, Mrs. Long, at least not at the moment, so let's be friends. Tell me what you've been up to."

Helen wondered how she could get back on the track of her worries about Jimmy. Apparently the professor could turn on that kind of intimate conversation and suddenly shift gears back to humdrum reality, but Helen couldn't. With a distinct numbness in her body and a steady ringing in her ears, she tried to focus on her relationship with Jimmy. She glanced at the professor, found him smiling warmly, and quickly looked away. She brought her folded hands to the top of the table and tried to control herself by staring at them.

"I have taken on something of a challenge," she said,

and quickly told him about Jimmy. He listened patiently. She found herself wishing he didn't have a full beard, realizing how it masked his face and hid his reactions.

". . . Well, his mother abandoned him. I just supposed that meant she'd given up. What else could it mean?"

"A lot of things. Maybe she knew she couldn't handle it. How do you feel about her?" She looked away from his eyes, which seemed suddenly quite intense.

"Feel? I don't know. Sorry for her, in a way. And angry with her, too, I suppose. To just walk off and leave a child in that condition—that seems, well, it's just unthinkable to me. A mother would have to be—it seems very selfish and very cruel."

He didn't question her further about that, seeming satisfied just to get her to state her honest reaction. "How does Jimmy feel about himself? Does he ever talk about dying?"

"Just once, in the hospital. I couldn't help getting into it because I had just heard his father say Jimmy didn't have a chance, and I was upset by that attitude. Jimmy told me he knew he was dying, had known it from the beginning, and he said it was okay. That was his word, it's okay." She felt a chill run through her as she said it, and could not help shuddering a little.

He noticed it. "At different ages there are different kinds of reactions to death. It's not my field, but there have been a number of studies of that. I'm not sure just how a ten-year-old would react, knowing he was going to die."

"He's not going to die! You can't just take that for granted!" She realized she had raised her voice, and went on more calmly, "I'm sorry, but you're just accepting it like the others."

He sipped his coffee and studied her in silence. Helen found herself decorating the lip of the styrofoam cup with little scallops she made with her thumbnail. It seemed very important to get all of them regularly spaced around the cup's edge. She glanced up and found him watching her hand. He grinned.

"Helen," he said, "you didn't have to accept Jimmy's proposition. You could have said no thanks, or something to let him and his father know you were not available for this dubious role of surrogate mother. Why did you agree to it?"

"Why? I—I've never asked. It wasn't like you say—something I could agree to. I mean it was never an actual decision on my part. It was there—Jimmy was there and I was there. He needed someone, and he picked me. Actually that was the way it was. He picked me."

"You could still get out of it." He said it very quietly and in such a level way that she couldn't tell if he was weighting his remark to influence her to do it or not to do it. Then he added, "It was and still is a decision on your part. You must know that."

She started to reply, then stopped as she began to consider what he had just said, that she had made a deliberate and conscious decision.

"I know that sounds strange, but I think the commitment to Jimmy came the first time he begged me to come back to the beach and see him, and I accepted." She hesitated, remembering something else. "My husband says I miss mothering my own child, my daughter who's in college."

"One child. Did you ever wish you'd had more? A son, perhaps?"

Helen laughed at the suggestion. "Oh, no, I don't think so. I was very content to have a girl. Boys always sort of scared me. The idea of having one of my own—no. I was quite relieved when they told me my baby was female."

The teacher leaned back in his chair, smiling. "I hope you'll keep in touch with me as you go through this thing, Helen. And I think I can offer you some practical advice. There is a woman you ought to meet, a teacher who is conducting a new class starting next semester, a class in death and dying."

"Death and dying?"

"It's a new field for this school. The idea is to train people to help those who are facing death."

"There's an actual course in it?"

"Not just a course, a whole field of study. Her name's Miller, Irene Miller. I think you should meet her."

"Even though I don't agree that Jimmy is dying, you think I should still meet her."

"If Jimmy thinks he's dying, yes. The question now is, what are Jimmy's expectations? What kind of contract is going to exist between you? If I were you I'd sit down with him very soon and make him state just what he expects and then tell him just how much you can do, and what you expect from the relationship."

Helen found herself wondering if the professor so carefully defined all his relationships. It all seemed very formal.

"So what are you going to do with the rest of the day, Helen Long?" he asked. "Back to the beach?"

"Yes. And I appreciate your help—very much."

"I hope this won't be our last talk. I'm very interested in this case. And in you."

Later as Helen walked to her car she thought, Case? Is that what Jimmy is to him, a case? Maybe that's the way he feels about me, too. The case of Helen Long, middle-aged female psychology student, mature woman with interesting problem, possibly frustrated wife of twenty years, possible candidate for quick roll in the hay? She found some satisfaction in replaying the dialogue and coming to that conclusion, because it quieted the butterflies in her stomach. It was very unsettling to discover all of a sudden, after so many years, that she was susceptible to that kind of direct sexual approach. She knew, of course, that her anger was not directed at Professor Mays, but at her own clumsiness and discomfort. Nevertheless, the anger felt good.

CHAPTER TWELVE

"Why can't you come to the beach and live here with me, like Jessica does?" They'd been having a lot of fun that afternoon, feeding the seagulls together, and Jimmy felt it was a good time to ask her.

Helen looked up from the sock she was sewing for him, then looked down again and bit off the thread. She was sure taking her time about answering!

"Couldn't you do that, Helen?"

"Jimmy, you have to understand. I have a husband and a home to take care of. We talked about that the other day, remember?"

"We didn't talk about you coming here to live." Not exactly, they hadn't. She had said something about expectations, and what he wanted from her. He'd said he didn't know what she meant.

"I agreed to take extra time on the Fridays when you have to go to the hospital for the tests, and to spend Thanksgiving with you."

"And Christmas!"

"Yes, and Christmas." Her face changed when she said Christmas, as though she didn't really want to do it. Then she went on to say, "My daughter's coming home from college for Christmas, I do have to spend some time with her. We talked about that, too. Remember?"

He answered yes, and Helen said, "I wonder if you'd let me take a picture of you to show my family."

"No!"

He wanted to get away from her for a while. The porch of the beach house just seemed too little for the way he felt. He started down the stairs and that weird sensation in his right leg came back. It was numb, as if it had gone to sleep. He stopped at the bottom of the stairs and looked back. She was watching him.

"Jimmy, what is it? Were you limping?"

She was getting to be just like Jessica, always watching him and worrying all the time. "My foot's asleep. I'm going to look at the gulls."

"Jimmy, I just can't come here to stay!" She was calling after him, but he just didn't feel like talking any more. He had to try extra hard to keep walking straight and not favor his right leg. He exaggerated the effort of trudging through the sand so she wouldn't notice anything.

They had taken a plastic bag of bread pieces down to the water's edge and had tossed the bread to the gulls about an hour before. The little one, the gull they had named Charlie, had been crowded away from the food by the bigger gulls, the way he always was. They finally got one nice big piece to the little guy and he'd gulped it down before the big guys could get it. Then Charlie had parked on the waves just beyond the surf and had looked as peaceful and happy as he could be.

As Jimmy walked up over a little mound of sand near the water's edge, he saw Charlie. The bird was running along in the wet sand where a wave had just been, but he wasn't looking for minnows as usual. Charlie was dragging one wing, making a little trail behind him in the sand. Jimmy spun around to call out to Helen and found her just a few steps away, coming toward him.

"Helen, Charlie's hurt!" He began running toward the wounded bird, and it flopped away from him. "Cut him off. Go the other way!" he shouted to Helen. She took a few steps toward the gull and it worked its way over the waves to the quiet water a few feet offshore. There Charlie sat, soberly watching them.

"It's his wing. Now the other birds will get all the food! We've got to help him!"

Jimmy plunged into the surf and began wading out toward the gull. Behind him, Helen shouted something that sounded like a warning not to go too far. But Jimmy had to go deeper because the bird moved away from him. The effort of fighting the surf was more than Jimmy had expected, and his right leg now seemed almost useless. What was the matter with it? He fought harder, and the water rose to his chest. The gull sat just out of reach now, watching him with one bright eye that seemed full of fear and pain. "I'm coming, Charlie. Just wait there! I'm coming!"

He heard a splash behind him and realized that Helen had come right in with him. He looked back to see that the water was above her knees, getting the legs of her pants wet. Then a large wave rolled in high and broke over his head. It knocked him down. Foaming white and green water poured over him and he could feel the sand getting into his mouth. Helen's arms came under him and when Jimmy came up she was almost crying.

"Jimmy! Oh, my God, you scared me! There's undertow here. Hang on to me tight now."

He threw his arms around her waist as the water pulled his legs right out from under him. Six feet away, Charlie rode the quiet water just on the other side of where the waves broke. Jimmy felt completely exhausted by his brief struggle with the waves, and Helen's arm around him and under his right arm felt very good.

"Let's go back, Jimmy," she said, and she reached right down and picked him up. He held on tight, feeling chilled to the bone. He noticed that he was getting her pretty blue blouse all wet.

"I'm making you all ugly," he told her.

She laughed, and she was breathing hard at the same time. "What a funny thing to say. You had me pretty worried, young man." They reached the beach and Helen didn't even put him down then. She kept right on going across the sand, still carrying him, and when

Jimmy looked up, Helen's face was right above his. She stopped walking and looked at him a moment, then she kissed him on the forehead. "Let's go to the house and get some more bread. Maybe we can coax him ashore. Okay?"

She set him down in the sand. But there was something in her face that came there just before she had kissed him, and it made him say, "I love you, Mom." Her arms went around him again and she sort of fell right down to her knees in the sand and hugged him.

"I love you, too, Jimmy. Oh, God how I love you." And her eyes were wet even though she was smiling like everything.

They went on to the house and found some more bread and came back to Charlie. In about two minutes he had come ashore, following a little trail of bread pieces they tossed. As he snatched up the last piece, Helen very carefully picked the bird up.

An hour later, with Jessica's help, they had it in a wooden box that was like a little cage. They found a place up under the porch of the beach house, not far from where Jimmy had hidden once to watch Helen with her book. He thought about that as he sat in the cool sand under the porch with her, watching the gull drink some water.

"Helen, do you think Charlie will die?"

"Oh, no, I . . ." was all she said, and then she stopped and seemed to think about it a while. Then, very carefully, she said, "I don't know, but he could get an infection or something in that broken bone, and if he did, well . . ."

"Where do you think birds go when they die, Helen?"

"What do you think?"

"I think they go up in the sky somewhere and they become giant seagulls, so big nothing can hurt them any more, as big as hang-gliders. Super seagulls."

"That may be, Jimmy. We don't know about the next life, about what it will be like."

"I do, Helen. I know what it will be like. I've seen it

in my dreams. People and birds and everything that lives goes to be with God. And it's a beautiful place. It really is!" This was something Jimmy had been wanting to tell her for a long time. About his dreams, all of them.

"You have dreams about—things like that?" she asked.

"Yes, and other kinds, too. Scary dreams."

"Do you want to tell me about them?"

"I guess so. I dream about how beautiful it will be with God, then I dream about something I can't even see in my dream, something terrible. I just know it's there and it's big and very black and it has big teeth, and it will hurt me. I just have the feeling it will hurt me more than anything. I feel it coming closer and closer and then I start screaming and I wake up, and I can't go back to sleep."

Her eyes were big as if she could see the dream thing herself, but she wasn't acting scared or crying. She just looked as though she wanted to hear more about it, and really cared that it bothered him. Jimmy decided he wasn't going to ask her any more about coming to live with him. That was up to Helen. Maybe she would be able to guess that the nightmares were one of the reasons why he missed her at night.

"Jimmy, I want you to know that any time you want to talk like this, about your dreams or your worries, I'll do my best to understand."

"Will you even let me talk about dying sometimes? Because that's what I think about a lot."

Her voice was so soft he almost couldn't hear it when she said, "Is that what you want to talk about now?"

It didn't have to be talked about now. What he had hoped she would say was that she would come and be with him at night. So he just said, "Not now, Helen." Then because he guessed she might be feeling bad, he told her, "I knew you would be a good listener. I knew that when I picked you."

CHAPTER THIRTEEN

When she returned to the beach house the following afternoon Helen gathered up Jimmy and the wounded seagull and they had a happy trip together to the local veterinarian's office.

Jimmy was delighted that the vet was able to set the broken wing, and that when the minor operation was finished the doctor had given a very hopeful prognosis. On the way back to the beach house they stopped at a Dairy Freeze for cones. Jimmy was able to eat only half of his before he began to feel a little nauseated, but even that was a boon because he hadn't been able to keep any ice cream down since his hospitalization.

The trip seemed to tire the boy more than their usual walks on the beach and he asked to take a nap upon their arrival. Jimmy had taken naps before and had shown weariness before, so Helen fought back an instant case of panic and kissed him goodnight with a smile.

"If you were here all the time you could kiss me goodnight every night," he said sleepily.

Jessica overheard it and when Helen settled into one of the lounge chairs on the porch, the nurse came out to join her. With a shake of her head she said, "That little con artist is still working on getting you out here full time, I see."

They talked for a while, keeping their voices low since the window to Jimmy's room faced the porch. Jessica was glad to hear about the ice cream, but Helen could tell there was something bothering her. She asked what it was and Jessica invited her into the kitchen.

"It's the tests. The last one showed that the drug isn't doing its job. His red cell count is down again, and if it drops much lower he may have to go back to the hospital."

Helen steadied herself against the sink. "Tell me about those tests, Jessica. Why do they have to take bone samples so often?"

"The leukemic cells grow in those parts of the body where blood is produced, the lymph system and the bone marrow as well as in the spleen. They can actually count the bad cells when they take a sample."

"I don't know how he stands it. Every week another trip to the hospital, blood tests, every few weeks another bone marrow sample from his chest . . . His courage just wrings me out."

Jessica smiled. "I know what you mean. It's enough to make you excuse the little tyrant when he gets on one of his high horses around here. But we have to help him stay balanced and normal, don't we? If we go and let him get spoiled, what kind of life is he going to have later on?"

She said it for Helen's benefit, and with a grin of conspiracy. Helen said, "Yes, we can't spoil him. But I'll tell you, sometimes I just want to scream. It's so unfair."

"My mama used to say, honey, God didn't make life fair, he made it rough so we'd all fall down sometimes and He'd have to pick us up."

"Do you believe that, Jessica?"

"No, I just believe it isn't fair or smooth or easy for anybody, and when it gets real rough I'd rather be caught by somebody who loves me—like Mama. What keeps me wondering is whether it was her religion that made her so good, or her goodness that made her religion look good."

Helen had never been in any kind of intimate association with a black person before. She felt a depth and breadth of experience back of Jessica's words unlike anything she had seen in any of her friends or acquaintances in the middle-class white suburb she and Arthur had lived in for twenty years. She couldn't help comparing Jessica's wisdom and quiet serenity with Katie's restless and never-ending search for some kind of packaged solution to all of her problems.

"There's something else," Jessica's quiet voice went on. "I'm going to tell the doctors about his leg."

"What is it? What's wrong?"

"I don't think he has much feeling in his right leg, and it worries me."

Helen carried that worry with her as she left at four o'clock. She was grateful that Jimmy was resting, because she had made an appointment that would have taken her away from him ahead of schedule. Jimmy definitely did not want her shortening her time with him, not even for a reason as good as this one.

The college campus was nearly deserted as Helen crossed the quadrangle and made her way past the student union building to the administration building. She found the second-floor office easily and entered to face a youthful secretary who sat at a desk surrounded by walls covered with clippings fastened to cork bulletin boards. The clippings included several articles about Dr. Irene Miller and her work. A newspaper photo showed Dr. Miller to be a small, foreign-looking woman with short gray hair. Helen thought her a slim version of Golda Meir, the one-time prime minister of Israel.

Dr. Miller appeared in the doorway of the inner office and smiled broadly. All feelings that she appeared too masculine or homely instantly vanished. The smile radiated charm and warmth.

"Come in, Mrs. Long. Come in! Right on time. Very good, I like that! Now you will sit down and you will tell me more about this wonderful child you've fallen in love with." She had a trace of a German accent.

Helen began by telling the story of their early encounters on the beach, and was surprised to find the doctor taking notes furiously. They had agreed on the phone that this would not be an "official" visit for which Helen would have been charged a small fee, yet the pencil flew over the pages of the yellow pad. She did not interrupt until Helen expressed some of her own feelings about Jimmy giving up on himself and being convinced he would die very soon.

"Has he talked much about this?"

"Briefly, a time or two, but today he told me that he would like very much to be able to talk to me a lot more about it."

"How does that make you feel? Inadequate? Frightened, or what?"

"Well, confused at the moment, because I just cannot think Jimmy is—is doomed. That's the way it feels to me, as if Jimmy and his father already think of him as dead and buried!"

"I see." She paused, staring thoughtfully at Helen for a long moment, then she seemed to brush something aside in her mind with a wave of her hand. "We will come back to that later. How old is the boy again?"

"Ten."

"What is it that worries you about this attitude of acceptance he seems to have? You feel he has given up too soon?"

Helen was relieved to have Dr. Miller say it. "Yes! Much too soon. I know he has a very bad case, and that it was allowed to develop far too long before treatment, but he should be looking forward. He should be back in school, for one thing, keeping up with his work. He should be seeing friends of his own age, meeting new playmates. He should be living his life, not waiting for—for . . ."

"Death," Dr. Miller said frankly. "You don't even want to say the word, am I right? Yet Jimmy says it, and he's the one who is facing it as a very real possibility."

Helen looked away from the smiling eyes of Dr. Miller, keenly aware of their directness.

"I wish I knew more. I wish, somehow, I were a

stronger person for Jimmy, smarter and wiser. I'm just a very average American housewife, Dr. Miller. My life has been quiet and sheltered. And now, all of a sudden, I feel way beyond my depths, responsible for someone and to someone I didn't even know a few weeks ago."

"So few of us have any experience dealing with dying people. You cannot be blamed for being uncomfortable, Mrs. Long. That is the problem, you see, that I try to deal with. No one really talks to dying people any more. What do we do with such people? We put them into a hospital somewhere and let the so-called professionals take care of their deaths, yah? So they get hooked up to machines and there they lie, like society's failures! Yah, failures, because the professionals, they are embarrassed by death. Death means someone has failed, they think."

Helen waited as she paused.

"Nobody wants to look squarely at death. This is a pity. The exit of a human being from this life, that is a time not without significance."

Helen was certain the woman had spoken these same phrases over and over in her speeches across the world, yet she was emotional as she repeated the ideas for Helen alone.

"We must get over the feeling that death is unnatural. But what about you and Jimmy? I must help you with him."

"If he wants to talk about death, I suppose I should let him, then," Helen offered.

"Of course, let him! Don't make him, or impose anything of your own. Let him have the choice. After all, he's the one who is dying."

"He's not—"

"I'm sorry. I meant that in a more general way. What I say is that it is up to the dying one to choose what to say or not to say. How many times have you heard someone around a dying person say, 'Oh, don't say that, Grandfather! Don't feel that way, Mama!' How ridiculous. It is their death and they have a right to say or do anything they please. So with your Jimmy, let him choose. The time, the place, and what he wants to tell you."

"I started to say that he's not dying," Helen reminded her. The woman insisted on seeing Jimmy just one way!

"I realize that, my dear. There are various stages in our reaction to death, our own or the death of anyone near to us. They have been repeated so often now they have almost become classical statements. But you should know them. And you can watch for these stages in yourself and in Jimmy. At the first stage we deny it. We say it cannot be—the diagnosis is wrong—the doctors don't know what they are talking about, and so on. Denial is followed by anger for a time, though not necessarily in all cases. A boy of ten may not have the same kind of anger and feelings of being betrayed which an adolescent or an adult may have. After anger comes bargaining, and also reactive depression where the patient grieves over things like losing his hair or his job. Finally comes a kind of acceptance, and this becomes very peaceful, and often leads to a kind of silent, holy waiting, and quietly saying goodbye."

"I should be taking notes," Helen said quietly.

"I'll have the secretary give you a little booklet I've prepared."

"Do you think I'm going through that first phase myself? Do you think I'm just denying the whole thing?"

"How would I know that, Mrs. Long? I'm not psychic. That's something you must ask yourself. But let me tell you, I share your feeling about the importance of hope. Hope must be maintained as long as possible. Keep fighting against anyone or anything that would rob your Jimmy of his wonderful courage, but at the same time you must be prepared to listen. Listen closely for all the clues Jimmy will give you about what's going on inside him. He obviously trusts you and loves you, and he will find a way to tell you what he wants you to experience with him."

The secretary came to the door and glanced at her wristwatch in an exaggerated fashion. Irene Miller jumped to her feet with surprising zest for what Helen thought must be her sixty or seventy years, "Ach, the time. I have to make a little speech to some faculty members. Have I been of any help at all, Mrs. Long?"

"Yes, oh yes. Thank you. There is just one more thing." Helen stood and talked fast as the woman gathered some notes from her desk and prepared to leave. "He wants me to move to the beach house with him. I feel terrible about saying no to him, when he seems to need me so much."

The woman stopped and scratched her thin, short hair with the eraser of her pencil. "There will be time for that later, will there not? If he gets better, you will not be needed. If he gets worse, you will go! And now, goodbye." She shook hands very briskly and smiled again with radiance. "Call me any time, Mrs. Long. My secretary always knows where I will be."

Walking to her car Helen realized that her own relationship with Jimmy was but one small event in a world where people were dying by the millions. Some had the comfort of professionals or family members who had been influenced by people like Dr. Irene Miller. Multitudes of others died in loneliness and pain with no one to talk to.

CHAPTER FOURTEEN

"A little more wine, my dear?" Arthur leered suggestively over the upraised bottle.

"Yes, please. I'm so glad I took some time away from there today," Helen answered. "It was just getting to me."

As Thanksgiving Day approached Helen had found herself increasingly morose. She had never been one to be depressed by holidays, but the mounting media campaigns for the year-end season against the reality of Jimmy's condition made the holidays seem more commercial and mercenary than ever.

There were other things, too, that dampened her spirits. Jimmy's situation was definitely worsening; now there was speculation about possible secondary tumors or something else that was causing the numbness in his leg. On the Friday after Thanksgiving he was to have X-rays of his spine in addition to his usual bone marrow and blood tests. Jessica had further terrified her by telling Helen about the incidence of brain tumor in leukemic children. In the past, Jessica said, the doctors had given Jimmy several injections directly into his spinal fluid. This was done to get the powerful cancer drugs past the "blood-brain barrier" and directly into the delicate structures of the brain itself. Apparently, as Jessica explained it, the brain guards the bloodstream and screens out any material its monitor identifies as poisonous, including the medications.

Helen had decided upon hearing all of that that she needed to get away for a while. She chose Wednesday, the day before Thanksgiving, and informed Jimmy that she would return Thursday morning to help prepare the turkey dinner. Instead of arguing or trying any of his usual ploys, Jimmy had very sweetly and quietly agreed with her—another indication to Helen of his deteriorating condition.

Now as she relaxed at home with Arthur on Wednesday night, enjoying an after-dinner drink at the end of a restful day, Helen nursed a small worry and wondered how to share it with her husband. As she had left the beach house on Tuesday Jessica had walked Helen to the car and told her, "Mr. Banning is coming for Thanksgiving. He called to ask if you'd mind."

Helen had said that of course she wouldn't mind, but had instantly begun worrying about how Arthur would take the news. Originally Helen was going to join Jessica and Jimmy to help brighten the day for them, and Arthur had agreed to letting her go. But how would he take the fact of Charles Banning's presence there? She had seen Charles only once since Jimmy's return from the hospital and then only for a few minutes, as the man had hastily said goodbye just as she was arriving, tossing his elegant leather suitcase into the trunk of his immaculately clean Mercedes and speeding away on another of his road trips. The Mercedes was new, bright red with white leather interior, and somehow that irked Helen. It seemed to go all too well with his mod clothes and gold chains and too-perfect teeth and precisely graying temples as the final touch to what she thought was a very contrived man-of-the-world impression.

Now Helen had to find a way to tell Arthur about Thanksgiving Day.

"When am I going to get to see Jimmy?" Arthur asked as he finished filling her wine glass. "Any chance?"

"I tried to get him to let me take his picture for you. He won't even agree to that."

"Does he look that bad?"

"No. But he thinks he looks very ugly. And he has

this fantasy, Arthur, that I'm his real mother. If he doesn't acknowledge you in any way he can keep that fantasy more real, somehow. I'm sure that's it."

"Well, what the heck," Arthur grinned. "Just tell him I wish him all the best, or can't you even do that?"

"He likes it better if I just don't mention you at all, or Sharon, or this house . . . I know it's strange."

Arthur shrugged it off and sat on the raised hearth of the fireplace facing her as she sat in their leather lounge chair. He seemed very relaxed as he said, "Just bring me some leftover turkey tomorrow night. I'll be fine. I'll spend the entire afternoon watching football. Meanwhile, my dear, here's to us and a quiet evening at home together."

He lifted his glass and she responded, then decided there would be no better time than this. She sipped her wine and said, "I just heard last night, as I was leaving, that the boy's father is going to join us for Thanksgiving."

There was no big reaction. Arthur merely asked, "What is it he does again, a salesman of some kind?"

"He sells panty hose, of all things. And he looks just like the typical flashy, shallow salesman. If he tried to sell you something, I'm sure you'd laugh. He's just so transparent."

"Just like his product?" Arthur joked. He leaned back and stretched his legs toward her, toying with the cuff of her slacks with the toe of his shoe. "Y' don't like the bum, eh?"

From the tone of that and Arthur's general look of total relaxation Helen surmised he was getting drunk. So am I, she realized suddenly. "Nope, I don't. I like you, and he's not like you at all."

"How about opening another bottle?" Arthur asked. Without waiting for an answer he scurried away from the fireplace and went to the wet bar in the corner. The clink of bottles seemed to Helen a warm and cozy sound. It was good to be with Arthur tonight, and to find him so agreeable about Charles Banning. She relaxed and looked about the room. This was her base, and she needed it tonight more than she had realized. The deep shag carpet, the panelled walls and the soft melodies from the stereo as Arthur turned it on near the bar all wrapped themselves around her with the feel of a familiar and beloved old dressing gown.

As Arthur returned with the wine Helen moved from the leather chair to the velvet couch. She stretched out on her side and slipped her feet out of her shoes as he approached, grinning.

"How about a fire?"

"Perfect," she replied as she carefully balanced her wine glass, sitting up slightly. She watched as he opened the fire screen and went about preparing the paper and kindling beneath the logs. How neat he is, Helen thought, not in a fussy, perfectionistic way, but just naturally and easily neat about his person and his life in general. As she watched his movements of striking the match and efficiently nursing the small flame to sudden growth, she felt a wave of appreciation for his patience and acceptance of Jimmy.

"Thank you, Arthur. I love you so much."

"Amazing what a little fire will do."

"You know I don't mean the fire. I mean for everything, and especially for accepting Jimmy into our life."

He placed the log at precisely the right angle for a good, slow-burning fire and carefully pulled the chain to close the wire mesh of the fire screen. His face glowed in the light of the flame showing that while he was silent he was thinking deeply about something.

"I've been wanting to talk this way for a long time, Helen. We need to talk." He sat on the floor, leaning his back against the leather chair. The leather squeaked beneath the weight of his back, and the silence seemed suddenly heavy between them as he stretched his legs out toward the crackling fire.

"What is it?" she asked, knowing instinctively that she would have to help him disclose what he was thinking.

"I just wonder, that's all. About a lot of things."

"Jimmy and me? Life in general? What?"

"We're different in some ways, Helen. I'll tell you what I mean by that. I've been thinking about it, and—it has to do with—with what a person wants out of life."

"You can be so indirect at times, Arthur. I can't tell whether you're groping for a way of telling me something, or being—I don't know, too careful of my feelings."

"I'm forty-two years old, Helen. My life is what I have made it, what I want it to be. I'm content. That's what I'm trying to say. I feel complete. I have you, my home, my daughter, my work and friends, and I'm happy. I know it sounds a bit old-fashioned these days, but I'm damn happy with my life."

He stopped there as if she must know exactly what he was leading up to. Helen felt herself tensing for some kind of criticism or blame.

"Arthur, please don't think I'm not happy, if that's what you're saying. Or do you still think I'm just restless? Do you think my involvement with Jimmy is just a meaningless little fling of some kind?" Her voice was rising in spite of her efforts to remain calm.

His tone continued to be cool and rational. "It's just that we're different. I can't figure out what you want any more. I'm not trying to be critical. It's just that I really don't know."

"You're afraid I'm changing."

"Maybe that's it. Are you?"

"I don't know. Maybe I am. Would that be so terrible? People do change. They grow, they learn new things, they develop new interests. They do if they're alive."

She saw him wince, and his quick smile was not convincing. "Ah, that's the current philosophy, isn't it. I don't think people change, not really. I think things they've kept inside for years suddenly come out, or tendencies they've had all along suddenly blossom into full bloom. But change?" There was bitterness in his voice. He was growing remote and tense.

"What is it, Arthur? I feel I've hurt you in some way, and I don't know how. All I've done is to take an interest in another human being, a child, Arthur! All I've done is to respond to his need for me, his love for me. I haven't taken time from you or from our daughter. I haven't really neglected this house or anything else that matters. How are you being hurt by my love for Jimmy? I would like you to tell me."

She was on her feet now, pacing, suddenly uncomfortable on the couch and too warm near the fire. Arthur remained seated, his legs stretched toward the hearth, staring into the brightly burning flames.

His voice was a bit too deeply laced with patience as he said quietly, "Did I say I was being hurt? You said that. I am just saying that you want something in life that I can't seem to give you."

She should have known that would be it. It was Arthur's way of being possessive. It was the one thing they had struggled with, one way or another for twenty years. Arthur wanted always to be able to be everything Helen wanted and needed. It made him dear and deeply caring and thoughtful; it also tended to make her life revolve totally in the orbit of Arthur Long. She had finally resigned herself to accepting that kind of affection over the two decades of her marriage, and had even come to think of it as protective and loving on his part. Tonight that possessiveness entered the room like an alien presence, sending a chill through her body.

"You can't be my whole life, Arthur. Not any more than I can be all of your life. We've made full circle, haven't we? Remember the second year of our marriage, when I first said I wanted a child? You felt then that I wasn't satisfied with you alone. We worked our way through that and had Sharon. Then when I wanted to take a job five years ago, no, you wouldn't have it. It was the same story—I wasn't content with you alone.

The same thing about my going back to school—and now this."

"This is not the same thing, Helen."

"It is. The same thing. I hoped I would never have to face it again, Arthur. I almost came to accept it as right, or if not right, at least the best I could expect, for a time. But I do not accept it now Arthur. I am not going to give into it this time. I am not going to see it as love and tenderness and somehow boyishly cute any more. It isn't cute! It is selfish and demanding and childish!"

"What are we talking about? Just because I don't want you to change? Because I happen to think our life here is pretty good and don't want it spoiled?"

"Spoiled? Not for me, for you. Is that it? It's your life that is important, your beautiful, neat and tidy little life! But if there isn't enough room in your life for me to show love for Jimmy, if there's no room for me to go to that boy and help him go through the hell he suffers every day of his life, if what I'm finding with him, the happiness that comes when I can make him happy, the warmth I feel when we reach some new understanding—if all that spoils your little packaged, happy housefrau image of your dear little Helen, then I'm not your dear little Helen anymore, and you darn well better get used to it!"

Arthur snatched up the wine bottle and the two glasses and marched them to the bar where he rattled them noisily, putting them away. Helen found herself reeling as she stared into the fire, knowing she had said far more than she'd intended, wondering vaguely where she had gotten the courage, and hoping it was not entirely the wine.

From the bar came the sound of a final spray of water from the tap followed by the noise of the sink swallowing, then Arthur's voice. "It isn't the same thing, Helen. I've gotten over a lot of those feelings I had years ago. I know it looks to you like the same thing, but it isn't. I'd like a chance to explain."

Happy for the chance to continue talking, to be able to hope for some kind of reconciliation after her outburst, Helen assured him, "Yes, please. And don't put that wine away. I want some more." She returned to the couch.

He returned with a glass for her, none for himself. He handed it to her and after a moment's hesitation, sat down beside her. "I ought to get you drunk more often," he grinned. "You really open up."

"Don't think it's just the wine. I meant every word of that."

He thought that over and nodded decisively. "Okay, good. Now let me have my say."

"Please do. Tell me it isn't just possessiveness, Arthur. I want very much to believe that."

"I am very proud of you for what you're doing. Don't you know that? I am. How could any man in his right mind not appreciate a woman who would see a child like that and respond the way you have—totally and beautifully."

It sounded lovely, and confusing. She set the wine aside after one sip, now wanting a clear head, if possible.

"Go on. I need to hear that."

"Do you think I'm surprised that the boy could be so attracted to you? It's no mystery to me why he picked you out on that beach. I know what he saw in you, Helen. It's what I have seen all along, and loved for twenty years. You are a very special lady."

"Oh God, Arthur, how I need to hear you say that tonight. Even if it's not very accurate."

"See. That's what you do. It is accurate, Helen. You just don't know the impact you have on people."

"You always say that, Arthur, and I can't see it at all."

"I've always felt a little outclassed by you, you know that."

"Arthur, no . . ." He looked so pathetic now and boyish that she took his hand and shook it as if to waken him saying, "Remember that I picked you, too."

Arthur continued, "Let me finish, dear. My problem is I'm always running scared. I don't always tell you, but the economy, my job, everything always seems like it's just ready to come down on me. Maybe it's my age."

"You're only forty-two years old, Arthur!"

"Okay—and that's not young, not any more. But, Helen, the way I feel about you, it's like you I can count on. Everything else can change, but you're there. You're my anchor. And I need that, Helen. I need to feel you aren't changeable like everything else in my life. I need to know our love, our home, all this is going to be here no matter what."

"I'm not going anywhere, Arthur. I need you, too, just the same way you need me." She leaned toward Arthur as he reached for her. There was something desperate in the way he clutched her, a hunger that reminded her in a way of Jimmy, and deep inside she responded in a fashion that was surprisingly intense. She wanted no more conversation, nothing that might spoil their closeness. Quietly she slipped a pillow from behind her back and dropped it to the floor as he held her.

He noticed the movement and drew away with a look of puzzlement. "What are you doing?"

She slipped from the couch to the floor and stretched out at his feet before the quietly smouldering fire. "Remember the first year we were married, Arthur? That funny little gas fireplace in the apartment?"

He slid to his knees beside her, his hand brushing the hair from her forehead, "The last time we did this your back ached for a week," he said.

Helen turned slightly so he could see the cushion she had dropped to the carpet. "But this time I've got a pillow."

Arthur came to her with a light in his eyes that had not been there for a very long time. But as they began to make love there was still tension in his voice as he said, "Helen, what in the world has gotten into you?"

I'm alive, she thought. For the first time in too many years.

CHAPTER FIFTEEN

Helen maneuvered her car off the busy Pacific Coast Highway, wondering if there were ever a day in Southern California when the highways and freeways were not crowded. She looked forward to Thanksgiving Day with Jimmy and to the happy task of preparing him a real feast.

In the carport next to the beach house Charles Banning's red Mercedes sat gleaming in the morning light. She parked beside it and noticed that Jessica's tired little blue Volkswagen had been shoved aside and parked out next to the traffic to make room for Charles's car. Like him, she thought, to make Jessica take the spot by the road.

"Jimmy's gone off with his dad," Jessica informed her. "And don't you look nice. I like that outfit. I wish I was tall like you. The way you wear clothes, umhum!"

Helen had not given the outfit much thought that morning, but she'd felt such a burst of energy and anticipation when she woke up that she had put on a nearly new pants suit of deep burgundy and gray that Arthur had picked out for her for one of Katie's parties. "You seem cheerful enough this morning, Jessica," she said in reply.

They worked happily over the preparations for the meal, both of them trying to make it extra special. The turkey, by prior agreement, was Helen's assignment, while Jessica was to take care of dessert and a special sweet potato dish her mother claimed she got in a dream, directly from heaven. "The angel Gabriel came down in a white robe and wearing a chef's hat, Mama said, and just laid the recipe on her, like the Ten Commandments. My mama was a kick," Jessica laughed. "You would have loved her."

Two hours later, with the turkey cooking at low heat, breast-down on a rack in the oven, "just the way my mama taught me," as Helen had informed Jessica, both women stepped out on the porch for a breath of air and a cup of coffee.

The November air was cool even though the sun was bright and the sky clear. "Not a soul in sight," Jessica said as they scanned the beach for Jimmy and Charles. "Good. I'd just like to put my feet up and lay back in the sun."

Jessica stretched out in one of the lounges and closed her eyes. Helen didn't feel like sitting at all. Somehow the night's conversation and love-making with Arthur had given her new zest. She felt freer about being with Jimmy now, able to concentrate all her energies on him.

"How's Jimmy today?" she suddenly remembered to ask. "I've been so wrapped up in the kitchen. Any change?"

Jessica kept her eyes closed. "No change."

It was not good news, but it was not bad news, either. No change meant the drug was holding to some extent. It meant he was not as energetic as before, but still able to get around. It meant, sadly, that he still reacted with nausea for most of the day after he took the pills.

As if she'd read Helen's mind, Jessica said, "I think he'll be able to eat, though. I'd hate to think we went to all that trouble just for ourselves."

When Charles and Jimmy had still not returned a half-hour later, Helen walked down the steps to see how Jimmy's wounded little gull, Charlie, was doing.

She walked under the porch, ducking her head beneath the heavy wooden beams that crossed between the huge telephone pole sections that held the porch up. How solid the house seemed when viewed from under there. She vaguely wondered if Jimmy had actually picked out the house himself, the way he had picked her. It seemed strange to her that Charles Banning would have let the boy make such a decision. The man must be very wealthy, she thought, or very easy about money. Yet Jimmy had made a good choice, if it was his. The house was not new, but it had a solid, honest kind of strength to it you could feel when you walked around inside it. It had substance, a kind of integrity that Helen had come to love. It was neat and honest, like Arthur. It wasn't as showy or flashy as the other houses on the beach, but she had the feeling it would outlast all of them.

The gull was walking around in its cage and watching her with a bright-eyed nervousness Helen attributed to good health. The listless look was gone from its round little eyes and it no longer held the injured wing low and away from its side as it had a few days ago. Jimmy had tended to Charlie's welfare with fanatical devotion, and his patient work was getting results. The bird's food cup was half empty, indicating that Jimmy had faithfully fed it, and also that Charlie was eating. The water dish was full. The bird's eyes appeared very bright and it paced the cage constantly, looking toward the sea. She knew the time was coming when they would have to turn it loose and wondered how Jimmy would react.

As Helen emerged from under the porch she caught sight of Charles far down the beach. He was striding toward the house, walking in the firm footing of the damp sand at the water's edge. And he was carrying Jimmy in his arms.

She hurried out to where she could see Jessica up on the porch and found Jessica standing, watching Charles with one hand on the porch rail and the other toying nervously with the tiny gold cross she wore at her throat. Helen began walking toward Charles as fast as she could in the stubborn sand.

She was relieved to find Charles smiling and Jimmy conscious, with both arms clutching his father's neck. "It's all right," Charles said, "he's just a bit tired. We walked all the way down to the pier to watch the big ships."

He set Jimmy down on his feet and the boy grinned up at Helen with that dazzling smile he could turn on at a moment's notice. "We put dimes in that big telescope out there and we saw a girl swimming off one of the boats with no clothes on!"

"Was she pretty?" Helen asked.

"I don't know. I couldn't see her face that well," was Jimmy's reply. Then he walked from her side toward his father again. Helen saw that he was favoring his right leg more than ever. It had become a definite limping movement now.

Charles was chuckling quietly over the boy's comment on the girl. He winked at Helen. "She was very pretty. A blond—all over." She felt herself blushing and angry that he enjoyed making her uncomfortable.

Helen played with Jimmy for a while as he rested in his room after the long walk. Charles had brought him three jigsaw puzzles, large ones that required the setting up of a card table in the bedroom. The room was small, with space enough for Jimmy's double bed and a small dresser and not much room left over for anything else. With the card table set up Jimmy perched crosslegged on his bed and Helen managed to squeeze in a canvas director's chair next to the closet door. They busied themselves with sorting out the pieces that looked easiest to put in, those with straight sides that would make up the picture's outside edges. The picture showed several cans of vegetables of some popular commercial brand. Not a very inspiring task, Helen felt, but Jimmy went about his work with enthusiasm. He snatched and clawed his way toward straight-edged pieces as if he were being timed.

In his haste he knocked the box toward the edge of the card table and Helen just managed to save it from spilling the pieces to the floor. "What's the hurry?" she asked.

"I want to get as much of it together as I can before tomorrow."

"We can take it to the hospital if you want."

"No, I want it to stay here, so I can come back to it."

Planning. He was always planning things, even what to do when he returned. Maybe it was Jimmy's way of assuring himself that he would return. She wanted to ask him, but her train of thought was interrupted as she became aware of Charles passing the door of the room and going to the telephone that stood on a small table in the corner of the adjoining living room. Jimmy went on digging for puzzle pieces, apparently content not to explain his feelings any further. After a moment she heard Charles laugh.

"Hello, Sherry, what did I catch you doing this time?"

Charles was talking to a woman. Helen could tell by the tone of his voice, intimate and flirtatious.

"Oh, you better believe it, sweetheart. It was a great trip money-wise, but a drag without you, baby."

She quickly glanced toward Jimmy and found him oblivious to the whole thing, concentrating on putting a corner group of pieces together. The tip of his tongue protruded from the right corner of his mouth as he tried to force two pieces together that just weren't meant to match.

She forced her attention away from Charles and his phone-mate. "Not those two, Jimmy. Look at the shapes again."

He tried again to force the two to join and the piece he held in his fingers suddenly bent. "The dumb thing!" he yelled and swept his hand to the side to throw the piece away. His hand hit the box and knocked the whole jumble of its contents to the floor.

His eyes turned immediately to her and his lips formed a hard line of angry defiance.

They had been through something like this before. Now he would cajole and plead and storm to get her to pick it up. "Jimmy, pick it up. All of it," she said, forcing herself to discipline him though everything in her commanded her to drop to her knees and relieve the child of the task.

"No. I don't have to. You do it."

"We've talked about this before, Jimmy. It's not good for people to have others do their cleaning up when they've made a mess."

"I don't care. I'm not going to do it. I'm tired. Dad had to carry me all the way back from the pier."

"Yes. And when he put you down you were able to walk well enough to climb the steps and come in here and jump up on the bed. So, I don't think you're all that tired."

His eyes searched her face for any sign of giving in. Slowly the line around his mouth began to soften and she knew she was right, he had been trying to con her again. Then Jimmy's eyes suddenly shifted to the doorway of the room where Charles Banning was standing.

"What's going on, Helen?" Charles asked, and his voice was edged with tension. He had apparently heard and seen enough to know.

"She wants me to pick all that up by myself, Dad."

Helen tensed, feeling caught in the middle and more than a little betrayed by Jimmy. Charles leaned his shoulder against the doorframe and smiled. "Well, Helen's probably right. I'll tell you what, Helen. Jessica needs your help in the dining room. I'll take charge here."

Relieved and a little surprised at the show of support, Helen slipped out of the chair. Jimmy stared at her in silence, then watched closely as his father sat down where Helen had been sitting. Charles had his back to Helen and she could only judge what might be transpiring by Jimmy's reactions. The look on Jimmy's face could only have been interpreted as one of smug satisfaction.

In the dining room Jessica looked up in surprise as Helen asked what she could do to help. "I'm all set in here. What's four plates and a little silverware?" Sensing something amiss in Helen's blank stare, she went on. "What is it?"

Helen took her aside into the kitchen. "Jimmy and I were having one of our little battles about his knocking the puzzle all over the floor and not wanting to pick it up. His father came in and said you needed my help."

Jessica shook her head and turned away. "That man. Did you believe that bit about Jimmy needing to be carried all the way back from the pier?"

"It didn't strike me as one hundred percent true, no."

With resignation in her voice, Jessica said, "Mr. Banning'll pick up the puzzle, too. If I was you I'd work around him, Helen. He spoils the boy, but you have to remember he's not with him a lot."

"I'm going to talk to him about it. It's not the kind of attitude Mr. Banning is going to appreciate in his son a few years from now."

Jessica opened the oven door and checked the thermometer that jutted from the turkey's thigh. "He doesn't think a few years from now will be a problem, remember?"

In spite of everything the dinner was a resounding success. Jimmy seemed suddenly famished and ate a plateful of turkey, dressing, sweet potatoes, broccoli, and salad with two extra portions of cranberry sauce. Charles Banning beamed upon all of them like a merry head of the family, bent on creating a mood of jolly celebration. He told stories of his travels that kept them all laughing. The tales all had the same theme of reckless adventure and bawdy fun including the colorful characters that made up his world of salesmen. Jimmy was holding his sides with tears of merriment streaking down his cheeks by the time dessert arrived, amid a tale of some length about a caper in Ibiza.

"So Mort had retired to Ibiza and wanted, of all things, to grow strawberries. So, Sam and Mort and I went down to a nursery there and the salesman really laid it on thick about these great strawberry plants he had. They were the greatest. They'd grow almost overnight, he said. With the soil and the climate on Ibiza, he claimed Mort would have giant strawberry plants in no time. Now nobody can be conned by a salesman quite like another salesman, that's a fact. It's an occupational hazard. So we're listening and we're watching Mort's face and he's buying the whole story. So we went back to Mort's place with the back end of his pickup truck loaded with strawberry plants. They were about six inches—about this high." And he measured off the height of the plants for Jimmy, whose eyes were glued on his father's face with a smile already dawning in anticipation of the punchline.

"So that evening, after Mort had made us help him set out the plants, Sam and I got together. We thought we'd play a trick on Mort, so we made some excuse, I forget what, and went downtown that night about ten o'clock. We found the nursery guy, got him out of a local pub, and made him sell us some really big plants he had where he'd been growing some berries of his own. And they were big, about this tall!" He lifted his hand two feet off the table. "We went back to Mort's place, took all the new little plants out of the ground and put in those great big ones. Then we went to bed. The next morning we managed to convince Mort he ought to take a look at his plants to see if they'd survived being transplanted, right? So we go over to the garden with him and when he sees the size of those plants, I'm telling you his eyes bulged right out of his head! He kept looking at them and saying, 'My God, the guy was right!' We had old Mort going for half a day before he figured out what we'd done to him."

Jimmy screamed with laughter and made his father repeat the look that was on his friend Mort's face when he saw the plants. Charles bulged out his eyes and gaped with his mouth and Jimmy roared with delight. Jessica was holding her sides and kicking her feet against the floor under the table, and Helen found herself aching with laughter.

The mood of dinner carried over through the time the table was cleared, with Charles Banning actually asking Jimmy to bring the dessert plates to the kitchen. As Jimmy set the plates down, though, his face turned suddenly pale and he hurried to the bathroom, where he lost most of his dinner. Charles rushed after him and stood by the door and his face underwent a total change. The great, loose grin was gone, replaced by a tight-lipped expression of deep revulsion. His glance to Helen who stood in the doorway to the kitchen was heavy with what almost amounted to rage.

Jimmy was put to bed, the dishes were washed, and Helen began to wonder if she should return home to Arthur. They had planned another quiet evening, with Arthur to share in the leftovers from Jimmy's banquet. He had been very understanding about not being invited even when she'd told him that Charles would be there.

Helen walked into the small living room and found Charles and Jessica watching a football game on the large color TV set. Jessica was totally wrapped up in it, while Charles seemed distracted. He paused every few minutes to sip from a large brandy glass and his attention would wander from the TV screen. He would scan the wall behind the TV set, or stare listlessly out the front windows toward the sea.

Helen moved toward one of the chairs near Jessica and his attention fixed itself on her. "That's a pretty outfit, Helen. And that was a great dinner. Thanks."

"I enjoyed doing it. Jessica did more than her half."

Charles fixed his eyes on hers for a brief moment and looked away, the smile that always seemed so ready to reach out and grab anyone he wanted to charm suddenly fading. As he stared at the game he said, "This game stinks. I need a walk on the beach. Any takers?"

Jessica waved him away with a broad smile, "There are a lot of my people in them uniforms. It wouldn't be right for me not to care which ones are gonna get creamed."

He chuckled and turned questioningly to Helen.

"Yes," she said. "I could use a walk, too. Let me get my sweater."

Helen felt a slight twinge of guilt about the time as she slipped into the sweatshirt she had started keeping at the beach house for her walks with Jimmy. She zipped it up to the throat and left the hood down, thinking, I should be going back, but I need to talk to Charles about Jimmy.

Since dinner and Jimmy's sudden onslaught of nausea Charles Banning had been a different man. His somber mood continued as they walked silently down the porch steps and across the sand.

Helen ventured to say, "I wanted to talk to you about what happened with the puzzle."

"Forget it. I got him to clean it up, with a little help." He trudged on beside her for a few steps and stopped. "You think Jimmy's going to live, don't you?"

She swallowed and hesitated, confronted suddenly with the very heart of the issue she felt to be a barrier between them. Carefully, she said, "I haven't been through all you've been through with him. But is it wrong to hope? Isn't it better than . . ."

"Than giving up? I'm not sure. I'm not great on theory. Let's keep walking."

He took her upper arm in his hand and his grip was almost rough as he led her a few steps toward the surf. Then, as if realizing suddenly that he was manhandling her, he dropped his hand. "It just makes me mad. Something in me boils every time I look at him. When I see him sick like that I want to hit something, or someone. I don't suppose you'd understand that. Jimmy's ten years old. He has pain that would turn me into a gibbering lunatic, pain I can't reach. When he suffers I feel so damn helpless I hate myself for being alive and well. I'm his father and I can't help him."

She wanted to say he couldn't blame himself for Jimmy's pain. She wanted to tell him that what Jimmy needed from him was just what she'd seen at the dinner table, and the love she knew the man had for his son. But the man's suffering, though of a different sort, was no less intense than the boy's, and it set him apart from Helen. She felt unworthy to instruct him.

"What you're doing, Helen, that's great. I can see a big difference in his attitude and in his behavior, thanks to you. Me—I have to get away from it. It's not that I would ever leave him, like his mother. But I do have to maintain some contact with reality. I would go down the bottle around here in about three days."

He was admitting a weakness, not asking for sympathy or even for understanding. He was just being honest with her. Helen tried to focus on the track of the conversation by getting back to, "I don't think I could function at all without some kind of hope. Not that he's going to live forever, or even for five years, but that he is going to live, and while he lives he should have something like a normal life."

"You have to do what you have to do, Helen. Jimmy picked you out and as far as I'm concerned this is all between you and him. I'll try not to interfere. We all have to do our thing. When Virginia, his mother, left, I had a hell of a time accepting it until I thought, somewhere in her genes or in her horoscope or in her potty training, whatever—somehow the way she got put together, that's the way she came out—a woman who couldn't come through the one time in her life when she was really needed." He stopped talking suddenly and plunged his hand into his hip pocket. He opened his wallet and took out a color photograph, stopped and handed it to her.

"That's Virginia."

Virginia Banning was breathtakingly lovely. She had the perfect features, the golden hair and flawless skin of a fashion model. She projected an air of serene superiority that made Helen think immediately of royalty.

"Her mother was Hungarian," he explained. "That picture, believe it or not, doesn't do her justice." It was said without enthusiasm, a bald statement of fact. Helen returned the photograph feeling she had acquired, in looking at it, some small sense of what Charles Banning had lost. He pocketed his wallet and looked away toward the ocean.

For the rest of their walk Charles turned on his salesmanly charm and told her stories. It was as if with the presentation of Virginia's likeness he had explained everything that needed explaining.

Driving home to be with Arthur, Helen looked back on the conversation on the beach and discovered that, for her, the mystery had only deepened. What was the connection between Virginia's leaving him, and Charles's giving up on Jimmy? She found herself wishing she could meet Virginia Banning in person. Was she so devastating that a man might give up on life entirely over losing her? Maybe a truly beautiful woman could have such an effect on a man, but she had her doubts. For all his charm Charles Banning didn't seem to her to qualify for the kind of romantic role that scenario called for. He didn't seem to be pining away for love. What about that phone call to Sherry and that trip he said was such a drag without her? Charles Banning was an enigma. No wonder Jessica had told her, "I'm not going to try to explain Mr. Banning. You've got to figure that one out for yourself."

Helen concluded that would take some doing.

CHAPTER SIXTEEN

"Marty's full name is Martin Luther King Taylor. He was born in February of 1968 right after the great man was killed." The cheerful black man Helen had met on her first visit to the hospital was standing with her just outside his son's room.

Helen stared at the plastic screen that surrounded the boy's bed within the special quarters his father had called "a laminar air-flow room." It was like a plastic bubble, and it lent to the room and the brave child alone within it an air of emergency, though the father seemed calm enough. Earlier she had seen him come out in a sterile gown, which a nurse removed and carried away. The man's toothy smile had not faded even though his son seemed to be battling for his life.

"We've got a habit in our family of naming everybody, boys and girls, after some important person. I'm F.D.R. Taylor. We usually end up with more initials than people consider kosher. Like my grandfather, named after W.E.B. DuBois!"

He grinned at his son, gave him a hang-in-there signal with his fist, then turned away. Helen walked with him toward the waiting room where they had first met six weeks ago.

"That room," Helen asked. "What's it for?"

"When the white cell count goes down, like it does with most leukemia, it leaves the patient wide open to infection. That room's as clean as modern science can make it. It'd be a damn shame to be beating the leukemia and have him chopped down by a cold or the flu, wouldn't it? He's gonna be fine, though, just fine. This is just a precaution. How's Jimmy doing?"

"I haven't heard yet. They're taking some X-rays."

At that moment she saw Charles Banning lounging near the nurses' station at the juncture of the two wide corridors that led into and past the children's ward. While Charles appeared to regale the nurses with one of his tales, a very tall doctor in a white gown was standing nearby at the very center of the intersection of the two corridors, talking to a lovely young Oriental woman with several files and a clipboard tucked under one of her arms. Charles finally caught sight of Helen and sauntered toward them with a wide grin.

"Hi, Taylor. How's Marty?" he asked as he shook hands with her companion.

"A little down right now and very mad. He thinks the coach is gonna replace him."

"Coach?" Helen asked.

"Marty's on the school swimming team," Charles explained. Then he patted the man on the shoulder. "How can they replace their star?"

"That's what I keep telling him. They'll get this new drug balanced out right and he'll be back in there in no time. What's this about X-rays for Jimmy?"

"A little problem with loss of feeling in one leg. Would you excuse us? I see you've met Helen."

"Oh, it's Helen? We haven't really been introduced." He nodded toward her and Helen immediately extended her hand.

"Helen Long. It's been nice talking to you—which one of your initials do you go by?"

"Frank. See you later."

He turned into the waiting room and Charles walked beside her toward the tall doctor who was now coming to meet them. Helen filed away that bit of information about Marty being in school—and on the swimming team. How about that!

Charles introduced her to the doctor who turned out to be the radiologist. His name was Lundquist.

"We have the pictures in here." He led the way to a small room adjacent to the X-ray lab. They entered and he pointed to three negatives lit by a glowing green light. Jimmy's lower back region was seen from three angles. How tiny and delicate the bones are, Helen thought. How vulnerable Jimmy suddenly seemed. Any idea of his being a swimming star like Marty began to fade as the radiologist talked.

"We took a myleogram. A die is injected into the system enabling us to photograph tissue we want to inspect. We were looking for something like this." He used a small pointer to indicate a dark shadow directly over the spinal cord.

"Is it a tumor?" Helen asked.

"No. It's a blood clot on the cord. You can see an area of compression on the cord itself. The result of local hemorraging. Dr. Jacoby will want to tell you himself . . . Ah, here he is now."

Helen had met Jimmy's chief physician during the hospitalization in October. A rotund little gnome of a man with a shining bald head and an energetic manner, Dr. Jacoby looked like a happy little Buddha who had spent too many hours in the sun. He was as red as a boiled lobster. Today he seemed more businesslike than she remembered him. His glance snapped from her face to Charles.

"Not good. Not good. You've seen these?" His arm swept toward the green glow of the displayed negatives in their cases.

"Yes," Charles answered. "How bad is it?"

The doctor's quick little eyes flicked toward Helen again and softened. He was checking to see if she was prepared and able to handle an apparently terrible piece of news.

"Jimmy will be—all right?" Helen blurted out. "He can be operated on?"

A signal passed between the head physician and the radiologist and the tall man slipped out, closing the door behind him. Dr. Jacoby shut off the green lights behind the translucent sheets of X-ray film, rendering them suddenly gray and lifeless.They seemed ever more threatening, somehow.

"The operation will have to wait until we can build him up a bit. He'll need a better red cell count and a lot more protection in the way of white cells. We'll go with whole-blood transfusions. A few days in the hospital to get him started, followed by a couple of weeks at home that I hope you can make some of the happiest, most active days of his life. He should be feeling well enough for the operation then."

He paused and Charles immediately asked, "It's very serious then?"

"Any operation on a leukemia patient is serious. The real problem is we have to drain off that infected area before real damage is done to both legs. If we let it go Jimmy will become a paraplegic, totally paralyzed from the waist down."

"It can be cured then?" Helen interjected hopefully.

"There is a very good chance we can save enough of the spinal cord to prevent paralysis, but he may lose the use of his right leg. It's almost certain he will."

For the remainder of the morning Helen was benumbed with shock. She managed somehow to get through an hour at Jimmy's bedside, chatting with him about the next several days when he would be receiving transfusions, resolving his worries about the condition of his wounded friend Charlie the seagull, promising to bring his vegetable puzzle to the hospital and thanking God that Jimmy showed no curiosity about the X-ray results.

Jessica arrived at noon, was told the news and volunteered to stay with Jimmy while Charles and Helen went out for lunch. Charles took her by the arm and led her past the nurses' station and a cluster of hospital volunteers chatting beside a lunch cart.

"No hospital cafeteria for you today," he ordered.

"You come with me. We're having a good lunch and then I'm taking you back to your car and you're going home."

She followed silently as Charles led her across the hospital parking lot to the Mercedes. With a prayer for forgiveness for past things she'd thought about the car, she sank into its luxurious white leather embrace with a grateful sigh. She glanced toward Charles as he maneuvered the car out of the parking space and across the lot. He was seething with that same rage she had seen at the beach house.

He turned right on Wilshire Boulevard, cursed the traffic and drove westward toward the ocean as if possessed with an urge to kill. Helen watched the speedometer climb to sixty in the spaces he found between clusters of cars and it seemed never to drop below fifty even in the heaviest traffic. Helen reached for her seatbelt and began buckling herself in.

Charles said, "Some kind of choice we've got." He slammed his fist against the car horn and drove a woman pedestrian with a shopping cart back to the curb in such haste a bag of apples tipped over in her cart. As they flew past the apples rolled into the street and the round little woman yelled something.

" 'A fire of zie treffen?' " was that what she yelled?" Helen asked.

Charles grinned for the first time and the car slowed to something less than breakneck speed. "Probably it's Yiddish. May the fires of hell entrap you, or something like that. Sorry about my driving. I told you how all this makes me feel."

Helen nodded, keeping one eye on the road ahead. Charles slowed the car even further and seemed to relax. She said, "Do you want to talk about it?"

"Not until I've had a drink."

He chose a restaurant that overlooked the ocean and they were shown to a table outdoors on a redwood terrace shaded by a yellow and white umbrella. Helen asked for white wine and sipped it while Charles drank a double vodka martini and ordered a second. As a bored-looking Mexican-American waiter sauntered away to fill the order Charles said that being able to put away quantities of booze was a prerequisite to the trade of the salesman. Then, he added, "I think the world stinks, Helen Long. It's not just a tale told by an idiot, as a very brainy writer once said: it's a tale told by a cruel idiot. Now don't get frightened. I'm not going to become maudlin and cry on your shoulder, or dangerous either. Unfortunately for you, when I drink I get philosophical."

"Why don't we stop evading the subject, Mr. Banning? I may cry. I may start screaming and throwing things. I'm mad too. But that doesn't change anything, does it? Jimmy has to have the operation to prevent being paralyzed for the rest of his life."

"It could shorten his life. In fact it probably will." The waiter returned with the martini and Charles stared at it without touching it. "It doesn't really matter what we do."

Helen swallowed an angry response and got herself under control. Then she expressed her honest opinion. "I think Jimmy should be told about it and be allowed to make his own decision. It's his life and it's his leg." When she said the word "leg" the table began to swim before her eyes as she envisioned Jimmy walking in the sand, dragging his useless limb. The tears came in a rush and she began to search her purse for a tissue. A clean handkerchief was pressed into her other hand by Charles. She wiped her eyes, straining to prevent the repetition of that sudden vision of Jimmy's future, and when she brought her free hand back to the tabletop, Charles grasped it and held it tightly.

"Do you still want to talk about it?" he asked gently.

"Yes, and thank you. I don't think I'll need this again." She freed her hand, aware that she was doing it with some haste. Charles took the handkerchief, folded it and returned it to his pocket.

"Jimmy," he continued quietly, "will do whatever

you tell him to do. So you have to decide. Do you want him to spend the little time he has left paralyzed, or to take the risk of the operation and end up dead—or, if we're lucky, with one bad leg?"

"I don't think you mean this. He's your son. What do you want for him?"

"Everything. I want him to play football. I want him to chase girls. I want him to go to college. I want him to marry a beautiful woman and have a house full of kids." The anger swept across his face like a cloud and he picked up his drink. When he set it down the glass was empty. "But I can't have any of those things, can I? And why not? Because in the mindless roll of the cosmic dice, Jimmy crapped out. And don't look so damned injured. I warned you, I get philosophical. I get to my true nature in which I very clearly perceive the shitty world for what it is." He looked away from her and glared across the crowded restaurant.

Helen suddenly wanted to be home with Arthur. The man sitting across from her looking sourly upon the people around them, his mouth twisted into a contemptuous sneer, made her ill. She could see none of Jimmy in him at that moment. He was not Jimmy's father, she felt, but an embittered stranger who tried to bend her vision of the world to his own. If this stranger wanted her to take responsibility for the decision about Jimmy, then take it she would.

"If I'm to decide, you know what my choice will be. Jimmy will have the operation. He'll have it in the hope that the doctors will someday find the right drug or the right combination of drugs that will stop the leukemia. In the hope and belief that Jimmy, alive and well, with one leg, is infinitely better than a whole team of football players and girl chasers, whether the world's as shitty as you say it is or not!"

And with that Helen found herself on her feet and walking out the front door. She arrived at the car and waited beside it, wondering whether he would follow or leave her to her own fate. Two minutes later the door of the restaurant swung open and Charles walked through it. He strode toward her and Helen could not tell what he was feeling. He bent down and unlocked the car door on her side, then straightened up with a sheepish smile. "Okay, Tiger," he said, "whatever you say."

As he climbed into the car beside her Charles said, "The doctor wanted Jimmy to have a great time when he comes home before the operation. Got any ideas?" The black mood of despair seemed gone, and he was Jimmy's father again.

True to his word, Charles drove her to the beach house instead of returning her to the hospital. She was grateful for his insistence that she go home and rest, though his seeming inability to relate to Jimmy well enough to tell the boy about the operation still bothered her.

"Are you saying you want me to be the one to tell him?"

"I wish you would, Helen. I don't think you appreciate fully just how Jimmy feels about you. To him you're his real mother. He's able to fantasize completely that you are exactly what he wants you to be. I think he even fantasizes about his death." He studied the road ahead as they approached the beach house, waiting for a break in the traffic so he could negotiate the turn. As the car moved forward and parked, he said, "It must be great to be able to do that—to make the world come out just the way you want it."

He was still seeing Jimmy as doomed. Depressed by it, and by the cold photographic evidence of Jimmy's problem she had seen in the hospital, Helen climbed out and began to turn away toward her car.

"Want to come in for a cup of coffee or something? We didn't eat lunch, remember? I think I'll just have another drink before I go back to the hospital."

"No, I do have some things to do at home. But thanks, Mr. Banning."

"Don't you think you know me well enough yet to

call me Charles? Or how about Chuck, or maybe Charlie?" His grin was broad and gleaming, the salesman's best. There was no doubt where Jimmy got his beguiling smile.

When she heard "Charlie", Helen remembered the ailing seagull. "Oh, I promised Jimmy I would look at Charlie to make sure he's all right."

"Good. I'll go with you. Cut through the house, it's shorter."

She followed him to the kitchen from the back entrance, through the small dining room and living room and to the front door. He opened it for her and as she passed close to him his face was near her hair.

"Nice perfume, Zen. I used to have that account. Made a lot of money on it." He continued chattering as he tramped across the porch behind her and down the stairs. Helen was suddenly conscious of his weight bearing down on her as the porch shook slightly and the stairs seemed to tremble beneath him. He was a solidly built man. She remembered the first time she had seen him crossing the sand toward her, confident and good looking. Many women would consider him handsome, those who liked that sort of flashiness and swagger.

They reached the sand and made their way under the porch toward the bird's little boxlike cage. Charles saw the gull first and stopped short. Helen could see only the bird's tail feathers, the rest hidden by the edge of the box. Charles, from a vantage point to her right was able to see the whole bird. Helen took another step and saw Charlie. He was lying on his side, and he was dead. Helen's first reaction was disbelief.

"He can't be dead! I saw him yesterday and he looked fine!" She fell to her knees and looked closely. The eye of the bird that only yesterday had appeared so bright now looked dull and lifeless like the X-rays of Jimmy's spine when the light had been turned off behind them. The shock of it now hit her full force, images of Jimmy and the gull mixing and mingling and sweeping through her, Jimmy and the gull as one, the sense of being betrayed by that gleaming round eye into believing in life and suddenly, without warning, stumbling into death, and feeling her confidence in Jimmy's future brutally shaken for the first time.

She stood quickly and felt herself swaying. Charles Banning's strong arm caught her and held her tight. She fell into his arms, weeping hot tears of shock and disappointment and anger. She felt angry at the bird, somehow.

"He shouldn't be dead! He can't be dead!" she wept.

Charles held her and seemed to understand the surge of emotion that coursed through her. As if he knew she was mourning the loss of her hope for Jimmy and seeing the boy's death in the bird's, Charles whispered, "It isn't Jimmy, Helen. It isn't Jimmy. Look up. Look at me."

He lifted her chin and made her look up at his face. Through her tears she saw his smile, and it was warm and genuine this time. "Don't stop hoping now, Helen. I need your hope. You don't know how much help you've been to me."

CHAPTER SEVENTEEN

"Helen, I think what you're doing for that boy is just magnificent. It's a wonderful thing to be involved. That's what you are, involved!"

Katie O'Donnell leaned across the table and forked another piece of turkey to her plate. Katie had questioned and prodded and coaxed until Helen had been forced to tell the whole story of Jimmy and herself and thereby give Katie's party something to chew on.

There were three couples at the O'Donnells' table, eating leftovers from Thanksgiving by mutual consent, Katie having reasoned that "beef's out of sight, and turkey is very good health food. So let's have a party on Friday night after Thanksgiving and we'll all pool our leftovers."

"What about that mother, though?" said Maureen Blaine, munching thoughtfully on a stick of celery. She was small and dark with large, lovely eyes that Helen noticed were glued a disproportionate amount of the time on Jim O'Donnell. The Blaines were younger than the other two couples. Winston, the short, fair-haired husband of Maureen, was an acquaintance of Jim's through his dentist's office, a patient who had been induced to become involved in one of Jim's real estate deals. They had discussed it earlier in the evening, the formation of some kind of "syndicate" to purchase an apartment house. Arthur seemed to be going in on it too, but Helen had lost interest in the conversation beyond that.

"Yeah, that mother must be some kind of bitch," Jim O'Donnell grunted. "To walk out on a dying kid—that takes a special kind of class."

"Now just a second," Katie mumbled through her turkey, paused to swallow, then, "Why does it have to be that way? How do we know she actually did walk out just like that, Helen?"

"Jimmy's father said it more or less that way when he told me," Helen responded. "He implied that Virginia couldn't stand to see the boy dying, that he was her whole life."

"That's weird, isn't it?" This from Winston, whose voice was so soft Helen had to strain to hear him at the other end of the table. "Why would she stay married to a man if she only cared for the boy? Why not just take the boy and divorce him? I think the two of them were probably having trouble, maybe a long time before the boy even took sick."

"That's it!" Katie shouted, in contrast to Winston's

near-whispers. "I'll bet they were already splitting up and this guy's ego is bruised. She's a beauty, right? This what's-her-name?"

"Virginia. And I've seen her picture. She's lovely, very beautiful."

"Okay, Virginia is a knockout," Katie continued. "He has lost her, maybe even to a younger man. That would do it. He's so mad he has to blame her. He has to find the worst thing he could say about her—and that's it. She ran out on a dying child. Male ego, pure and simple."

"Bullshit, Kate!" Jim shouted above her, his heavy voice almost rattling the chinaware. "Everything has to play into your fem-lib obsession. The man always has to be the villain, right? I say no way. Look who's taking care of the kid now. Look who's paying the bills. Look who's donating his own blood, for God's sake. The man has been left to do it all, and he's doing it. Have you seen any young broads around there, Helen?"

Helen recalled the phone call to Sherry but shook her head silently. The speculation going on around her was raising some questions she had not been able to voice herself. Even though it was shocking and bizarre, she wanted it to continue.

Arthur was toying with the water glass near his plate, sliding the edge of a knife up and down on its side, like a sculptor shaving the surface of a clay figure.

"From what Helen's told me," Arthur said, "I think the woman may be in a mental state. Wasn't there something about them taking the boy to a faith healer or something?"

"I'm not sure of the details, but the nurse, Jessica, she said they tried other treatments, and yes, a faith healer of some sort. To tell you the truth, the woman's part in this is a mystery to me, too."

"Maybe they tried Laetrile," Winston said quietly.

Arthur continued, picking up on that. "Laetrile, a trip to Mexico, maybe. But suppose the woman is really fragile, maybe just barely in touch with reality. Whether she's having problems with her husband or not, whether he's playing around, or even if she's playing around herself, the boy could be all that's holding her together. When she hears he's dying of leukemia, something snaps. Where is she now?"

"Now? I don't have any idea." It had never occurred to Helen to ask where Virginia was. "It seems odd, I know, but I haven't even asked. Maybe I didn't want to know—I'm not sure."

Maureen, her eyes wide and speculative, said, "It really is a mystery. All kinds of scenarios are possible. This is like that party game, isn't it, where someone tosses out an idea about something and each one adds something to the story? Haven't you ever played that? Let's try it with this!"

"Great!" Katie exploded. "You start, Maureen and Winston'll go next. We'll go right around the table and let's see—Helen, you'll have the finish. Go ahead, Maureen!"

Helen was beginning not to like this. Maureen seemed to take a ghoulish sort of pleasure from it by the look of her as she licked her lips for a moment, then said, "All right. I know a woman who was very, very beautiful and was married to a rich, attractive salesman. The man was gone on the road all the time and the only company she had was her fair young son. She loved the boy, but when her husband was gone she was very lonely. So one day . . . Okay, Winston."

"So one day," Winston's whispering voice continued, "when she was very lonely and the boy was in school, she accepted an invitation to lunch from her hairdresser, who wasn't a big macho salesman type like her husband, but a very sweet and understanding, and safe man, or so she thought. The hairdresser came on strong and the next thing you know they were in bed. This went on for several weeks and she never noticed that her boy was getting sicker and sicker. By the time the father got back from one of his long trips the boy was almost dead with leukemia. The father immediately . . . Okay, Katie."

"Oh, I don't like this a bit. Now let's see—long trip—hairdresser. Okay—the father immediately called up one of his girlfriends. Hah! Yes! A cheap little broad! And he went over and cried on her shoulder about the boy, and immediately felt better. Then he went home and took the boy—and, wait a minute! He was so mad when he learned from a friend that his wife was seeing the hairdresser, even though he had a lot of women of his own, he took the child and left her. He just walked out, and he left no forwarding address. There it is! I'll bet that's what happened! He moved the boy to this beach house and put him with that nurse, then he shacked up with one of his girlfriends! Where does he live, Helen? At the beach?"

Helen was confused. Where did Charles Banning live? "On the road, I guess. There's a spare room at the beach house, but I don't think he uses it. Maybe he has an apartment somewhere. But I don't know! All this is just speculation . . ."

"Score one for me," Katie said. "Now where was I? He's shacked up and the mother can't even find the child. That's what's really going on. The mother is looking for the boy. Now, Jim, what can you do with that?"

"That's too much. The boy could be traced because of his illness. He's had the same doctor all along, from what Helen says, and goes to the same hospital. The other kids there even know him. Let me think a second." Jim leaned back in his chair and imitated a writer staring off into space looking for inspiration, hand raised to his forehead as if in pain. Maureen giggled.

"All right. She is looking, but not very hard. In other words, the guy has solved her problem for her. She moves in with the hairdresser and says good riddance to the kid and the husband and goes on screwing."

"Ugh. God you're vulgar," Katie groaned, loving it.

"Now," Jim continued, "a little time goes by. The hairdresser gets tired of her and throws her out on her pretty little behind and she immediately thinks of money."

"I knew it would come to that," Arthur grinned.

"She lays a heavy settlement deal, with the aid of a very smart lawyer, who she also lays. This action takes the money the father needs to take proper care of the boy. So, almost destitute, the father turns to religion. He goes to a faith healer, broke and on his knees, and says, I understand you won't accept a fee, just a tax-deductible donation. Okay, Arthur, let 'em have it."

It was Arthur's turn and Helen found herself hoping he would end the game or put the whole thing back on a more serious track. The fun and games had started just when Helen felt the discussion might throw some light on things. Now it seemed cruel to continue.

"He didn't actually go to the faith healer. He only thought about it. But he was having a bit of a financial problem. His wife was suing him for a divorce—Is she, Helen?"

"I don't know about that either. Do we have to do this?"

"Back to the hairdresser," Arthur looked away from her and continued, "She tires of him and wants to go back to her husband. It wasn't that she didn't care about the boy. She had a temporary lapse because she was, or thought she was, in love. Now she isn't and wants to come back. She tries calling the house and gets a tape, all the time, saying her husband is on the road, please leave a message. She gets frantic and starts blaming the hairdresser. Then he throws her out. Without husband, child or the lover boy, she cracks up, just like I said. I really do think the woman is in a hospital somewhere. I can just feel it. I cannot believe any woman in her right mind would do what she is accused of doing."

Arthur turned to Helen as if expecting her to go on. Katie called out, "Now wait. We have to finish the game. You're not supposed to get serious about it, Arthur. You have to give Helen a funny line to pick up on."

"The game's over, Kate," Jim said loudly. "There's nothing funny about it when you stop to think of it. It's a damn crime, what that woman did. And look at Helen. The boy's dying. What the hell's funny about that?"

Jim's remarks silenced them all. He had placed it squarely in Helen's lap to decide how to get everybody out of feeling uncomfortable. Grateful to Jim, she said, "I think we've talked about it enough. There are a lot of unanswered questions about Virginia and Jimmy's father. I'm not sure how much I need to know, or how much I want to know. Something happened and Jimmy was left without a mother when he needed one very much. I came along, and I'm it. So—okay. I admit I'm curious, probably more now since all this came up tonight. But tomorrow morning I have to tell that boy he has to have an operation, and after the operation he won't be able to walk without crutches for as long as he lives. When you look at it that way, where his mother is, or where his father is living, or why she left him in the first place doesn't matter all that much. Does it?"

Arthur didn't talk about the party all the way home. He was thoughtful until they entered the house. Then he said, "I'm sorry about all that. You are one fantastic lady," and kissed her very tenderly.

CHAPTER EIGHTEEN

Jimmy felt that his mom was too distracted. She asked too many questions about how he was feeling and how many transfusions he'd had, and whether he had a good night's sleep, and how he liked his nurses, when she should have known that he'd been here so many times that none of the hospital routine mattered to him very much. He wanted to talk about some things he'd been thinking about that he couldn't say to Jessica or his father or anyone else but Helen.

"What's wrong with you?" he finally asked, hoping he might be able to get her attention and stop her looking around the room and talking about a lot of unnecessary things.

"Nothing," she said, but he could tell by her look that something was wrong.

He immediately thought of Charlie. "How's Charlie doing?"

"Jimmy . . ."

"Is Charlie sick again?"

"He's dead, Jimmy. I didn't want to tell you."

She could have lied about it. His father would have, and maybe Jessica, but she didn't. He liked that. "What did you do with him? Did you bury him?"

"Your father and I dug a little grave for him under the beach house. We put him in a shoe box and we marked the grave with two sticks we tied together to make a cross."

She was watching his face very closely as if she expected him to cry or something. He didn't feel like crying. "I'm sorry about Charlie, Mom, but I think he was in a lot of pain and he was just tired of it and wanted to rest. He's in heaven now."

"Yes," she answered. "He's a super seagull now, big as a hang glider."

"Thank you for not lying to me." She had taken his hand and there were tears in her eyes, for Charlie. She patted his hand, blinking the tears away, then dabbing at them with a Kleenex. "Don't ever lie to me, Mom. About anything. Okay? Other people do, you know. The doctors lie, and the nurses. They tell you something isn't going to hurt when it does, or it isn't going to taste bad, or it isn't going to make you as sick as the last drug they gave you. They try to make it easier by lying to me. I don't like that."

"They don't mean any harm by it."

"I don't care. I'm used to it, but I don't want you ever to lie. Promise?"

It took her a long time to get around to answering him, and he wondered why. She fidgeted with putting the tissue into her purse and closing the purse up and laying it down, and for a moment he began to wonder if she was lying about something already and couldn't figure out how to get out of it.

Finally she said it. "All right, Jimmy, I promise. I will never lie to you. Never."

Good. Now he could talk about what he'd been thinking about. "Mom, Virginia is a Catholic. My father is a Protestant of some kind. I was baptized a Catholic so I'm all right. But when I am in heaven with Virginia, my father won't be there, will he?"

She smiled quickly, then got sober again when she saw that Jimmy really meant it seriously. "God loves everyone, Jimmy, even Protestants."

"But won't they be in different parts of heaven, like they're in different churches here?"

"I don't think so."

"I've been very worried about that. You're a Catholic, aren't you?"

"No. My father was Scandinavian. Most of my people were Lutherans."

"Do you mean there's a chance, I won't see you?" A feeling of panic went through him, then quickly subsided. That couldn't be! Of course Mom would be in heaven! "Why do people say all those things about God and religion and stuff if they don't mean it! They make such a big deal, like my mother did, and when it comes down to it, God just loves everybody the same! Lies! That's what I'm talking about, Mom. There are so many lies!"

"People don't start out to tell lies about things like that, Jimmy. I really don't think they do. The different religions, maybe they're just different ways of looking at God. Some people like to see God one way, some another."

"Charlie wasn't a Catholic or a Protestant, was he? And I know he's in heaven. So I guess that's okay."

Why didn't people just always tell the truth like Helen? They were even lying about something else Jimmy knew about. He tugged on her hand and pulled her closer.

"Marty's going to die soon and they aren't telling his dad. I heard two of the nurses. He's still in the clean room and they're pretending he's going to make it, but he isn't."

She looked very surprised, and he wondered why. She said, very quietly, "Are you sure, Jimmy? His father says this is just a temporary setback. Do you know that Marty is the champion of his school swimming team? He's very strong."

What a silly thing to say! Jimmy thought. What difference did that make? "It's okay, Mom. Marty knows it. We talked about it one time when I was here. I tried to tell him not to get so mad about having to die, and he yelled at me for a long time, then just before they let him go home he came around to my room and said, just don't tell my dad. So I won't tell him, but I think the doctors should, don't you?"

What was wrong with Mom? She kept looking away from him and biting on her lower lip and looking as if she was going to cry again as if she didn't understand what it was he was trying to tell her at all. She even let go of his hand and got up from her chair beside the bed and started to walk out of the room!

"Mom?"

She stopped at the door and turned back to stare at him and she looked as if she was going to faint or something.

"I'm sorry if I upset you, Mom. I didn't know . . ."

"Jimmy. Listen to me, please." She walked back to the bed and sat down again and took both of his hands in hers. How warm her hands were!

"Jimmy, I don't know how you—how you face things the way you do. I don't understand where all of this comes from. I have some—some news for you, and it isn't good."

"It's about the X-rays, isn't it?"

"How did you know?"

"Because they took them. They don't take them unless there's something wrong. So what is it?"

"You have to have an operation. You'll be in here a while yet, and then you'll come home for a week or two, and then . . . There is something wrong with your back. That's why your leg has been feeling funny."

"It's okay. I'm not afraid of operations. They just put you to sleep and you don't feel anything at all. I've had things a lot worse than that."

"You're so brave. I don't know how you do it."

"Is that all, Mom? Just that I'm supposed to have an operation?"

She was looking into his eyes pretty hard now. He could tell she had something else to tell him. He saw her swallow and look away toward his feet.

"You probably won't be able to use your right leg any more, Jimmy. Maybe not ever."

Her eyes were pleading with him now, and he quickly said, "That's okay, Mom." Then he tried to picture in his mind what it would be like. He remembered Charlie limping along the beach dragging his wing in the sand. The worse thing was that he would look ugly, not just being crippled. How many years or months did he have ahead of him, anyhow? There wouldn't be a lot of bad days with kids laughing at him and stuff. It was just that he would look so terrible—and how it might make his mom feel about him. He studied her face for any sign of revulsion and all he found there was a loving smile that gave him a moment of hope.

"Mom, would it matter to you? It wouldn't make you leave me, would it?" His heart was beating so hard he almost couldn't hear his own voice.

"Oh, Jimmy, no! No, my darling. Nothing could make me leave you!"

Then she was holding him and hugging him tight, and he felt one of her hot tears running into his ear.

After she hugged him for a while, she pulled away with her eyes shining. "Jimmy, it will be a couple of weeks at least before the operation. Is there anything you would like to do before . . ." She seemed to need help.

"Before I can't use my leg any more?"

"Yes. There must be something very special you've always wanted, someplace you'd like to go or something you've always wanted to see. While you're still able—we'll do it. Whatever it is. We'll do it together."

When she first started saying it, nothing seemed to come to Jimmy's mind, because it was as if she was talking about taking a trip or something, but by the time she finished, he knew.

"I want to fly on a hang glider! That would be great! And don't say I can't, Mom, because I've seen other kids do it. That's what I want, and you promised! You said whatever it is, Mom, and that's it! I want to learn to fly on a hang glider and take a ride right off the cliff down to the beach! Wouldn't that be fantastic! "And you said we'd do it together!"

CHAPTER NINETEEN

With the coming of December the winter rains arrived. The sky was overcast with a gray mass of dripping clouds that seemed glued in place, so immovable and changeless were they. It had been raining halfheartedly for three days and a chill wind off the sea had kept Jimmy inside the beach house with a mood as foul as the weather, alternately staring at the soggy beach and the half-hidden tops of the cliffs as he complained about not being able to start getting his wish.

Now Helen sat in Dr. Irene Miller's small office on the college campus, gazing absently at the rain drops that coursed down the window. She had called for an appointment the day before and Dr. Miller had remembered her, showing an amazing recall of the story Helen had told her almost a month before. They had arranged for Helen to stop by the office after class the following day.

"Ach, Mrs. Long. I'm sorry to be late. The students ask so many questions after class." Dr. Miller bustled across the room and dropped a heavy notebook on the desk before she turned to Helen and extended her hand. She pumped Helen's arm vigorously. "And how is our Jimmy? Bring me up to date."

Helen told about the decline in Jimmy's condition since the last visit, about Thanksgiving, about the loss of Charlie the seagull, and about the coming operation. "And now I'm stuck. I promised him a chance to ride on a hang glider and the weather won't let up long enough to give us a chance."

Dr. Miller's round little eyes looked puzzled. "What is this hanging glider?"

Helen explained that they were like giant kites that people ride on.

"He wants an adventure then. Good for him. He's a brave boy, this Jimmy. And he accepts everything, does he not? The death of the seagull, the loss of his leg, his young friend's death as well as his own. Does this make you wonder?"

"Yes, it certainly does. I don't understand it at all. That's what I wanted to talk to you about. It doesn't seem—I don't know how to say it—realistic? It's as if he doesn't realize what these things mean, or even worse, that he's suppressing his natural reactions—trying to be too good. I think that's it, that he's trying to be just too good about it all. I think I would like to see him more rebellious somehow, fighting back more."

"Ahh, you must remember his age. Adults fight back, and teenagers, oh my, even more. They protest and defy and cry out against the horrible injustice of it all, because the adolescent has just come into his own, so to speak. He has just taken adult life in his hands and felt the glow of it, and now it is being snatched away from him. Adults have so much to leave behind, yah? But this is not the way it is with a child of Jimmy's age. They react completely differently."

"So he's all right."

"Of course he's all right! It is perfectly natural for a child. Jimmy is able to fantasize about death as no adult or teenager ever could. And you need to understand this. Most of a child's life is fantasy, is it not?"

"I haven't thought of it that way. In the hospital when we talked about his operation, he seemed so—mature about it. He was unbelievably wise and beautiful about it all, while I was just coming apart."

"He will not come apart, not about his death. I do not think that is to be expected. I think he felt, and still feels, his mother's departure far more. That is something a child can feel as part of the real world. Most of the rest of it is still a mystery. And remember what a wonderful thing it is to see the world through the eyes of childhood! The whole world is a wonderland! A child can lose himself in the contemplation of a butterfly or a seashell. The taste of a ripe, red apple, can you recall what that was like when you were small? Everything is alive in a child, all the senses. Electric! Totally aware of the feel of the wind and the passage of a cloud in front of the sun. Do you remember feeling that way as a child?"

"Oh, yes! I can still recall the smells and feelings of one special day I spent up in the attic of our house on a rainy day when I was eight or nine. Beautiful, just beautiful."

"Yah! And today it is raining, and it no longer makes the whole world feel and smell brand new, does it? No, because you and I have seen too many rainy days. We have smelled too many flowers and seen too many butterflies. But Jimmy is capable of all of this, and such a sensitive child as he, think what he sees and feels as he goes through the experiences of his own illness."

"It isn't just grim and awful to him then? That's what keeps me so fearful for him. Thinking of his suffering and the bleakness of what's ahead for him. Losing the use of his leg, having to walk on crutches . . ."

"Mrs. Long, may I say something a bit shocking? I will tell you that Jimmy is capable of living the adventure of his own death with the same verve and excitement another child might get from being lost, or another may find in being involved in a tragic accident. Their lives are not mapped out and programmed as our lives are. They are able to take it as it comes. I think you should take comfort from this. I think this is very important for you to think about."

"This is why he can talk about it all so easily?"

"Not just easily, but eagerly. He wants to share it with you. And I tell you, if the boy dies, you will be a very privileged person indeed. You will see and hear all of it, and you will share his dying, every splendid moment of it. And now I *have* shocked you."

Helen felt a chill on the back of her neck, something primitive and reflexive that whispered death should be ugly; it is not splendid but awful and unnatural. What is this woman doing, talking about dying as if it is some kind of game, some kind of trip to the park for her and Jimmy to share? A taste, bitter as gall, rose in her throat.

"I—I'm sorry, Dr. Miller. In the first place I am not ready to say Jimmy is going to die. And in the second place—I just can't see it that way. I just can't. It is a horrible thing to me that Jimmy has to be ill at all. And to think of—of what you're talking about . . ."

"Mrs. Long, may I tell you a story?" Dr. Miller raised one bushy eyebrow in question, and did not wait for Helen to answer. "Many years ago, before I became so deeply involved in my present work, I began to practice medicine in Vienna. After about a year, one of my patients who had been admitted to the hospital for routine surgery turned out to have cancer. It happens all the time. To me it was a personal disaster. I, the great Doctor Miller, was about to be beaten by death. When I got over the shock to my exaggerated sense of self-esteem, then I began to realize I would have to tell the patient and her family. Then I was in real trouble. I had no idea how I would relate this news to them. It happened my little niece, a girl of seven, was a guest in my home at the time. So I shared my problem with this child. I talked about it, largely because she wondered what was wrong with me, and why I wouldn't play with her. So, I told her, and that little girl, with all the innocence in the world, just said, 'Well, you just say that her dying is part of her living.' Unfortunately, I didn't have the nerve to put it quite that way. I muddled through it with that family. But I never forgot what my little niece said. Now I am still learning everything that is implied in that dear child's words. Dying is part of living. It is! It is not unnatural. It may be terrible to contemplate. It may be impossible to admit, that it will happen to me, and to you, Mrs. Long. But it is not unnatural. It is as natural as birth, which we have not always talked about with perfect ease either, until recent years."

Helen left Dr. Miller's office with a piece of paper on which the doctor's secretary had written the title and author of a book. At the college library Helen checked it out. It was a book about dying children.

As she drove toward the beach house the sun broke through the leaden clouds, and by the time she arrived it was shining gloriously. As she parked at the rear of the house Jimmy came bounding out the door. His face was glowing with excitement and the new sheen of health the whole-blood transfusions had imparted to him. He looked the picture of youthful strength and vitality.

"Helen, the sun's out! This is Friday, and tomorrow's Saturday, and I'll bet the people with the hang gliders will be up on the cliffs! Dad called, and he said he'll be here tomorrow and if they're up there, we can get started! Isn't that fantastic?"

He ran ahead of her, through the kitchen and on out to the front porch. He was out there jumping up and down, cheering the sunlight and yelling for the rest of the gray clouds to disappear as Jessica stopped Helen in the kitchen.

"You're all going to get yourselves killed," Jessica told her. "Do you really mean to take lessons and fly one of them things yourself like Jimmy says?"

"I sure do, Jessica. You don't think I'm going to let him have all the fun himself, do you?"

"You aren't scared?"

"I'm scared to death, for myself as much as for him. But we're going to have an adventure, Jessica. An adventure!"

CHAPTER TWENTY

At eleven o'clock on Saturday morning Charles drove Jimmy and Helen to the top of the cliffs. It was necessary for them to go north on the coast highway for a couple of miles, then cut to the right, away from the ocean and up into a tract of luxury seaside homes. They wound upward, the tract gradually thinning out around them, until near the top they passed a sprawling mansion with tennis courts, a riding stable, and a huge swimming pool. Charles called out the name of the house's owner, some movie producer Helen had never heard of. Then the road leveled and began to run parallel to the ocean. From that immense height with the car moving at some distance from the brow of the palisades, Helen could not even see the horizon of the sea beyond. She began to have goosebumps thinking of the sickening sensation of leaping from such a height with no other support than those gossamer hang glider wings.

"Look, there they are!" Jimmy cried. He pointed ahead and to their right where a meadow of short green winter grass ran toward the lip of the cliffs. Three colorful hang gliders were moving about on the grass like giant triangular beetles with human legs as the people under them worked at readying them for flight.

Jimmy was hopping up and down in the back seat of the Mercedes as Charles parked the car. As soon as Helen opened the door on her side Jimmy squeezed behind her seat and dashed across the grass toward the grouped gliders, shouting, "Hey, hi! Bobbie! Frank!"

Charles looked at Helen with amazement. "He knows these people?"

Helen remembered the day the gliders had landed on the beach. "Apparently he does. I saw them land near the house the first day I saw Jimmy. He seems to know them very well!"

A tallish young woman was waving Jimmy nearer and welcoming him as one of the men disengaged himself from the harness of his kite. Helen recognized his orange and green as the first of the two kites that had flown over that day on the beach. The green letters FR on its bright orange wings now suggested initials.

"Frank Reynolds," the handsome young man said as he introduced himself. "And this is Bobbie, my wife. We met Jimmy a couple of times on the beach."

They were two picture-book California young people, tanned and outdoorsy, with the easy manners and openness that characterized what Helen had come to think of as the best of the younger set. They looked to be about twenty years old. Their blue jogging suits with gold stripes down the sides set off two very trim and athletic-looking figures.

"Can I go over where the other man is, Dad?" Jimmy asked. "I want to see over the edge! I bet I can see our house!"

Bobbie accompanied Jimmy a few yards away to meet the other flier and Charles quickly explained the situation. Frank Reynolds listened to the story of Jimmy's condition with a look of deep sympathy. An enthusiast, he had no trouble accepting the fact that a boy might want more than anything to go aloft on a glider as his last request, but his face darkened as Charles declared the intention of all three of them to fly off the cliffs.

"No way. It's not the hardest thing in the world to learn, but nobody would let you take off alone from here after a week, or even a month's experience."

Helen felt instant relief for herself, since she hadn't

been able to get over the queasiness she felt just being that high up, even on the ground. But she knew Jimmy would be disappointed.

"What he wants," she explained, "is to fly up there with the seagulls, like you do. Isn't there some way he can do that?"

The young man turned away to watch Jimmy. He was running back and forth from the other kite pilot to the edge of the cliff, terribly excited. His shouts of pleasure and enthusiasm could be heard over the steady whistle of the wind and the distant throb of the coast traffic.

Reynolds turned back to them, pondering the situation. "He seems to move all right. Limps a little on the right leg, but he can run okay, can't he."

"And he's strong in his arms, too," Charles added. "He's in the best shape now he may ever be. They gave him transfusions of whole blood last week to build him up. He'll never be fitter than he is now."

"Is he subject to fainting spells, anything like that?"

"Only when his blood count is down," Helen put in quickly. She sensed that Reynolds was forming some kind of answer to the problem. "Not now, though."

"Well, I'll tell you what." Reynolds stroked his lean chin with a muscular right hand and paused. He ran his eyes over both of them, then: "Suppose we give the three of you some instruction." He paused again as if doing some kind of mental calculations before going on. "Then after about—how long did you say you've got?"

"We lost time because of the rain. Only a week now," Charles said.

"Well, just a second. Let me talk to Bobbie and Jack. This takes some thought." He walked away at a brisk pace, caught up with Jimmy, took him by the shoulders and whispered in his ear, then sent him racing back toward Helen and Charles. Reynolds watched Jimmy run, undoubtedly checking again to see if the child would be able to do whatever it was he had in mind.

"Are they going to let us, Dad? Mom? Are they?"

"It may not be the way we thought, Jimmy, but I think he's working something out."

"Boy, are we ever up high! Our house looks about as big as a shoebox from up here! Come and look!" He took Helen by the hand, led her past Frank and Bobbie and the man who had been referred to as Jack, and up to the very brow of the cliff.

"Not so fast, Jimmy! This is close enough!" She felt herself teetering on the edge, though on closer, saner inspection the cliff proved to have a lower shelf that jutted out another twenty feet or so before the sheer rock of its face plummeted toward the highway below. Clutching the child's hand tightly, she backed away three steps just for an extra margin of safety, and backed into Charles Banning. He caught her elbows from behind and steadied her.

"It was a bad idea," he said. "Definitely a bad idea. Not the part about Jimmy, but the part about you and me going along!"

"Boy, won't it be something, Dad?" Jimmy's upturned face glowed with the joy of his dream. "It'll be better than Disneyland or Magic Mountain or anything!"

To Helen it was a nightmare. Amusement park rides had ended at puberty for her, had vanished behind her in a miasma of nausea when she reached age thirteen. She was immensely relieved when Frank Reynolds called them away from the cliff's edge.

Frank and Bobbie walked toward them with their arms around each other, both of them grinning widely, showing teeth like toothpaste ads. "We've worked it out," he announced. "It took some doing because Jack, our real veteran flyer, has a steady nine-to-fiver. Jack!" He waved to a short, muscular man in his fifties, wearing a tank top shirt and shorts, who seemed impervious to cold ocean air. His taut figure rolled toward them on powerful legs covered with black curly hair. His eyes were dark brown and as they were introduced he twisted the ends of his bushy, gay-nineties moustache. Helen thought of the classic portraits of the man on the flying trapeze.

"Jack Newcombe is the best hang glider instructor on the West Coast," Bobbie informed them. "He taught both of us."

Jack seemed a no-nonsense type of man. He shook hands with Charles and got down to business immediately. "What you want is to go tandem. That means two people to one kite. The way I see it, I'll take the boy, Frank can take Helen, and Bobbie can take Charles. That way the two women, who are lighter, will be paired with two men." He surveyed Charles. "How much do you weigh, about two hundred?"

"Thanks." Charles stroked his rounded paunch. "Two twenty. Is that too much?" Charles almost sounded hopeful that he might be disqualified.

"Nope. But the thing is we'd have to work at it every day for the next week, and I'd have to cut work. Could you come up with, say, a couple hundred just for my time? The boy goes free, of course."

"Two hundred. No problem. You're sure we can learn it that fast?"

Helen felt the blood draining from her head. They were actually going to do it! Why didn't Charles balk at the money, or something! She felt the ground sliding away under her feet as if the clifftop was melting and dropping her toward the highway while the others laughingly went on planning her doom!

"Oh, it's not that hard," Bobbie assured Charles. "Do you know that when one of these things is really soaring and the winds are just right we can stay up for an hour or more?"

"Oh, wow, Dad! An hour! My gosh, I don't believe it!"

Jack Newcombe smiled and patted Jimmy on the head. The boy's new growth of yellow blond hair was past the crewcut stage already, Helen noticed. How fantastically well and happy he looked at that moment.

"Now don't get it in your head we're going to soar around tandem for an hour. She was talking optimum conditions. How about ten or fifteen minutes?"

"I was expecting more like about a half a minute!" Jimmy grinned. "That would be super!"

For the next half-hour, with Jimmy pestering Frank for a full explanation of every principle of the construction and operation of the kites, they settled on a program of training. By the end of the negotiations Helen's fear had been transformed into a kind of jellied commitment, not unlike the feeling she always got when taking off on a jet just as it started down the runway and she knew there was no way to back out. From listening to and mostly looking at Jack Newcombe, she finally felt a slight glimmer of trust, just barely enough to keep her from throwing up on the way home.

The lessons were planned for every afternoon of the following week starting Sunday. The actual flight from the cliffs would take place on Thursday and Jimmy would re-enter the hospital on Friday to be prepared for his operation.

Helen arrived at home in mid-afternoon, anxious to share the story of the coming adventure with Arthur. She was disappointed to find the house empty. Arthur had been talking about going out with Jim and Winston to look at the plot of land selected for the apartment house investment and had shown some displeasure with her for spending weekend time with Jimmy. Saturdays and Sundays, with few exceptions, Helen had managed to save for home and husband. She didn't know how Arthur would take the news of her being gone Sunday as well.

There were several Christmas cards in the mailbox along with the usual bills, and Helen felt a twinge of guilt. She had made no holiday plans yet and the UNICEF cards she had ordered late had not yet arrived. It seemed a good time to call Katie and get busy on the domestic scene.

"Well, there you are!" Katie's voice greeted her.

"Maureen and I were just talking about you last night. She's going with me to my consciousness-raising class now."

Helen prepared herself for one of Katie's sales talks. "Is this the same thing you were telling me about when was it—in October?"

"Oh, no, dear! That was a fluke. The Swami collected everyone's money, gave two lectures, and took off for Katmandu in his personal jet. Too bad, because I was really getting a lot out of those sessions. I liked what the nerd had to say. You know we have to make a distinction between what a man says and what he may be in his personal life. Remember what the priest used to say, don't do as I do, do as I say!"

"I wasn't a Catholic. But I've heard it." It was comfortable listening to Katie rattle on again. Helen settled back and led her on a bit. "So this is something different. What did you call it?"

"Consciousness raising! Don't tell me you haven't heard of it! There are levels of consciousness, my dear. Most people just drift along in total unawareness of themselves and others, don't you know that? Then there are those who have trained their senses, both conscious and unconscious, to full awareness. Full! At the highest level it even reaches into the extrasensory! And this teacher is an actual ninth-level sensate being! She can tell if you are feeling bad just by looking at your aura! She tells me I could be at least a seventh level, which includes telepathic powers. Imagine, Helen, being able to actually read someone's mind! Of course, you know I have some of that ability anyway. I'm really a very psychic person, as you've seen over the years."

Helen could recall no time at which Katie ever manifested more than a spark of interest in the psychic, let alone possessing any kind of gift. But now she had convinced herself she did.

After a half hour of ecstatic pronouncements about the total wisdom, beauty and charisma of Lucinda Scaritt, "who only charges at the end of a class and then only if you say you're totally satisfied with what she's given you!" Katie finally ran down.

"I need to catch up on my Christmas shopping, Katie. How are you doing?"

"I hate Christmas because it always catches me a day late and a dollar short. Don't tell me you've got time for shopping!"

They set a date for a night visit to the closest shopping mall on Tuesday. Just before she broke the connection Katie's voice took on a confidential tone and she said, "I believe you and I should have some real sister talk, Helen. I can't go into it now, but I expect a full report on *all* your activities Tuesday. Bye now."

All? Why had Katie put it that way, "Sister talk?" and "All your activities" said with a kind of smirk that implied almost that Helen was up to something.

When Arthur came in at dinnertime he seemed distant. He listened to her tale about Jimmy and the hang gliders with an occasional grunt of polite acknowledgement, but she could tell he was not really interested. When she probed for information about his land deal, he shared little more than the bare facts. Yes, the land looks suitable. Yes, they might go through with it. Yes, Jim thinks it will make a pile of money.

After dinner Arthur stationed himself in his easy chair and pored over an issue of *Business Week*. When she announced that she was tired and going to bed he did not even look up. "Fine," he said. "I'll be up later."

The bed felt cold and empty. After the excitement of the morning and the joy of seeing Jimmy so buoyed up about the week that lay ahead of him, home seemed almost unfamiliar. Katie had sounded like a moonstruck teenager. And Arthur was a silent, tight-lipped stranger who was either indifferent or angry. Katie's final, unpleasant remark had left an ugly taste. What had the woman been implying?

Dreamy scenes of the morning's experience came drifting into her half-sleep. Jimmy beaming with delight, his rosy cheeks aglow with good health. The lively, happy couple, Bobbie and Frank. The orange and green hang glider. Now the glider was bearing her skyward with Frank Reynolds by her side, the ocean and the highway slipping away beneath her with a curious seagull passing, looking very much like the departed Charlie. And finally the face of Charles Banning, looking much more relaxed than she had ever seen him, trying to use his almost unnoticeable paunch as an excuse to keep from going along on their adventure. Charles seemed a welcome presence as she drifted toward sleep. She never would have thought it possible that she could come to like such a man.

CHAPTER TWENTY-ONE

At eleven o'clock on Tuesday morning Arthur Long punched the button on his desk intercom with a trembling index finger.

"Janice, cancel my lunch appointment with Paul Burke of Atlas Electronics. Something has come up. I'll phone him later. Thank you."

He knew the secretary would wonder. No phone calls had come in during the morning from home or from any of his personal friends, so she would be a bit suspicious. The hell with it. Arthur had gone through the most miserable two days of his life and had decided to resolve something. He put away the file he'd been working on, straightened up his desk, and left by the side door to avoid Janice's inquiring eyes.

He sat in his car actually shaking as he contemplated what he was about to do. The simple physical action of starting the car and driving out of the parking lot seemed to exact a particular toll of guilt, and as he drove toward home the feeling grew. It was a sensation he had known only once before in his life. When the first explicit sex movies had hit the theaters, just after Helen and Arthur were married, his chums had gloated over the films to such an extent that Arthur had begun to feel it wasn't masculine not to be acquainted with what was going on on the sexual frontiers of the society. After several weeks of hesitation Arthur had driven one afternoon to a remote X-rated movie house far away from the area where he lived and had sat in a musty, litter-strewn room where scratchy images of copulation danced wearily on a dirty screen. The whole furtive caper had filled him with the kind of feelings he had now. He had trembled then with the same sense of betraying himself and Helen, and he had been driven by the same kind of irrational, instinctive urge he felt now. He had felt like a creep. Just as now he knew he was going through with it, and he hated every step that took him in that direction.

He stopped at home and picked up his binoculars, carefully avoiding the mirror over the dresser in which they were stored. He tossed them onto the front seat of the car and drove toward the beach. His stomach churned into nausea under the impact of warring emotions.

The problem had started on Saturday when Jim O'Donnell dropped a remark about Helen. "Kate says she hears this Charles Banning is quite a guy, Arthur old buddy. Does Helen talk about him much? They're together every day now, aren't they? Flying kites or something?"

No, she doesn't talk about him, Arthur steamed. She won't let me in on this thing at all, no way. Won't show me pictures of the boy, says he's ashamed of the way he looks. And no mention of Banning, oh no! Too flashy, she says. Separated from his wife, on the loose, probably on the make all the time. A salesman, the bastard. Arthur pictured the look on Jim O'Donnell's face as he'd said, "If Kate was off with a guy like that, I'd know what the hell is going on."

As he drove up the Coast Highway from Santa Monica, he scanned the cliffs for any sign of a spot where gliders might be seen. What if Helen saw him driving around in the area? That really made him ill. He would tell her Jim O'Donnell had mentioned a piece of land down there by the ocean and he'd been trying to find it. Jim would cover for him if it came to that. Jim would understand what Arthur was doing. Damn, it would be tough if he had to let Jim in on it, though. How Katie would feast on that one! He and Helen had had a good relationship, up to this. It would be so goddamn rotten to have it spoiled, if the whole thing was really what Helen said it was.

That thought made him pull off to the side of the road. The road had climbed and bent around on a jut of high land overlooking the ocean. Arthur stopped the car and sat there for a while. He thought, if only I could see what this guy looks like. If only I could see them together, I'd know. I would be able to tell in an instant if there is anything between them. And if I saw that boy, somehow it would give the whole thing some substance. I would know who this little character is who has come into our lives like this. I know he's sick, probably dying, and that he loves Helen and needs her. But damn it all, I need her! I feel like I'm losing her, like we're going in two directions now.

Far out on the face of the sea near the horizon a black oil tanker was heading in. Closer in a small private fishing boat moved slowly northward. He lifted the binoculars and scanned its deck. Three men were in the boat, their three fishing rods angled up at the rear of the open deck of the trim white craft. The waves were rocking them gently and the guys were laughing as they fished. One of them rummaged about in a cooler and came up with beer cans he passed to the others. The sun was bright and warm and the three men seemed to be having a hell of a good time.

Arthur lowered the binoculars and laid them on the seat beside him. He glanced away from the sea and let his eyes roam the edges of the hills where lovely homes lay nestled into rich, expensive-looking landscaping, their wide windows facing the ocean. Suddenly he caught a glimpse of something bright orange moving along on the top of a small hill that lay in a valley below his vantage point. Then he saw something white. Their shape was unmistakeable. They were hang gliders. Helen had described them and told him, though he was busy pretending not to listen, or not to care, on Sunday morning just as she was getting ready to leave the house. And there they were. Arthur could see all three of the gliders now, one orange, one white and one blue. All he had to do was to lift the binoculars and he would be able to do precisely what he had traveled out here to do.

He watched them for a while with the binoculars lying unused on the seat beside him. Apparently the teacher had taken them to a small practice hill. All the while Arthur watched, for perhaps five minutes, the group seemed to be standing there fooling with the kites and equipment, or waiting for the wind to come up. They were so far away they were like black stick figures on the landscape. He couldn't tell which was Helen or which might be Charles Banning. There was one tiny figure that would have had to be Jimmy, but from that distance Arthur could not distinguish even what the people were wearing, let alone the details of their expressions or actions.

He glanced down at the binoculars and knew suddenly that he would not use them. To lift them to his eyes and spy on Helen would kill something precious between them. Their friendship would be damaged. Just to sit here as he was, knowing she was all right, that she was enjoying herself and that Jimmy was getting his wish, that was enough. His conscience could tolerate that. Somehow he began to feel he owed it to

Helen and he owed it to that almost invisible little child beside her not to pry any further.

After another minute of watching the silent scene on the distant hillside, Arthur started the car and drove away.

CHAPTER TWENTY-TWO

"The only way they'd get me up on one of those glorified kites is if I was stoned out of my mind," Katie groaned. She lifted a pair of transparent bikini panties for Helen's inspection. "These? Nuts." She dropped them carelessly into the pile of undergarments on the store counter. "Jim laughs every time I try a trick like that. It's gotten so I can't do anything to get his attention. Why couldn't I have got lucky and married a man ten years younger than me instead of the other way around?"

Helen bit her tongue and fought down an urge to find a chair on which to wait out Katie's painfully slow selection process. Every buying decision for Katie seemed to involve a major effort. They had tramped through at least twenty establishments from specialty shops to department stores and Katie had bought two gifts. Helen's arms were loaded with presents for Sharon and her husband as well as gifts for her sister, her uncles and cousins, and even two for Jimmy. It had been a successful shopping spree, except for Katie's indecision.

They abandoned the lingerie department and Katie headed for the perfume counter. As Helen struggled up beside her and balanced her load next to a display of the latest erotic scent which bore the blatant title of

"Come On," Katie sprayed a hefty fog of the substance around herself and said, "You haven't told me yet how you like this Charles Banning."

The scent was overpoweringly musky. Helen coughed slightly and was amazed that Katie had to sniff the air to detect the stuff.

"Well?" Katie queried. She turned to Helen with a look that was almost a leer. "What's he like? Ugly? Pretty? Tall? Short? Dark? Blond? You know, you're so secretive about this man I'm beginning to wonder."

"He's rather good looking, I suppose. He's trying to be a good father to Jimmy. That's what I care about. You're not going to spray more of that stuff, are you?"

Katie blasted the air with another cloud of "Come On" and Helen watched the tiny globules alight upon the glass counter. "It's subtle, but nice, don't you think?" Katie asked. "Musk turns men on, brings out the animal in them," she growled.

They left the department store with Katie carrying her two packages and one large bottle of the perfume. She carried it clutched in her right hand like a weapon. "Wait til Jim gets a whiff of this!"

"Wait til he gets a whiff of the price!" Helen countered.

As they moved toward Katie's car, angry shoppers were blowing their horns at each other in the holiday battle for parking space. A large red-faced woman in a Cadillac raced past them, almost running them down, hand on the car horn, trying to blast a little Honda away from a tiny space that had opened up at the end of the row ten car widths away. The Honda was already nosing into the space when the Cadillac slid to a stop, the horn still blaring. The large lady lumbered out of her luxury vehicle and bore down upon the driver of the Honda, cursing like a muleskinner.

"Christmas," Helen sighed. "Peace on earth."

"Well, it's exciting though. It's something to do, isn't it? And speaking of something to do, Helen . . ."

"Yes? You were saying?"

"I have to tell you something. I just feel it's my place. Let's go somewhere for a drink and I'll tell you."

"Tell me what?"

"Well, not here, dear. It's—well—personal."

"About me or about you?" Helen had heard enough innuendos on the phone and during the shopping trip to begin thinking that Katie was leading up to something. She had no patience for further hints and delays.

"What is it, Katie? What's on your mind?"

"Let's get in the car."

"If you have something to say to me, Katie, I would like to hear it now."

"You don't have to get so tense about it. It's no big thing. In fact I think it's exciting. I envy you a bit."

If Katie envied her it could only mean one thing. Helen turned away, feeling a little nauseous. "All right, Katie, let's sit in the car."

Katie bustled to the door of her Continental Mark IV and let herself in. She touched an electric switch on the inside of her door that unlocked Helen's side and as soon as Helen had closed the door behind her, Katie laid a hand on her arm.

"We're friends, Helen. This is all in friendship."

"I understand, Katie. What is it?"

"Well, people talk, you know. I just feel I ought to warn you, about you and that Charles Banning."

Helen felt herself turning to ice. "Go on."

"A friend of Maureen's works at the hospital over at UCLA, as a volunteer. She saw you over there one day with him. Your story and Jimmy's—well, it's gotten around the hospital. The volunteers were there with the lunch cart one day and they saw what a terrific hunk of man this Charles is. They got to talking, and watching, and you know how people are!"

"No, I don't know how that kind of people are, Katie. Suppose you tell me."

"I'm not sure I appreciate that attitude, Helen. I'm trying to help you."

"Tell me what they are saying."

"That the two of you appeared to be very chummy, that's all. Now is that such a big thing? It's just that I worried when Maureen told me. I know you're over at that man's place all the time. And now with this kite flying, or whatever it is . . ."

"Does Jim know about this? Have you said anything like this to him? Because if you have and this gets back to Arthur . . ."

"Would I share something like this with that bum? He'd go right over and use it to put Arthur down. You know how Jim is. It's just that I want you to be—well, careful. I mean if there *is* anything between the two of you, well, honey, I say hooray. You know me!"

"No, Katie, I don't think I do."

"Oh, come on, Helen. Just between us girls. I mean, from what I've heard the man is fantastic. Am I supposed to believe you're out there every day and half the nights . . ."

"Whoa. I have never been to the beach house or even to the hospital at night."

"Details. That's not the point, is it? Does this man mean something to you or doesn't he? It's just that—well, I feel kind of sorry for Arthur. I mean he's in a peculiar kind of bind, isn't he? If he protests, he's against that poor, sick child you're trying to help. It would make him look like a heartless slob, wouldn't it, if Arthur said you had to stop going out there, or spend more time at home or something?"

Katie's words began to blur together as her voice went on and on. Helen sank back in the car seat, her own thoughts swirling as her temper rose dangerously. She dug her nails into her palms and fought off wave after wave of revulsion and anger.

". . . and there's poor Arthur spending his evenings and weekends staring at TV or mowing the lawn, or God knows what else. I'm not putting you down for it, but . . ."

Helen clamped down hard on an urge to throw the door open and run blindly into the night, leaving Katie talking to herself or thinking whatever the hell she might want to think. She was surprised at her own self-control as she mastered the impulse and let Katie continue.

"And we're friends, dear. That's what counts. So if there's anything at all, I just want to share it with you. Don't you see?"

Yes, I am beginning to see very clearly, Helen thought. I see how pathetic and empty your little life is, Katie O'Donnell. I see how desperately you run from guru to guru and hobby to hobby and study group to study group, all on some kind of endless pursuit of a reason to be alive. I see you are so hungry for love that even the chance to be a parasite on someone else's supposed affair feeds your appetite. I see you are terribly sad, Katie O'Donnell, and in spite of everything I wish I could help you.

"If you don't want to tell me, Helen, I suppose I'll just have to assume whatever I assume, won't I? I thought we were friends, dear. I really did."

Helen kept her voice as steady as she could under the circumstances, and measured her response very carefully. "Katie, I feel sorry for you."

"Sorry? For me?"

"I wish I could help you. I really do. I really wish I could tell you some wild story of a passionate affair to warm your bed at night. I wish . . ."

"Helen!" Katie drew back as if Helen had slapped her face.

"I wish I could recite some magic formula for you, Katie, one that would give you the instant happiness you spend so much time and money trying to find, running from one crazy new idea to the next . . ."

"Well, this is the thanks I get. I was just trying to be a friend and this is my reward!" Katie's upper lip was trembling and at the same time drawing back spasmodically from her teeth, baring them like fangs. Her whole face twisted into a grotesque imitation of offended charity, as Helen went on.

"I wish I could be your friend, Katie. You offered me your little token of friendship. And now I offer you mine, and it is far more sincerely well meant. I wish you a younger husband, or a lover, or a dozen of them if it will help."

"Get out of this car. Get out!" Katie screamed.

Helen's anger was mixed with a sense of pity for her friend. She began to gather up her packages with a sense of remorse and loss.

"I'm truly sorry, Katie, that it has come to this. I'm not mad at you, honestly. I just feel so sorry . . ."

"*Get out!* You two-faced bitch! You slut! Pretending to be helping that boy while you play around with his father! Do you think I don't know what's going on, you pious sweet-talking hypocrite?"

Helen rolled out the car door, slammed it shut and felt herself reeling as she turned from the car into the chaos of the parking lot. As horns blew and shoppers quarrelled, Katie O'Donnell spun the tires of her car and sped away. Helen propped her bundles on the trunk of the car next in line, laid her forehead on top of them and wept uncontrollably. Somewhere above the senseless din of the parking lot and the sound of her own sobs she heard the music of church bells playing, "Joy to the World." The bells clanged on and on and on.

When Arthur arrived a half-hour later the store had closed and the parking lot contained only a handful of cars belonging to the store personnel. Helen stood inside the recessed entrance of the store, hugging her gifts and feeling chilled.

The car was warm inside and Arthur's smile was reassuring.

"So you and Katie finally had it out," he said, and he patted her knee. "Are you all right?"

"No, I'm not. I'm miserable and cold and feeling very sorry for myself. And for Katie, darn it."

Arthur leaned back and Helen glanced at his face to find him looking both relaxed and exhilarated. "I want to thank you for getting those two off our backs, Helen. I've never liked Katie, and I think Jim is a number one horse's ass."

She felt the strain and sadness draining out of her, and sensed once again the strength of Arthur and how much she depended on him. "You really mean that?" she asked.

"You know, Helen, when you're a good couple, when you've got a relationship going for you, like us, people like the O'Donnells are like creatures from another planet. Katie and Jim are not friends. That's their problem. But we are. We're friends, sweetheart, and that's something—with all their mod attitudes and condominiums and gurus and their redwood tub and their big real estate deals—that's something they'll never have."

They drove along in silence for a long while. The lights of Wilshire Boulevard swept by them. In Arthur's presence the gaily-colored Christmas decorations with their bells and candles and twinkling green lights somehow seemed less gaudy. Helen began to feel that Arthur was waiting for her, letting her take her own time about telling him what had transpired with Katie. On the phone she had said only that they'd had an argument.

"Want to stop for coffee somewhere?" he asked.

"No thanks, Arthur. I would just like to go home."

"Good. Me too." He smiled and winked at her. "You're getting tougher. A few months ago I couldn't have imagined you telling anyone off. Now it seems perfectly believable."

He was being very patient, and she felt she was being a bit cowardly. "Arthur, what Katie and I were fighting about—I think we should talk about it. She was implying that I'm romantically involved with Charles Banning. Implying—that's an understatement. She ended up calling me a two-faced bitch!"

Arthur whistled. "Whew—that's pretty low even for Katie. Let me save you the trouble. Jim laid the same thing on me on Saturday."

"Oh no!"

"All very indirect and cool, and in the spirit of true friendship, of course."

"Oh, you got that too? Out of the same mold, those two."

"They deserve each other," Arthur grinned. "Let's not even do them the honor of discussing it any further. Unless you want to."

"There is nothing going on, Arthur. I want you to know that. I do feel I've hurt Katie, though. She's really a very sad and lonely person."

"You've got enough sadness to deal with, sweetheart. Let's talk about Jimmy. How are the flying lessons going?"

By the time they reached home Arthur had completely soothed her frayed nerves and settled her worries. She wondered how she had ever thought of him as jealous and possessive.

After dinner Arthur cleared the table and said he would do the dishes for her. He bundled her into an easy chair in front of the fireplace, and placed a snifter of brandy in her hand to ward off the possibility of her catching cold from the evening's exposure to the elements. On his way to the kitchen he kissed her on the cheek and said, "You've got to stay in shape if you're going to go flying around on those kite things. And it wouldn't be the same for Jimmy without you there."

She heard him whistling to himself in the kitchen as he washed the dishes. She thought, he really is my friend; Arthur was so right when he said that. We're friends.

CHAPTER TWENTY-THREE

It had seemed as if Thursday morning would never come. Jimmy had lived the experience over and over at least a thousand times in anticipation of flying off the cliff with Jack Newcombe. And now they were actually getting ready to go!

Jimmy and Jack were going to use the same kite, Jack's blue one, that they had practiced in, but the other two kites were different this morning. They were larger, and he listened as Frank explained the change.

"The more square footage in the glider, the more lifting power. With the weight factor right at the margin, we talked it over and Jack decided we should go for the two hundred and thirtys." Dad was nodding his head as if he understood exactly what Frank was saying, but his Mom just stood there quietly beside Frank looking a little bit pale and scared.

"It'll be super, Mom! Don't be scared. It's even safer than driving a car, Jack says!" Jimmy tried to cheer her up and she did smile, but not very much. Frank was buckling the harness around Helen and Jimmy could see that her hands gripping the control bar of the hang glider were both clenched so hard her knuckles had little white spots on top where the blood was squeezed out.

"Remember to let me do the driving," Frank smiled, kidding Helen, trying to get her to loosen up a little. She was all buckled into the harness, which was like a little hammock made of wide straps of nylon and went completely under the front of her.

"You can't fall out, Mom! Look at all the straps! Remember how easy it was on the little hills?"

"Jimmy," she called out, "I'm going to have my eyes closed. You'll have to tell me what you see!" As she said it Frank finished buckling his harness, laughing, and the two of them started toward the edge of the cliff where Jimmy's dad and Bobbie were already standing, holding their kite pointed right into the wind and right at the ocean horizon. Dad was lucky, Jimmy thought. He was actually going to help guide it a little. His dad was side by side with Bobbie and he didn't even have to put his arm around her as Helen had to do with Frank and Jimmy would have to do with Jack.

Jimmy wished they all could have used the same kites they practiced with. The colors of the new big ones were both dull gray with red trim, very military-looking like jet fighters, not bright and circusy like the smaller ones. He was glad Jack hadn't changed his kite, because in his imaginary flights he had always seen himself with the beautiful dark blue with JN-1 in gold above him as he soared among the clouds.

"All right, we're ready!" Jack called out as he finished checking Jimmy's harness and buckling himself in. "Any time you're ready, Bobbie!"

Bobbie and Dad would go first as soon as they felt the wind was just right. Then Helen and Frank, and finally Jimmy and Jack. Why didn't they hurry up? Jimmy would have liked to go first, but Jack had been very firm about it. The others would test the wind for them. Jimmy didn't like being babied that way, but all the others had agreed with Jack and that's the way they were doing it.

Jimmy looked away from his dad and Bobbie for a moment to see if he could see the sun coming through the wings above him. There was a bright glow coming through the blue and gold, and it was just as he'd imagined, except that the letters were much bigger than he'd remembered. Around the edges of the wings the sun created a halo as it glanced off the bright metal tubes of the kite's frame. When he looked back toward the cliff, Bobbie and his dad were gone.

"Where are they?" he cried, fearing that they had dropped straight down.

Jack lifted his chin upwards and tilted the kite back so Jimmy could see the sky. His dad's kite was already far off the ground, riding the strong up-drafts from the cliff that Jack had told him about. The two riders lay in their hammocks under the gray wings and rose higher and higher into the glorious blue sky.

Jimmy looked back quickly toward Helen and Frank, just in time to see their feet leave the ground. The kite seemed to poise for a moment, five or six feet in the air, then Frank nosed it forward just a little and it caught the updraft. Away they went like two people on an elevator! Jimmy could hear Helen's voice crying "Whoooo," and he wondered if she had opened her eyes.

"Okay, Jimmy. Remember what I told you now. You keep your arm around my shoulders like we practiced. Okay? Are you comfortable? I don't want you to change your position just as we start taking off."

"I feel fine. I won't move, and I'll let you drive," Jimmy said. His mouth felt all dry and sticky and the words came out funny, but he didn't have time to even think about that because they were standing right on the edge of the cliff. He could see the beach house far below and slightly to their left. On the Coast Highway there were just a few cars moving along, looking like toys, and there was one miniature red and white truck. He lifted his head to get his balance just right as Jack had taught him and let his legs hang loose off the ground and still. He was glad that he'd been able to keep his breakfast down and that the new drugs weren't making him too nauseous, because otherwise . . . and then they were going up!

"Whooo!" just like Helen said! That little drop down at about six feet off the ground followed by a sudden swoop upward was really something!

"That's the hard part, Jimmy!" Jack called out after a moment. "From now on we just ride and enjoy the sights! You can loosen up on my neck now. You're choking me a little bit."

Jimmy quickly loosened his grip and found himself relaxing a little. It was so much easier and so much more beautiful than he'd even imagined it would be!

"You can breathe, too!" Jack grinned at him.

He let his breath out and relaxed even more. "Where are we going to go?"

"Wherever the wind lets us go, Jimmy. We're following the air currents, just like the birds. Look over there!"

Off to their right the other two kites were completing a beautiful circle that had taken them far out over the water, and were heading back toward shore. A flock of seagulls were playing with them. The gulls would circle, following them for a while, then dive down and come up on the other side of them. Jimmy could see Helen looking at the gulls, then he saw her hand waving at him. Jimmy loosened one hand from the control bar and waved back.

"Is that okay, waving?"

"As long as you keep that arm around me to keep the kite in balance. A little movement's okay."

For five minutes they rode the winds without losing any altitude at all. There was no sound except the wind itself whispering around them. All three kites, circling and climbing, made a beautiful sight. Jimmy thought, I know how Charlie felt, being a bird. I know why birds always seem happy, too. Nothing can bother them up here. Thc sun is warm on their wings and the wind lifts them like a pillow made of air, and all they do is play. Then it occurred to him, no wonder Charlie looked so sad when his wing was hurt. No wonder he would stare out at the sea and once in a while look up at the sky with such longing and regret. Having your leg taken away from you couldn't be as bad as losing a wing, because you would still have the ground, and your home and your friends, and everything you loved even if you only had one leg to walk on. But without a wing Charlie had lost the sky. He had lost his home and friends, and most of all this feeling of being as free and light as the air itself, the happiness of the sun on his wings and the joy of seeing all the houses and people and noise of the human world far, far away. He felt tears in his eyes for Charlie and what he had lost.

Jimmy felt the kite banking to the left, away from the shoreline and back toward the sea. Then all of a sudden he noticed that the other two kites were continuing on in the other direction toward shore. Jack was taking him on a special ride of his own!

"The others will be going down soon," Jack reported. "How would you like to see the Santa Monica pier from up here?"

"My gosh, that's a long way down the coast! Can we make it?"

"I think so! Look at that flock of gulls out there!"

Jimmy looked at a spot in the sky about a half-mile away, and there he saw about twenty gulls circling and rising. Some of them were almost out of sight, they were so high.

Jack said, "Watching the birds is one way a kite flyer can tell where the best wind currents are. The birds know!"

They moved toward the gulls and caught the air of a strong rising current under their wings. Jack banked to the right, just the way the birds were going, and they began to climb rapidly. Jimmy kept his eyes on a sailboat about a mile away and saw it grow smaller and smaller. As they made a circle that let him look back toward the shore, he could see the other two kites dropping down in a long glide along the beach, going down.

"They're finished, and we're still going! Yippee!" he cried. "You're a very good flier, Jack! I'm glad I got you!

Jack was beaming as if it was the best thing anybody had ever said to him. Then his serious look came back again. "Do you think you can take another ten or fifteen minutes?"

"Are you kidding? I could stay up here forever!"

They reached the top of their climb, and now the sailboat was just like a little white speck on the water. The surface of the ocean seemed not to be moving at all, as if the waves formed another pattern when seen from so high up. Each riffle on the blue-green face of the water seemed fixed in place. The surf was a white band that didn't flow in and out at all, but just stayed the same. This was something new, something that he wanted to share with Helen. It went with his idea about things not being opposites. Everything depends on the way you look at it, he thought. When he came to the time of dying, he would try to tell Helen that, to make her feel better. He would have to try hard to get Helen to see dying the way he saw it, so she wouldn't be so frightened of it, and so she wouldn't keep him from talking about it the way she usually did. Dying would be just like going off the cliff, he would tell her. A moment of panic and then the thrill of a brand new adventure, like flying toward the sun on his own wings, rising alone and unseen, past the gulls and the clouds and even past the sun. He wouldn't like leaving, and he would be a little scared at the first step, but that was what dying would be like, just like flying.

CHAPTER TWENTY-FOUR

To Charles Banning the hospital waiting room was too much like all the other anterooms in his life. In the Navy he'd cooled his heels in an anteroom while a superior officer in the next room drank gin and chatted with the Admiral about how much time Charles should spend in jail on a drunk and disorderly charge. A bare anteroom at the Santa Monica police station had once held him for two hours with his head spinning and his stomach in knots when he'd been booked on an involuntary manslaughter charge that his laywer, when he could be reached, had gotten him out of. The lawyer, for that matter, had also kept him waiting in his leather-padded anteroom when Charles had gone to him about Virginia's indecent demands in their property settlement.

Some people could sit in waiting rooms and actually read magazines. Charles couldn't. Waiting was one of the things he did worst. Virginia had never understood that side of him. She was the passive type, the kind of person who could wait. But Charles had charged past so many secretaries and office flunkies to make a sale with their boss, that his fellow salesmen had dubbed him O.J. He felt that waiting demeaned him somehow, as if he were being put in the same category with losers and beggars.

He was standing in the doorway of the hospital waiting room, not allowing himself to sit down and give in to it. He preferred company when he was nervous, and the room was empty. Down the corridor at the nurses' station everyone was busy. He wondered if hospitals had a rush hour at this time every morning. It was eight o'clock and Jimmy was already under the knife. Under the knife. It satisfied the realist in him to think of it that way. Helen, he knew, would be along within a few minutes. She would be company, but he never felt free with her. The situation with Helen was unfamiliar to him and made him damn uncomfortable. It called for him to be respectful and keep his hands off, to appreciate what she was doing for Jimmy but to keep his distance, to be in close association with her, close enough to smell her perfume, but still try to think of her only as a friend. Never in his life had he been friends with a woman.

He bestirred himself and strode purposely past the

nurses' station as if he had something important to do. At the end of the corridor he passed the elevator and swung open the door to the stairway. He trotted down the concrete steps, aware of the scratchy echo of his leather soles on the grit left by the feet of too many poor suckers.

Morbid, that's the way he felt. Damn morbid. He swung into the employee's cafeteria for a cup of coffee and glanced at the clock on the wall as he paid the cashier. Eight-ten. Jimmy had been in there for over an hour.

He turned with the cup in his hand and spotted a familiar face. The young Oriental girl who worked at the X-ray lab on Jimmy's floor was sitting alone along the side wall. She had her head down over the morning paper and there was a coffee cup by her elbow.

"Good morning. You're—" Charles purposely looked away from the name plate on her white jacket as he sat down, to show her that he knew the name without looking—" Miss Tsusumita, from X-ray."

"Yes," she smiled. "And you are Mr. Banning. Have you any news yet of Jimmy?"

Her accent was charming. How totally feminine and vulnerable Japanese women are, he thought, as he said, "I never read a paper before six at night, and never without a drink." He reached across the table and folded the paper after carefully lifting her elbow to remove it.

Her smile only broadened. "And Jimmy?"

"Nothing yet. I hate waiting rooms. I hope you don't mind. I don't even like coffee much. What I really like is good company. It's like a morgue up there."

She continued smiling, as she quickly extracted a cigarette from a very expensive-looking silver box and leaned toward him. If Charles was fast with anything it was with a light for a lovely lady. He was even faster in gauging female interest. Her satiny black eyes locked onto his as she drew back, enjoying the cigarette.

"Sherry told me about you," she purred.

"Oh—well, you have me at a disadvantage then. I know nothing about you beyond what my dazzled old eyes perceive."

"She's working in surgery now, did you know that?"

He paused, disoriented for a moment by the sudden jerk back to reality. "You don't mean she's in there with Jimmy."

"Yes. And don't worry. She's really very good at her work. I think with men she may be a bit of a fleabrain, but that's just an act. I know. We're good friends."

"It was no big thing between us," Charles quickly assured her. "I understand she's found herself a doctor now. Tell her I'm glad for her."

The smile faded a little and the girl lowered her eyes, suddenly the picture of the classical Geisha, demure and secretive. It was like a physical withdrawal, but it only served to stimulate Charles to a little more overt action.

"I hope Sherry didn't tell you anything too incriminating."

"Why would you care what I think?"

Very direct. Charles liked that. "Because I would like very much to take you out some time. I am a super dancer. I enjoy music, both classical and contemporary. I meet people easily . . ."

"Oh, I can see that."

"And I bathe regularly." It was an often-used line that usually produced a bit of reaction. Again she looked away, and this time she actually glanced at her watch.

"Good for you," she said. "Very healthy habit. I don't like music much, of any kind. I am a terrible dancer. I am quite shy with people, and I am due back upstairs in two minutes." In spite of the explicit rebuff she smiled again, even more sweetly than before.

She began gathering up the folded newspaper and her purse and cigarettes. Charles stood and tried his best to think of a parting shot that might leave some opening for the future. She turned away before he could collect his thoughts, then she stopped and looked back over her shoulder at him.

"What do you do for a living, Mr. Banning?"

"I'm in sales." He felt dumb saying it.

She replied with a toss of her black hair, "Good. At least you're not a doctor." And without the slightest hint of whether he had offended her or not, or whether on the other hand she might be interested in further negotiations, she walked out.

Charles dropped back into his chair and stared at the surface of the black coffee stagnating in his cup, already showing a film of oil building up as it cooled. He pushed it away and there beside the cup on the table was an elegant little calling card she had managed to leave behind. He tucked it into his inside coat pocket and patted it, then picked up the coffee. It tasted just fine.

Helen had arrived by the time Charles returned to the floor by eight-thirty. He found her standing in the corridor near the "clean room" formerly occupied by Frank Taylor's son, M.L.K. Taylor. To Charles she looked haggard and a bit more carelessly dressed than usual.

"I couldn't sleep at all," she informed him. "Any word yet?"

"Not yet."

She turned to watch two young black orderlies come out of the clean room carrying bed linens, which they loaded on their utility cart. "Will Jimmy be kept in there?" she asked. Her voice carried small signals of anxiety, though she was apparently trying very hard to remain composed.

"I think so. Would you like to sit in the waiting room? Could I get you something?" Charles would have felt better if Helen dropped the brave front and leaned on him a little.

"What happened to Marty Taylor?"

"I checked as soon as I saw the empty room this morning. He's been sent home in good remission."

Hearing that, Helen relaxed. Apparently the question about Marty was what had been troubling her. She turned to him with a much more cheerful look and said she would like to sit down in the waiting room.

Helen selected a deep lounge chair near a reading lamp and a corner table. Charles sat on the end of a small couch at an angle to her, their knees almost touching. He glanced at her long slim legs outlined by charcoal gray wool slacks with a narrow cut that showed her thin knees and trim thighs to very good advantage. She crossed her legs and glanced down at her fingernails as if inspecting them.

"I feel like a mess this morning," she sighed. "If we could just be sure he'll come through the operation all right . . . Surgery always worries me."

He didn't know how to reassure her, and decided that a change of subject would be better for both of them. "We had a great time with those kites, though, didn't we? I'll never forget the look on Jimmy's face when Jack landed and let him out of that harness. It was like he'd been to heaven and back."

"It was worth everything we went through," Helen smiled. Her blue eyes held his for a moment and her smile faded. "Charles, I'm glad we have a chance to talk here for a while. It may not be any of my business, really, and I want you to tell me honestly if you don't want to talk about it—but I would like to ask you about Virginia. And before you say anything, the reason is Jimmy. Now that he's facing this—I mean the possibility of being crippled for life—I just feel he needs his mother. He needs her—his real mother. That's what was keeping me awake all night. Oh, yes, I worried about the operation, but as the hours went by I started asking myself—what am I doing? Am I really helping Jimmy, or am I standing in the way of Virginia possibly coming back? I need to know something about her."

"What is there to tell? We're divorced, officially and messily and finally, as of three weeks ago. She's living in the house in Encino, which I gave her, being only too glad to see it go. I got the Mercedes and Jimmy. She got most of what was left."

"And she doesn't ever talk about coming back, not even to see him? She must have visitation rights."

"I can see that this has been a problem for you, Helen. You should have come right out and asked me these things long ago. You find it pretty hard to believe that she could just turn her back on Jimmy, don't you?"

She hesitated a moment, her forehead puckering between her lowered eyelids as she examined her hands again. "It was enough for me just to know Jimmy needed me. But now . . ."

Charles hated seeing her torturing herself over Virginia. He decided to dispel any doubts. "Helen you are a good human being. Somehow I get the feeling that you've never really met a genuinely selfish person, so you find it terribly difficult to believe what is actually true. Virginia left Jimmy because a sick child cramped her style. With me on the road most of the time the care of Jimmy would have been squarely on her. Sure, we could afford a nurse, but that meant taking money away from some of the other things Virginia's little heart desired. And if you think I'm stretching a point, just consider this, Helen. The judge granted custody of Jimmy to me, the father. Do you have any idea how unusual that is?"

"I've wondered about that," Helen replied.

"Not only did she prove herself unfit by deserting Jimmy when I was on the road, leaving him with a neighbor and going off for a week without telling anyone where she was—not only did she do that, but she also neglected to take him in for his checkups and medication. The judge considered all that, plus the fact that she didn't even ask for custody."

"I guess I just can't comprehend it. Was she terribly unhappy, or mentally unbalanced by Jimmy's illness, or what?"

"It wasn't real to her. Maybe that is a kind of mental

problem. The pain or inconvenience or distress of other people Virginia always treated lightly, but let her have a headache or a hangnail or a mosquito bite and she would drive you crazy with her complaining. Haven't you ever known someone like that?"

"Not intimately. Arthur is almost too sympathetic. I have to be careful not to let him spoil me when I come down with anything. But I guess the hardest thing for me, Charles, is to believe that anyone could be just plain cruel, that she could intentionally neglect Jimmy and finally just walk away from him." Helen shuddered visibly.

"Have you ever known a person who gave back or traded in every Christmas present she was ever given? That's Virginia. She was my second wife, I don't know if you know that. The first died after just five years of marriage. My only defense for loving Virginia was and is that she is so incredibly beautiful. I felt like a king with her by my side. However selfish or spoiled I knew her to be, I couldn't get out from under her spell. In a way her inability to cope with Jimmy's sickness was the salvation of both of us. Jimmy and I are better off without her. And don't you ever doubt that, Helen. You are ten times the mother Virginia was, and a hundred times the human being."

Now that was enough. Charles had said all he cared to say on that topic. He studied Helen's face and found the lines of anxiety disappearing from her forehead and the corners of her mouth. Helen smiled briefly in response to his attempt to cheer her up, then her eyes shifted to the doorway. Doctor Jacoby had entered.

The rotund doctor greeted them with a quick nod of his round, bald head as they both stood quickly to their feet.

"How is he?" Helen asked quickly.

Still nodding his head and wiping beads of perspiration away from his eyes, Jacoby did not try to soften the news. "We found the problem. A hematoma—blood clot. But we did a thorough job."

"It was just the way you thought then?" Charles asked. "You had to damage the spinal cord?"

"There is some damage, yes. We had to drain the clot, and we found pretty much what we expected. His right leg will be affected—permanently."

The doctor walked with them to the recovery room, which was the newly made-up clean room where little Marty Taylor had lain a few weeks before. As he left the doctor informed them that Jimmy would need more whole blood.

Charles said that he would donate again before he left the hospital, and as he turned back from saying goodbye to the doctor he found Helen studying him with those incredibly soft, mothering eyes of hers.

"How often have you given your own blood?" she asked quietly.

He had to be honest about it without seeming to sound heroic. "I lost count at twenty."

Helen just looked at him, her eyes resting on his for a moment, then turned away to stare silently at the empty bed standing behind the plastic screen.

They brought Jimmy in a few minutes later. The wheeled stretcher rolled to a smooth stop at the door of the clean room. The orderlies politely asked them to stand aside as they moved into the curtained section of the room. There they put on the sterilized garments, sterile gloves and white masks, and shifted the unconscious boy to a sterile cart. They nodded toward Helen and Charles, signaling that it was all right for them to enter the small antechamber in which they could stand without sterile protection. Charles and Helen watched as Jimmy was lifted toward the bed. One of his legs, the right one, lay exposed as they slid their hands from under his unconscious form. The limb was pale and so thin and fragile-looking Charles felt his vision blur with anguish. On the leg were two prominent skin sores at least two inches in diameter, raw, angry-looking, purplish blotches.

Charles heard a gasp from Helen. She looked up

with her wide eyes showing pain. "I've heard about those bruises leukemia patients get. I've never seen them before."

Charles could not comment. Seeing his son so helpless he felt a wild surge of anger sweep through him, blinding him to Helen, Jimmy, the hospital, everything. He wanted to get away from there, to drink, to scream, to smash something, to find someone to absorb the rage that exploded within him. He excused himself hastily and rushed away from Helen to stride rapidly down the corridor and not stop until he reached the door to the X-ray section and Miss Tsusumita.

CHAPTER TWENTY-FIVE

It was the most miserable Christmas Helen had ever known. At the hospital Jimmy began acting as if he had given up for good. He went through Christmas in a mood of stubborn resistance to all efforts to cheer him up. As if unified by his iron will his whole body seemed to respond with negative reactions. He was nauseous continuously and his white cell count stayed dangerously low, making it necessary for him to remain in the clean room days longer than planned. Every toy or gift that was to be admitted to that room had to be disinfected completely first, with the result that most of his Christmas gifts, those that could not be boiled or sprayed could only be shown to him through the transparent plastic sheet that surrounded his bed. He would glance at them listlessly and turn away. Worst of all he adamantly refused to begin the physical therapy routine necessary to starting to walk on his crutches. Helen pleaded with him on Christmas Day to make everyone's happiness complete by trying to take just one step. Jimmy lay stiffly against his pillow, staring straight up at the ceiling, and said, "I'm just going to die anyway, so why should I?"

The situation at home was not much better for Helen. She managed to find time enough to cook a Christmas turkey to serve to Arthur and Sharon and Mike, the young man Sharon brought home with her from college. But beyond that the holiday was a disaster. Arthur tried to assure her that he was not disappointed in the least and had never cared much for all the fuss of Christmas anyway, but Arthur's helpful attitude only made her feel more guilty. She felt guilty for getting her cards mailed out late, for buying the few gifts she managed to find on that one unhappy trip with Katie, all of which proved to be the wrong color or size, for failing to get the house decorated, for not helping Arthur with the tree, and for her own mood of despair about Jimmy.

Sharon did not stay at home for long, and Helen would have blamed herself for that too if Arthur had not cut her short. "Look, Helen," he said. "She did the same thing last year, remember? She just wants to know we're here so she can check in, drop off her laundry and catch up with her friends."

Two days before New Year's Day Helen dragged herself back to the house after another horrible day with Jimmy to find Arthur holding some tickets in his hand. He explained that Mike, Sharon's boyfriend, had managed to get tickets to the Rose Bowl game. Helen could see his pleasure in having such a prize.

"This boyfriend has some connections! Do you realize how hard these are to come by?" Then Arthur said, "Helen, I want you to go with us. It will be good for you. And I won't take no for an answer. This is one time when Jimmy will have to play second fiddle."

Helen would have preferred to think about it a bit, but Arthur insisted on an immediate answer, saying, "We can't let that seat go to waste. If you don't want it, then Mike has a friend he will take along, but he has to let his friend know right away." He paused and his voice dropped to a tone that was a bit more demanding. "Helen, I want you there with me; and I think you owe it to Sharon."

"I need time to think about it, Arthur."

"Can't Jimmy spare you for one day? Will it make any difference to him in the long run?"

"He expects me to be there. You wouldn't think so to hear the things he says to me, but he wants me with him. I know he does."

"So do I. So does Sharon." Arthur tried to take the sting out of his statement by grinning at her, but Helen felt he was forcing her to a choice between Jimmy and the family.

"You're not being fair, Arthur. It's just because Jimmy is so down and so blue that I feel he needs me. The child talks about nothing but dying. He says he doesn't care if he never walks again. He's just given up completely."

Though Arthur greeted her comments with silence, she knew he was not accepting her refusal. He laid the tickets on the dining room table, fanned out so she could count them.

"I think it would be good for you to get away from Jimmy for a while, Helen. Maybe he'll think again about things if you're not there for a day. Please, let me talk you into it just this one time."

"How will I explain it to Jimmy?" Helen asked. That was the heart of the matter. She tried to help Arthur see the problem. "Jimmy does not want to hear anything about this part of my life. He tries to think of me as his own mother, can't you see that?"

Arthur shook his head stubbornly. Jimmy's possessiveness was one of the things about the boy he found hardest to accept. He said, "That's just a fantasy he has. Maybe it would be good for him to be more realistic."

Helen pointed out that such a thing was easy enough

to say, but reminded Arthur that fantasy was about all Jimmy had in his life. In the end, though, Helen did give in, on the condition that she would be able to go to the hospital early on New Year's Day and the others would pick her up there on the way to the game. Arthur agreed, though the possibility of arriving late at the Rose Bowl and having to park several miles away because of the Rose Parade crowds in Pasadena was not a pleasant prospect.

She arrived at the hospital on New Year's Day to find that Jimmy had been transferred out of the clean room and into a semiprivate room. His release from the confines of that plastic cocoon environment helped to raise Jimmy's spirits, and to her great relief she found him enjoying his Christmas gifts when she arrived. One present in particular held his attention. It was a toy model of a hang-glider given to him by Frank and Bobbie. He was sitting up in his bed hunched over a lap tray on which he had begun assembling his gift. He greeted her cheerfully and Helen promptly told him about her plans for the day.

"That's okay, Mom," he smiled. "I'm going to be busy with this neat glider anyway."

Relieved, she sat down next to the bed and offered to help.

"No, you just sit there," he said. "Talk to me while I do it myself."

He concentrated on his task with the furious single-mindedness of which he was so capable when his interest was aroused. Helen found herself thinking again what a terrible waste it was for a boy of such active intelligence to be kept from school. She determined, with a kind of New Year's resolution and promise to herself, that she would do everything she could in the coming year to stimulate and nurture his keen young mind.

Still directing his attention to the task of clipping together the small plastic parts that made up the frame of his model, Jimmy quietly said, "Mom, when I die I know it's going to be just like going off the cliff on the gliders."

She caught herself starting to contradict his statement, with her usual instinctive rejection of such talk, but remembered Dr. Miller's advice. It required a real effort of will power for her to say, "That's an interesting way to think about it, Jimmy."

"It came to me when I was up there with Jack. You remember that first second when you left the ground? It was scary, but it didn't last long at all, did it?" He looked up and grinned at her. "I heard you go whoooo!"

"It was scary. I thought we were going to drop right down the side of the cliff."

"But we didn't, did we? And when I die that's the way I know it will be. A little scary at first but just like flying up into the sky, right past the sun and clear up to heaven. Remember that bad dream I told you about?"

"Yes."

"I've only had that dream once since I thought about how it would be like flying. That was here in the hospital the night before my operation." He finished assembling the part he was working on at the time, and lay back against his pillow. His eyes were closed. Helen could see that his eyelids were almost transparent. His skin was still very pale. A stray lock of his newly grown straight blond hair drooped toward his right eye.

"Are you all right, Jimmy?"

"Yes," he replied, opening his eyes. "I was just feeling what it would be like to have my body lying in the ground. It would be the same as being asleep, wouldn't it, Mom?"

"Jimmy . . ." Again she had to force down the impulse to reject such a vivid picture of his death, and in an instant found herself wondering: why do I react this way? He touched her hand.

"Wouldn't it be like sleeping?"

"Yes, Jimmy, I think it would."

"Sometimes, Mom, I almost wish . . ."

He glanced up at her as if weighing the decision whether to share it with her or not. She took his slim right hand in hers and squeezed it gently. "What do you wish?"

"You won't get mad?"

"I'll give you an honest reaction. If I feel mad I'll tell you why. Okay?" Helen tried to keep her tension from communicating to him through her hand.

"Sometimes I wish I would go to sleep and just not wake up any more." His eyes searched her face. "Is it bad to feel like that?"

"No, Jimmy. Nothing you feel could be bad. Not if it's an honest feeling." Helen felt herself drifting into what was deep water for her. A course in elementary psychology and the rearing of one incredibly healthy youngster had not prepared her for this. Cautiously she added, "We all have a right to our feelings."

"Once I thought about doing something to myself so I wouldn't wake up again."

"Oh, Jimmy, no!" Helen felt the uncertain psychological ground she was treading grow suddenly treacherous. She wanted to grasp something to hold onto. She knew it was a cliché when she said, "You may feel discouraged, Jimmy, or even in pain, but don't ever think of that. You must not do that."

"Would that be bad?"

"Yes, Jimmy. It would be very bad."

"Why?"

Helen grasped both his hands and held them tight as she struggled to find the words. "Jimmy, it would be bad for you, because our lives, they're not just ours alone. There are people who love you and are trying so hard to help you. Think of your father, of Jessica, and your doctors—and me, Jimmy. I just wouldn't be able to stand it, if . . ."

"Don't cry, Mom. I'm not going to do it. I just thought about it one time when I was all alone here in the hospital and I was so sick of the shots and the medicine and the pain. That was before you came along."

He smiled his angelic smile and pulled his hands away to reach for the unassembled glider.

As Helen searched her purse for a tissue, her vision swimming in tears, Jimmy bent over his toy to begin working again. She dried her eyes, thinking how easily he could take her from the heights to the depths. "Before you came along" he had said, with that smile of his. It warmed her heart like a flame, and encouraged her to pursue the matter yet one step further.

"Jimmy, I feel sometimes like you've given up too soon." He looked up frowning. She went on quickly, "For some reason, maybe because Virginia left you, maybe for some other reason, you seem to have made up your mind that you are going to die. I want you to know that I do not believe that."

"I know that, Mom." He said it very matter-of-factly, and went back to concentrating on his work.

"I just think it would be better for you, Jimmy, if you started really thinking about living. Really living. About things like the future—and maybe even going back to school one of these days."

He did not look up. "No, I won't ever go back to school. Because I'm not going to be able to walk right."

"A lot of boys and girls have to use crutches. Some go to school in wheelchairs, and can't use either one of their legs."

"No. Hand me the glue, will you, Mom."

His voice told her his decision was final. She picked up a tiny tube made of dull lead-colored metal. He took it from her fingers and removed its cap.

"Jimmy, you mustn't let your mind get set like that glue. Our minds have to stay free to grow and change. This idea of dying has just gotten stuck in your head, and I want to help you unstick it."

"Are you saying you don't want me to talk to you about dying any more?" He looked up suddenly, very wistful, a small child expecting punishment. The look in his eyes wrung Helen's heart.

"No, Jimmy. It's all right to talk about it, if you feel

that way. I'm not saying that. Please understand me. I'm not saying you're bad or anything like that. It's just that I'm trying to help you see that there is another way to feel about what you're going through. Do you understand that?"

He looked puzzled. "I just feel what I feel."

"I know you do." Helen's mind raced to find a way of holding on to the progress she felt they had made. It was the longest conversation she'd had with him about dying, and the first time she had tried to alter his fixed view that the future had already been determined. She needed something that would keep the matter open between them. After a moment of further thought, she said, "Jimmy, I promise that I will let you talk about dying any time you want, if you will make me a promise, too."

"About what?" His curiosity was aroused.

"You must promise me that you'll let me talk about living. And you'll listen and think about it the way I do when you talk to me."

"I'll try," he answered. Then he looked away from Helen and his forehead wrinkled as he stared at the pieces of his beloved toy. "But it's not easy to think a lot about something you know you can never have."

Helen suddenly realized that there in one stunningly simple statement Jimmy had answered everything. It was so direct and so obviously from the heart that it was beyond further question. He simply could not think about living and all it implied of happiness and growth and new experiences because it hurt too much. It hurt less to think of death. Helen sat back and watched him intently working, now understanding his way of concentrating so hard on whatever occupied the present moment, seeing it now as Jimmy's way of fully living each moment he was sure of. It was a painful insight he had given her, one that made part of her want to wrap her arms around him and tell him not to worry, not to let his child's mind linger on the dark terror of death. But another part of her knew he was beyond easy consolations and trite explanations, knew that Jimmy was living in his own kind of world, the one he inhabited daily and had fully explored, within which he had made his own kind of peace. To lead him back toward life now might mean shattering part of his strange truce with death.

Throughout the day and night that followed, Helen moved as if in a daze. As soon as the four of them entered the car for the drive to Pasadena Helen found herself having to force an interest in the family outing she did not really feel.

Sharon's boyfriend, Michael, was surprisingly clean and healthy-looking compared to other boys Sharon was in the habit of bringing home. He was slim and tall and rather scholarly in his appearance. His hair was cut to a nice length, over his ears but not too long, and rather high cheekbones gave him a slightly exotic, almost oriental look. He was dark-skinned. Sharon explained that his father had once been connected with one of the maritime unions in San Francisco. When he spoke with Helen or Arthur he was polite, but seemed perfectly at ease and not trying too hard to make a good impression, which impressed Helen, though she sensed that Arthur was a bit tense with the young man.

Arthur spent a good deal of the time preening himself on the arrangements for parking and getting to the Rose Bowl he had managed to contrive. A group of engineers had gotten together and secured parking permits on the grounds of the Jet Propulsion Lab. The world-famous center for space exploration was located just north of the Rose Bowl in the same huge canyon, and lay no more than a mile from the site of the game.

They parked and entered a small van with two other couples, all but Helen laughing and waving USC pennants and getting an early start on the thermos jugs of martinis that seemed to be something of a tradition for this group.

The pageantry and hoopla of the game passed Helen by as if it transpired on another planet. She sat between

Arthur and Sharon and tried to concentrate on the scurrying figures far below as they chased and battered each other. They were so far away and their actions so indistinguishable that Helen finally came to see them as red and white cells struggling for dominance. The red jerseys would sweep the white ones down the field, then the white would recover their strength and slowly but surely move the red ones back. Red cells against white cells. In the case of the game it did not matter to her which side won.

At halftime Sharon accompanied Helen to the rest-room. As they stood in line with fifty others, Sharon said, "Mom, how do you like Michael? You haven't said."

"I like him. I think he's very nice."

"Very nice! Mom, he's very special to me."

There was something in the way Sharon lifted her chin and glanced up at Helen, then quickly away, that made Helen ask, "How special?"

"Very. I want to talk to you about him—and me."

Helen sensed that Sharon was approaching one of her revelations, as usual, in a very roundabout way. Sharon had always found it easier, or more convenient, to talk to her father when there was something she wanted. The distance between Helen and her daughter had grown during the late teen years, and just when she was getting to an age when Helen thought there might be a chance for them to become good friends again, Sharon had decided on college. Helen wasn't sure just how close their relationship was now, not when it came to something really significant. From the way the lines of doubt were forming between Sharon's eyebrows, Helen felt this might be a real test of just how close they would be in the future. She waited for Sharon to speak first.

"It's been a long time since we had a real talk, Mom."

"Yes, it has. I've missed the times we used to have together."

"Well, life goes on, as they say." Sharon fidgeted and glanced over the heads of seated spectators between them and the halftime show. The Rose Parade Queen and her court were being paraded around the field seated on the back of a white Cadillac convertible. Sharon grinned. "The queen. Want to see her?"

"Who could see her?" Helen responded. "She's a half mile away from here. What is it, Sharon? There's something you wanted to tell me."

Sharon kept staring at the tiny figures of the girls in their white formals on the white Cadillac. Her voice trembled a little as she said, "All white, with roses. Do you think they're all virgins, Mom?"

Helen wasn't sure whether Sharon was trying to shock her or not. There might have been a time when such a statement would have. Helen was pleased to find herself laughing. "If you're trying to shock me, dear, I'm afraid it won't work. I may be forty but I'm also going to college now, learning psychology and all kinds of things. I would even be willing to say that whether they are virgins or not is up to them. Now tell me about you and Mike."

She had opened the way for Sharon and could see the relief in her daughter's eyes. "We're going to live together, Mom. Lisa's moving out of the apartment we've been sharing. Michael's moving in."

They were within a few feet of the restroom door. Helen felt she ought to have some kind of ready answer for Sharon, but she wasn't sure just what her reaction should be. She took the easy way out. "Let's discuss it when we come out. This hardly seems like the place."

Sharon laughed explosively, with evident release of built-up tension, and led the way into the ladies' room.

When they emerged a few minutes later, Sharon seemed to have done some thinking of her own. She took Helen's arm and squeezed it to her side. "Mom, I was really afraid to tell you. But I did want you to know. Somehow keeping it a secret would have made it wrong for me."

"You weren't asking me for advice then, were you?" Helen knew the answer to that before Sharon grinned and shook her head. "What you want is a reaction. Am I going to think less of you, or worry about you, or not speak to your father for you, right?"

"Right!" Sharon beamed. Then she suddenly stopped and pulled Helen aside out of the stream of moving bodies that was sweeping them back toward their seats.

"Why are we stopping, dear?"

"Mom, do you really want me to live with a guy?"

Helen took a deep breath and held it for a moment as she looked into her daughter's inquiring and somewhat puzzled eyes. "You are twenty years old, Sharon. I trust you. I think that you have been given all the values and all the love your father and I could give. Now it's time for you to decide what your life is going to be. I won't say no, if this is what you feel is right for you. But I won't turn handsprings, either, and boast about how liberated my daughter is. I'll be worried—but I'll have faith in you. I don't know what else to say."

Sharon's eyes suddenly glazed with tears and she threw her arms around her mother and hugged her close. Helen felt herself momentarily overwhelmed with memories of Sharon's wild, spontaneous displays of almost violent affection when she was a small child. Then she would fling herself at her mother's neck and cover Helen's face with kisses. Now she hugged her tightly and in an almost comradely fashion and quickly released her. "You know, Mom, you and I ought to have a long talk about this boy of yours, Jimmy. He's bringing out something terrific in you."

They returned to their seats with Sharon clinging to her arm. As they sat down, Sharon whispered something to Michael, who leaned out around the girl and smiled broadly at Helen. Sharon squeezed her arm and gave her a kiss on the cheek.

* * *

Arthur said nothing about the situation with Sharon until they were preparing for bed that night. He was already under the covers with the light on on his side of the bed when she emerged from the bathroom.

"Sharon told me the news, Helen. She said she'd talked to you and you told her to do whatever she wants. Is that right?"

"Yes. I think she has to make that kind of decision herself."

He stared at her, tight-lipped and pale. "They're not even planning to be married, did you know that?"

"I didn't ask."

Again he was silent. He stared at his feet beneath the covers, shaking his head. "I don't know about you. I just don't know you any more."

"Is it so wrong, Arthur, what she's doing? At least she came to us openly and honestly and like a grownup. The fact she's so open about it could mean she may be ready for something like this."

He rolled over, turning his back to her. "If she gets hurt, you have to live with it."

There was a time when his silence would have tortured her into capitulation. On nights like this in the past Helen would lie awake half the night worrying about Arthur's feelings and punishing herself toward some kind of compromise solution. But now she felt none of that old sense of guilt and inferiority. It pleased her to remember what Sharon had said about Jimmy. "He's bringing out something terrific in you!"

Helen could not determine in any direct sense just how her relationship with Jimmy was affecting everything else, but it was. It was as if in responding spontaneously to him she had opened the gates to her inner self. There wasn't much that really frightened her any more. It was as if with Jimmy she spent entire days staring death in the eye and in the process finding new planes of understanding within herself. Jimmy was taking her somewhere, toward something inside herself that she anticipated with a kind of breathless impatience. It was something she could share with no one, not even the wise child who was bringing it to her like a gift. But from now on she knew, she would attend to Jimmy's gift of wisdom in a new way. She would sit at his feet like a disciple and learn as one learns from a perceptive traveler whose eyes have beheld another country.

CHAPTER TWENTY-SIX

Jimmy's father was taking him home from the hospital. It was the fifteenth of January. Everybody seemed to be mad at him. Even his mom scolded him when he wouldn't use the crutches. The look on her face, around her mouth, reminded him of Virginia.

"Jimmy, you're just being bad. Didn't you hear what the preacher said? He said God would heal you if you just believed hard enough. You're not trying! Now this time when we get to the tabernacle I want you to sit right there in the first row and listen to every word Reverend Malgrove says, and you believe!"

He had never been permitted to call her mother, or mom. She always wanted to be called just Virginia, and she even used to get after Jimmy's father for not making Jimmy call him by his first name. But Dad didn't mind being his dad.

Jimmy lay back in the tilt-back seat in his father's car and watched the UCLA campus recede from his view. His dad wouldn't argue with him about not using his crutches. His dad always let him do or say anything he wanted. Jimmy knew that his dad felt sorry about the Thing, and about the way Virginia had turned out, and he was always trying to make up for it.

Virginia had to have everything perfect around her. The clothes she wore were always new, and the closets were jammed to overflowing even in the big house in Encino that had so many rooms. Cleaning ladies came in twice each week to make sure the house looked perfect. Virginia would follow them around as they worked and caution them about being careful of the antique furniture and the expensive oil paintings and her precious cup collection. She was always firing the cleaning ladies and getting new ones. Then she would follow the new ones and scream at them if they made a mistake and make them so nervous they would be sure to scratch something or drop something and break it, and they would get fired too.

Jimmy used to look perfect before the Thing came along. He would never forget the time he had heard Virginia talking to one of her friends on the phone. He could hear her voice now, high-pitched and tight like a wire stretched to the breaking point, saying, "Charles just expects me to do everything. I just can't stand it. He's not the same boy at all. No, he's not. I can't even think of him as my son, he's so changed. You know how they get. His hair has fallen out, and he looks so ugly I can't stand to look at him. And his teeth, you know how their gums bleed, and he's pale and tired all the time. And cleaning up after him! I mean he throws up everything he eats, and it's not my fault! I feed him well, follow all the diet things they've given me, but vomiting—ugh, dear God. I mean right on one of our priceless antique chairs! How much can a person be expected to take? I work with him day and night! Oh, of course there's the nurse and the cleaning people, but so much of it falls on me. Charles? He's off on his so-called selling trips all the time. And I'm getting lines around my eyes. Oh yes! And dark circles. It's taking its toll, I'll tell you. And I just don't know how I can go on. It's too much to ask of any human being. I think the boy ought to be put into a hospital somewhere and just left there until he's better. This idea of home care being best for them is just a farce. Can we afford it? Of course we can, only Charles is too cheap to do it. He expects me to get some kind of special delight out of taking care of Jimmy, as if it's a privilege of some kind. I'd like to see him do some of these things!"

Jimmy thought, people can love you when you're perfect, but not when you're ugly. He felt his ugliness more than ever now, with his useless leg flopping around. He'd just started getting some hair back and putting on a little bit of weight, and now this. He thought, I'm just going to get uglier and uglier until I die, and not even my new mom will be able to love me.

The day Virginia left she came into his bedroom at home and told him, "You're going back to the hospital again, Jimmy, and when you come home, I won't be here any more. Your father and I just don't love each other any more. He's been bad to me, selfish and cruel, and I just can't take it any longer. And he's going to be taking care of you. He doesn't think I'm doing a very good job of it, so we'll just see if he can do any better."

Jimmy glanced at his father's face. Charles turned and looked at him as if he could feel Jimmy watching him. His dad winked at him and said, "How're you doing, Champ?"

"I'm not a champ."

"Oh yes, you are. You're beating everybody over this business of not walking on your crutches."

His dad had a way of making things seem like a game sometimes. Sometimes it was fun, but this time it just made Jimmy mad.

"I can't help it, Dad."

"You're the only one that can help it. It's your life, Jimmy. If you want to spend the rest of it lying around in bed, that's up to you."

Jimmy didn't answer. He was thinking how different his father was from Virginia. No matter what his dad said Jimmy knew his dad liked him. Virginia had never seemed like his real mother, not even before he got sick. She was always dressing him up and fussing over him and getting mad at him if he got dirty. Once he had run into the house when his puppy got hurt in a dog fight and when he threw his arms around Virginia he got her white slacks dirty. It didn't matter to her that his dog was hurt or that he was crying, because she could only yell at him about her pants.

Jimmy had never talked to his dad very much about Virginia. He decided this might be a good time. "Dad?"

"Yeah, Champ?"

"Was Virginia my real mother?"

His father waited for a while before he answered. The expression on his face as he drove the car was like the way people look when they've just tasted something they didn't like very much. Then he said, "Depends on what you mean by real. She gave birth to you."

"Why was she always afraid of getting dirty? She used to yell at me a lot about it."

"She was afraid of a lot of things." His dad kept driving, and Jimmy didn't know whether he realized it or not but as soon as they started talking about Virginia he started driving faster. After about another minute his dad said, "You're better off without her. You know that, don't you?"

"I guess so." One of the things Jimmy thought about sometimes was whether Virginia would ever come back. He wasn't sure how he would feel about that. "She's not ever coming back is she, Dad?"

"Not if I can help it."

"She left because I got ugly, didn't she?"

All of a sudden the car went through a crossing on a red light. His dad finally slammed on the brakes, and with horns blaring on both sides of them, he backed up to get out of the way of the traffic. While they waited for the light to change he said, "Jimmy, I've told you before. That isn't it. She left because she felt I made her unhappy. It wasn't your fault, son. Maybe I could have tried harder, I don't know. But Virginia is just an unhappy person to start with. No matter how she's treated, believe me, she's going to be unhappy, because she's unhappy with herself. I'll tell you a secret, Jimmy. If you don't have happiness inside you, nobody can give it to you. And you can't make another person be happy if they haven't got some of it on their own. It's like Virginia was missing a happiness button. You didn't make her lose that button, and I didn't either. She lost it somewhere when she was a child, I think. Her mother used to dress her up and push her out in front of people all the time, in beauty contests, things like that." His father laughed all of a sudden, as if he'd seen something funny. "That was it. One day she got all dressed up to try out for Miss Junior High School of nineteen hundred and whatever, and they were so worried about her dress and her hair and her eye makeup they lost track of her happiness button, and it's been missing ever since!"

They went on through the light and his dad drove slower as if he'd relaxed. There was a big, loose smile on his face.

Jimmy thought about something that he felt would make both of them a lot happier. "I wish you'd marry Helen, Dad. Then she'd be with us all the time. I think Mom's got a happiness button."

His father chuckled. "You're right about that. But Helen's also got a husband. And don't start riding her about coming to the beach to live with you. She's doing more than we have any right to expect as it is."

Jimmy didn't answer that. He was beginning to feel tired out by the trip, and the idea of his new mom not being with him all the time depressed him. There wasn't anything to look forward to in being home. His seagull, Charlie, was dead. He wouldn't be able to walk on the beach any more, or fly again on the hang glider. He would just lie in his bed, missing Mom, looking out the window at the water, and waiting until he had to be taken back to the hospital again. It occurred to him that maybe he didn't have a happiness button either.

CHAPTER TWENTY-SEVEN

"The milk's sour." Jimmy folded his arms across his chest and glared up at Helen.

She took a spoonful of the milk in which his favorite breakfast cereal floated and tasted it. "It tastes all right to me."

"Well, it's not. They never gave me sour milk at the hospital."

She tried to cheer him up. "Maybe they use a different kind of milk there and it tastes different. But this isn't sour, Jimmy. It's just your first week home and you have to get used to changes again."

"I don't care what you say, Helen, it's sour. And the orange juice tastes funny, too." He pushed the tray away, almost making it spill onto the bed. Helen caught it and carried it to the kitchen. She set it on the sideboard of the sink next to Jessica.

"He's been in a rotten mood ever since he got home," Jessica informed her.

"Could the new drug affect his taste buds somehow?"

Jessica smiled. "Did he tell you that?"

"No. I just thought . . ."

"Last night he said the bed was too hard. When I finally got him off of that he tried to think of something else to complain about and decided the ocean was making too much noise for him to sleep. He stayed up half the night and made me play Monopoly with him." Jessica yawned as if the memory induced immediate boredom. "Then when I beat him at it he threw the money and the board and all the pieces all over the room."

"He's never been this bad before. It's his leg, Jessica. It's hard to get mad at him."

"Not at four o'clock in the morning, it ain't. I had to crawl around on my hands and knees and pick all that stuff up." Jessica rolled her eyes and did a fairly comical imitation of a put-upon servant. Then she sobered and shook her head. "I'm only kidding. If I'd suffered what that boy's suffered, Lord knows I'd be harder to live with than he is. Our biggest problem isn't going to be his tantrums, it's gonna be getting him out of that bed and on his crutches."

Helen returned to his room and found Jimmy staring out the window toward the sea, his head turned away from her. She spoke his name and he ignored her. After a moment of hesitation she walked around the bed and stood between him and the window. He turned his head the other way.

"Jimmy, this is silly," she said. "Is this the way it's going to be now? You're not even going to look at me any more?"

"You don't care about me." He kept his face away but there was a catch in his throat that conveyed to Helen a message of real hurt.

"Jimmy! I know you don't mean that. Look at me." She sat on the edge of the bed and laid her hand under his cheek to turn his face toward hers. He raised his eyes to hers and his tears were real. She kissed his cheek and his forehead, then his closed eyelids tasting of salt. Jimmy, usually a bit reserved with her and standoffish, brought his arm up around her neck and clung to her. A lump rose in Helen's throat as she laid her cheek against his and their tears mingled. He brought the other arm up and held her with both of his thin arms locked around her as one anguished sob after another began to wrack his emaciated frame. Helen's own tears flowed and it soon became a storm of weeping for both of them, one that tore at Helen's heart. For minutes it continued until Helen feared he would wear himself out with it, and just when she felt he was finished it began again. His arms did not loosen their hold for perhaps a full five minutes of unleashed grief which Helen shared in waves of tears. The harder Jimmy cried the more Helen released her own pent-up sadness. At the end she was sobbing as if she had carried the burden of his sufferings for a lifetime. As the storm finally began to subside they clung to each other in silence, communicating in a closeness and joining of grief that was too profound for speech. At last his arms relaxed and Helen drew away to look at him. Their eyes locked on each other's faces, silently questioning, examining, loving, and then finally enjoying each other.

"Boy," Jimmy said.

"Whew," Helen agreed.

"That was something, Mom. I'm sorry I said you didn't care about me."

"And I'm sorry, Jimmy, just for everything. Maybe now that we've done all that we can start this day over in a new way, okay?"

"I'm just sleepy, Mom. I'm so sleepy I can't even talk any more."

She patted his shoulder and tucked him in. As she turned to leave his muffled voice followed her to the door.

"The reason I was mad was because I knew you were going to leave me and go to school. I'm sorry, Mom."

"You sleep now, and by the time you're awake for lunch I'll be back." Helen softly closed the door and looked up to find Jessica standing in the corridor near the kitchen, drying her eyes with a corner of her apron. The black woman opened her arms to Helen and hugged her to her bosom, and Helen thought the whole thing was going to start over again with Jessica. After a moment of thumping Helen's shoulder blades with both her hands and leaning her face against her shoulder, Jessica pulled away.

"I couldn't help hearing all that," Jessica sniffled. "You get me started bawling and nothin's gonna get done around here." She extracted a tissue from her apron pocket and blew her nose in one quick, business-like spurt.

"I'm not sure what brought it on," Helen said. "It was just there all of a sudden. Now he's going back to sleep."

Helen made her way quickly to the small bathroom and freshened her face with cold water. As she passed through the kitchen toward her car to leave for school, Jessica said in her soft drawl, "As far as I know that's the first time Jimmy's really cried. I'm a great believer in crying. I think you just did him a world of good."

An hour later, during Professor Mays's lecture, Helen felt completely drained by the experience with Jimmy, yet oddly refreshed by it. It had been a catharsis. Her attention kept drifting away from the classroom and back to the beach house. Just before the end of the class she was mulling over schemes for getting Jimmy to use his crutches, when she suddenly became aware of the students around her looking in her direction with amused smiles.

Professor Mays's voice came through to her. "Wouldn't you agree, Mrs. Long?"

She felt a flush of embarrassment. "I'm sorry. I missed the question."

"Too bad, and it was such a brilliant question," the professor grinned, sensing her distraction. "We'll start from there tomorrow, class." He dismissed the class, thus saving Helen further discomfiture. Helen remained in her seat as the room around her exploded into youthful activity. She needed time to recover.

Professor Mays gathered his books under his arm and made his way up the stairs of the lecture hall to her seat, his grin gradually giving way to a look of amused inquiry as he reached her side and the last clamouring sophomore left the hall. He stood over her, stroking his full, red beard.

"Well, Helen. How are you? I'm sorry I caught you

off guard like that." His apologetic grin shone through his beard with unmistakeable warmth.

"I've had quite an unsettling morning. Thanks for getting me off the hook by letting the class go."

"There were a couple of minutes left, but at this age they're already halfway out the door fifteen minutes before the period ends anyway."

As she gathered up her purse, notebook and text, he continued casually, "At the prices their parents are paying for this you would think they might feel deprived of their rights to be let go ahead of time. Unfortunately, most of them feel they have far better things to do than listen to a lecture."

She walked beside him as they came out of the building into the sunlit quad that fronted it. Helen's awareness seemed heightened by the emotional storm with Jimmy. She felt as never before the coolness of the leaping fountain, the crisp green of the lawn and the graceful sweep of red tile that paved the Spanish-style courtyard. It made her want to breathe deeply and lift her face to the warm sun.

"You seem to be holding up rather well," the professor commented. "How about a cup of coffee?" He took her arm as if sure of her assent and smilingly escorted her toward the faculty lounge.

Inside, the atmosphere contrasted sharply with the student cafeteria. "My, this is classy," Helen observed. "I'm joining the faculty today."

The teacher maintained his jovial mood as they seated themselves in deep leather chairs in a small side room that seemed designed for issues of great academic import. Paintings of former college presidents adorned the paneled walls and a large fireplace in Spanish mosaic and stucco dominated one entire side of the room. The couches and deep chairs were grouped in conversation areas, each grouping with its own solid oak coffee table, and each area lit by the soft glow of a heavily shaded wrought-iron floor lamp. Helen and Mays were alone.

Professor Mays leaned back, savoring his coffee and studying Helen.

She suddenly yawned. "Oh, I'm sorry," Helen said. "I feel so relaxed here. And something happened this morning that has just unstrung me completely."

She went on to tell about the scene with Jimmy, which led to his asking for a complete summary of her situation. He listened very attentively, seeming to get a great charge out of the story of Jimmy's and Helen's flight on the hang gliders, then showing deep sympathy over the operation on his spine. Helen felt encouraged to share with him the problem of Jimmy's unwillingness to use the crutches.

"He just won't consider getting out of bed again, and he's unbelievably cranky with everyone. I think his attitude is he's going to die soon so why bother."

"How do you feel about that?"

"Just as I've felt from the beginning. He is going to live, at least we have to carry right on as if he is. We must not give up."

"Has Dr. Miller been any help?"

"Some, yes. But I haven't talked to her about his problem now, about not wanting to walk again. Do you think I should?"

"Maybe I can help. I'm very good with children."

Helen suppressed a smile as she saw a familiar look in the professor's eye. She knew he would probably give generously of his time for Jimmy, but was not sure what the man might expect in return. She was flattered somewhere inside among all the warning alarms that were going off, but she really wanted his help with Jimmy. "He doesn't like strangers," she said. "But thanks for offering."

"You don't like strangers much either, do you?"

"I don't know what you mean."

"Oh, come on, Helen. Relax. You can be open and honest with me. I find you very attractive, and I think you should know that."

"Professor Mays . . ."

"Now you're reminding me of my official title, as a not-too-subtle warning for me to back off. Can't you talk to me as a man?" His tone had turned harsh, almost angry.

Confused and tense, Helen replied, "I don't handle things like this well at all. I'm not one of your campus teenagers."

His smile curled within the beard. "What you need is a good group experience."

"What kind of group—experience?"

"Something to free you up. I can't believe you. Did you just come out of a convent or something? Where have you been during the sexual revolution?" Before she could think of a reply, he went on, "There's a group that meets right here in Santa Monica. They work on interpersonal communication through touch—they work in the nude."

Helen almost burst out laughing, but the psychologist was not smiling. The anger she had sensed in him was obviously smouldering now and he positively sneered as Helen answered, "I don't work in the nude."

His tone suddenly changed and became comforting in a way, though beneath it all ran a current of contempt that truly frightened Helen, as he said, "I could help you, Helen. You are trying to get out of your shell and you are at the same time afraid of what you're going to find. Sex is basic to your whole problem. It would be irresponsible of me not to point that out to you."

She snapped, "How very generous of you." Then she caught her breath as he stiffened, glaring down his nose at her.

"Why in God's name did you take a psychology course, if I may ask?"

"To learn about myself—and other people," Helen weakly replied.

He stared at her, shaking his head as if his contempt had turned to pity. "You want to get a lot of little tricks and secrets and catch phrases in your head, right?

That's not what it's about, dear lady. It's about change and growth and turning on the woman in you. I'm prepared to lead you through a personal revolution and you want me to crochet you a little sampler to hang on your wall, a tidy little thought-for-the-day."

Helen suddenly wanted out of there, and out of his classes forever, but there was still Jimmy. "I wanted to ask your help with Jimmy. That's all I wanted."

Professor Mays suddenly reached out and grasped Helen's wrist, squeezing it tightly. "Don't tell me any more about that boy, Mrs. Long. I can tell you precisely what's happening with him."

He released her arm and actually smiled again, demonstrating that almost mechanical ability he had of going from intimacy to business as usual in a single breath.

"All right, tell me, if you want," she stammered.

"He's changed. Since he's been home he's totally uncooperative, given to rages over nothing, and blames the adults around him for everything."

Helen waited, amazed, as he continued.

"His rage comes from his vulnerability. Without the use of his leg on top of all his other problems, he feels you've let him down. He is more dependent than ever and he thinks you've failed him. What he needs is reassurance."

Her head swimming, Helen said, "Reassurance? I've tried to tell him . . ."

"To tell him!" the professor laughed. "Oh, yes, I'm sure you have." He stopped laughing and almost snarled at her, "He needs more than that, but to tell you the truth, I doubt he's going to get it from you."

Helen reeled under the cruelty she saw in his eyes. "I'll do anything to help Jimmy. Why are you talking to me like this?"

"Because I think you're faking it, Mrs. Long."

"Faking it! With Jimmy?" Helen was on her feet and was well aware that she was about to walk out on another ugly scene. Mays leaped to his feet and stepped in front of her.

"Avoiding confrontation is one of the things phonys do best. Are you afraid to hear what I have to say?"

Helen backed one step away and halted, her breath catching in her throat, her gaze swimming with the impact of the shot of adrenalin that was coursing through her. "All right, tell me then," she challenged.

Again he smiled! It was infuriating! What a power complex this man had! "Mrs. Long, if you want to be a mother to Jimmy, then stop playing at it. For God's sake be a mother. Go down there and live with him. He had one mother who let him down, and believe me he can't stand another." He turned quickly away and hissed at her from over his shoulder as he left, "And I'd advise you to drop the class. I don't think you can cut it."

Helen collapsed into her chair and stared at his stiffly moving shoulders until the professor was through the lounge door. Trembling with shock and dismay she stared at the empty coffee cups thinking, "My Lord, I took psychology because I thought they knew something about dealing with people!"

She glanced about the room to see if anyone had seen them and was relieved to find herself quite alone. She exhaled deeply and relaxed for a moment, pondering the man's final parting words. He thought she was only playing at being Jimmy's mother! God, if he only knew what she had gone through, had only listened! She tried to shrug off the comment, but found that it stuck, burrlike, in her mind. Go to the beach house and live with Jimmy? Arthur had been very understanding up to now. What if she confronted him suddenly with this? It was just impossible.

She stood and began to walk slowly toward the door, still smarting from her teacher's harsh treatment. The man was cruel and manipulative and power-hungry—but was he right about her and Jimmy? The answer stopped her in her tracks. Perhaps he was. If there was anything Jimmy had been trying to say to her over and over, it was just that: please come and live with me.

As she walked through the door and out into the bright afternoon sunlight she knew she was faced with a decision that could change her life. The fact that it had been suggested by Professor Mays did not alter the truth of it; it only made it harder to swallow.

CHAPTER TWENTY-EIGHT

Later that afternoon Helen told Jessica about the conversation with Professor Mays. She listened gravely. Jessica's features betrayed every emotion she felt, and Helen could see that she was troubled by the decision Helen was contemplating.

"Don't you think I should do it, Jessica?"

Jessica heaved a deep sigh and bent over the pile of clean laundry she was sorting on the kitchen table. "You're getting in awful deep, Helen. I can't say one way or the other, it's got to be your choice."

"But is it the right thing for Jimmy? The more I think about it the more I believe the professor was right. But I trust your judgment, Jessica. I need to know how you feel about it."

"If you ask him, you know what Jimmy's going to say." Jessica extracted a clean white bedsheet from the laundry basket and Helen automatically reached for the edge of it to help with the folding. The sheet stretched between them as they brought the corners together, working at the familiar domestic chore with practiced skill. Jessica added, "I wouldn't tell Jimmy, though, until you're sure."

"I have to talk it over with my husband first." Helen

took a step toward Jessica, handing her the corners of the folded linen that dropped between them. Jessica gathered them with her fingertips and finished the last fold as she asked, "How's he gonna feel about all this?"

Helen leaned against the refrigerator and thought for a moment. "I'm not sure. Arthur changes."

Jessica nodded, smiling. "Don't they all?"

"Well, not Arthur. Not really. He's always been very steady and predictable, until now."

"And now?"

"For a while he was sort of caught off balance by my relationship with Jimmy. It surprised him, I think, that I could be so—well, independent. Even my going back to school set him back on his heels a little."

"I would guess you've always been pretty predictable. You don't strike me as the fly-by-night type."

Helen smiled, impressed as always by Jessica's common-sense wisdom. "Arthur liked me that way, at least he thought he did. Now I honestly think he likes me better, respects me a bit more."

"Good for you! Then what are you worried about?"

"I'm just not that sure he's consistent! Coming here, I would be asking him to accept quite a dose of independence. If I could only get him more involved with Jimmy . . ."

Jessica shook her head, pursing her lips as she smoothed the creases out of one of Jimmy's T-shirts. "Ummm—you know how Jimmy is about that. You know he doesn't even want to think about you having anybody else at all!"

"Now you can see my problem." Helen paused, thinking of another side of the situation she wasn't certain she was ready to share with Jessica.

Jessica straightened a stack of washcloths as she added the final bit of laundry to the folded things on the table. "It's a good thing your husband's not the jealous type." Her lovely almond eyes flicked up to Helen's face and Jessica instantly grinned. "Or is he?"

Helen nodded, acknowledging Jessica's intuition.

"You amaze me, Jessica. He has been known to be a bit possessive sometimes, yes."

Jessica began gathering armfuls of stacked clothing, and as she did so she whistled softly, some tune that Helen did not recognize.

Helen said, "Jessica, what do you think I should do?"

"I think you'd better have a long talk with yourself. What if your husband happens to hear about Mister B. hanging around here, and starts to get worried?"

"He already has."

Jessica gave her a cautionary look and walked away. She resumed her whistling out in the corridor by the linen cupboard. The tune had the flavor of an old blues number.

Jimmy seemed to be in a more pleasant mood later that day. He and Helen spent the afternon hours playing backgammon. Jimmy won three games to her one, and was cheerful even when she was victorious, which was something for him. Seeing him more cooperative and relaxed she began to wonder whether there was any real need for her to change their arrangement. She began to feel that she had been a little hasty, that perhaps she had communicated to Professor Mays more of a sense of panic and distress than the situation called for.

After the fourth game she began suggesting that they put the board away, that it was time for her to go home. Jimmy's back stiffened and he leaned away from her.

"It's not time for you to go yet," he said, and he extended his slim arm to show her his watch.

"It's four o'clock, Jimmy."

"It's five minutes to. I don't know why you always have to go sooner and sooner." He looked away from her to stare out the window. "You're always in such a big hurry to leave, I don't know why you come in the first place."

"I come because I want to, and I leave because I have to." Helen kept her voice level though she was stinging with hurt. Jimmy did not answer. There was only one thing he wanted to hear, and that she was not prepared to tell him yet. She pushed her chair away from the bed and began gathering up the game pieces. She tucked the red and white plastic discs into their notches in the gameboard and folded the lovely hardwood box closed. Jimmy did not turn to look at her as she placed the game on the shelf in the room.

"I'm sorry you feel that way, Jimmy." She walked back to the bedside and bent over to kiss his cheek. He still would not stir from his rigid position, looking away from her as Helen asked, "Are you saying you don't want me to come any more?"

"I didn't mean that." His eyes rolled up toward her, though his face didn't move. He was checking her expression out of the corner of his eye to see if she meant it. She smiled and caressed his cheek.

"I didn't think you did."

He rolled over to face her and his expression softened. "I just wish you didn't have to go at all."

She wanted to tell him right then, to take him in her arms and say she was coming there to be with him always. As she hesitated on the brink of voicing her decision, the corners of Jimmy's mouth drew down and he turned his face away.

She came as close as she could to saying it. "It would be wonderful to stay here with you, Jimmy. Maybe someday I could." His only response was to turn his shoulders and silently present his back. "Some day" was not what he wanted to hear.

By the time Helen reached home at four-thirty the sky had become overcast and a light rain was beginning to fall. The car radio had informed her and several thousand Superbowl fans that the rain was going to dampen their enjoyment during the following weekend and for a considerable time thereafter. Helen found her first opportunity to use one of her Christmas gifts, the one Arthur was most proud of, an automatic garage door opener. She poked the control button and sat gloomily watching the garage open its mouth. Helen thanked Arthur silently and wondered how she was going to tell him about her decision.

Inside the house she went automatically through the procedures of turning up the thermostat, taking a frozen entree from the freezer, sliding it into the microwave oven to defrost (not without a familiar stab of guilt) and setting the table.

By five o'clock she had her meal preparations completed, timed for dinner at six-thirty. Arthur's vodka martini was in the freezer, and her cup of hot tea sat steaming on the corner of the kitchen table as she listened to the steadily increasing wind gustily blowing sheets of water against the kitchen window. Out of long habit she pictured the clogged Southern California freeways Arthur would be facing on his way home, his passage rendered suddenly hazardous by nothing more than a normal winter storm. She glanced quickly at the kitchen clock, then stood and peered through the window. The rain was pouring down and the driveway was awash with debris blown from their pepper trees. She glanced toward the shrubs and grass of their well-kept lawn and thought of Arthur's patient care of the house and yard for all the months she had been preoccupied with Jimmy. Without one word of complaint Arthur had tended to everything inside the house and out. Helen had suggested that they hire someone to take care of the lawn, but he had protested that he enjoyed it and needed the exercise. Helen had managed to keep up with the basic house cleaning, but there were dozens of little tasks which Arthur had cheerfully assumed, including stopping frequently at the market on the way home, which she knew he detested.

None of these thoughts was helping her prepare to face Arthur with her decision. The rain did not help either; Arthur was easily depressed by it. In one way the inclement weather would help her cause; Jimmy could only be expected to be further depressed and Arthur might understand that.

When he had still not arrived by his usual time of five-fifteen or five-thirty, Helen decided to take a shower and change her clothes. Waiting with nothing to occupy her mind was only making things worse. She found the hot water relaxing and refreshing, and she stepped out, after lingering far longer than usual, to find Arthur standing beside the shower stall holding a towel.

"Hello, beautiful. Rotten night." He grinned and hoisted his martini glass with the other hand as she took the towel. "Can I fix you anything?"

She began drying herself off and his eyes took it all in with evident appreciation. She said, "No thanks," grateful for his cheerful mood. "I'll be down in a minute. Was it really bad coming home?"

He winked at her. "Not now that I'm home."

Good so far, she mused as Arthur closed the bathroom door behind him. Then she began looking for something suitable to wear. She rejected the sexy peignoir he had given her for Christmas, deciding that kind of suggestion would be just rubbing it in on top of what she had to tell him. She settled for a dark blue turtleneck sweater and warm wool slacks to match.

She found Arthur watching the TV news. A truck had spun out and flipped over on one of the freeways, residents of a hillside tract were preparing for the inevitable mud slides, and the sportscaster was certain a muddy field was going to aid Minnesota's Superbowl hopes. She decided to wait until dinner.

Arthur was on his second glass of wine and halfway through his second helping of noodles romanoff when he looked over, stared at her plate a moment, and said, "Why don't you just go ahead and tell me what it is you're thinking about. Then maybe you'll be able to eat."

"Am I that obvious?"

"You are tonight. For one thing you haven't said a word about your day with Jimmy. He still won't get up and get going?"

She exhaled and took the plunge. "That's part of it, but it's even worse than that, Arthur. He's just in terrible shape since his operation." Then step-by-step, Helen went from the incident Jessica had witnessed the night before to a carefully edited version of her conversation with Professor Mays, to what she had seen during the afternoon. She did not, however, mention the suggestion her psychology professor had made about her going to live at the beach house.

Arthur finished his meal, shaking his head in consternation and real sympathy; then he pushed his plate away and reached for his wine glass. "The poor kid. I think your teacher's probably right, too. Jimmy must feel nobody gives a damn about him. But what can you do?"

"The professor did have one suggestion, Arthur. But I don't know how you would feel about it. He thinks I should go and stay with Jimmy for a while." There. She had said it. Now she watched as Arthur looked steadily at her, trying to compose his face and not show his surprise.

"He thinks that will help? What do you think?" he asked.

"I think he's right, Arthur. That's what I've been trying to find some way of telling you. I think I should go and live with Jimmy. I feel it just has to be. Up to this point, I don't know—maybe I've just been playing at it. Now I really have to come through for Jimmy. I have to try to really be his mother."

His voice was constricted, his jaw tight, though he still tried not to show it as he asked, "How long will it take?"

"I don't know. If he comes through this, then not long. But if he doesn't . . . if he gets worse . . ."

Arthur sat back in his chair and reached for a cigarette. He never smoked at the table, considering it bad manners. Now it was an automatic reaction. He blew the smoke away from the table over his right shoulder. "It might be the worst thing you could do, Helen." He paused and laid the cigarette in an ashtray. "Because once you're there, and once he's had you with him all the time, isn't he going to be hurt that much more when you want to leave again?"

She had thought about that on the way home in the car. "I don't think we should try to predict Jimmy's future to that extent, Arthur. In a matter of days his attitude could change completely, and he could be ready to accept my coming home again. Or he could get into good remission and be ready to go back to school. Or he could die. There's no point in trying to predict it. I think what I should do is to react to this spontaneously, just say okay, and go."

"With no way of knowing for how long. Just go?"

"Go because he needs me, and face the future when it comes."

"That's what you want to do? You're sure?"

"Yes."

"When?"

"As soon as possible."

"Tonight?"

She sensed anger starting up in him like a coiling spring. "No, I don't think it has to be tonight. Let's be reasonable, Arthur. I'm not going to rush out of here and . . ."

"What's reasonable? If he needs you, he needs you. If not tonight, when? Tomorrow? The next day?"

"What are you saying, Arthur? I thought I would go tomorrow."

"How bad off is he, Helen? That's the point, isn't it? Or is it? You make it sound as if the boy is desperate—that he's drowning and only you can save him. Then you say you can take your time about throwing him the rope?"

"Arthur?" Helen was confused. She sensed the feeling behind it and knew Arthur well enough to know he could be in a murderous rage and not show any more emotion than he was registering now. His attitude irritated and frightened her, but she did not want to go to

Jimmy with this kind of feeling between them. She tried to control her irritation and calm him down.

"Arthur, please. You know I don't want to go. I don't want to leave you. God knows you've done enough already. I was just thinking before you came home, how much you've sacrificed. And to ask this of you . . ."

"Don't put it on me, Helen. I can take it. I'm getting a little more independent myself." This time he did not try to hide the bitterness. "You've made up your mind to go whatever I say. So go. Get it out of your system. Do your thing."

So that was it. The same old Arthur, still trying to keep her from changing, still annoyed that she was doing something on her own, still trying to hold his little dream of happiness together. Sensing that, her own anger flared.

"I'm going, Arthur. I was hoping it wouldn't come to this, but I can see you really haven't changed. You've been patient, sure. You've let your little Helen out of this cage of a house a few times, magnificent! But, by God, you don't like it! You hate what I've been doing! Oh, not Jimmy—of course you can't hate a helpless little boy who needs a mama! But you begrudge every moment I spend with him, every hour I'm there and not sitting here keeping your cozy little picture of domestic bliss firmly intact!"

"My God, you sound just like Katie!" he sneered. His face went white with anger as he stood to his feet and swept the empty wine glass off the table and across the dining room into the kitchen where it shattered on the floor. He shouted, "I saw Jim O'Donnell today, and do you know what he asked me? If you had moved in with that salesman yet!"

"Dear God!" Helen struggled to her feet and ran out of the dining room and across the living room toward the stairs. "I'm going now, Arthur. Right now!"

He stumbled after her, knocking against the coffee table in the living room, screaming as he pursued her,

"So don't give me all that crap about the boy, Helen! I know what's going on! I've known it for months! What the hell do you take me for, a total idiot?"

She slammed the bedroom door behind her and locked it. She jerked open the closet and threw her luggage on the bed. Hot tears of anger and humiliation dripped down onto her beautiful matching leather suitcases like rain.

Downstairs, ten minutes later, she found him gone. The garage door gaped open and Helen's car stood alone. She rushed to the trunk of the car and hurled her luggage in, then stopped for a moment. Her heart was pounding in her chest and her breath was coming in choking sobs. The cold rain was driven against her legs by the blustering wind, chilling her as she stood there thinking, dear God what am I doing? Arthur's jealous wrath had changed everything. Suddenly she wasn't leaving home on an errand of mercy; she was leaving Arthur. Her decision was opening a rift between them that might never be healed. Benumbed with that realization, she stumbled into the car and collapsed wearily behind the wheel. For a brief moment she wondered what might happen if she simply returned to the house and waited for Arthur to come home. The memory of his sneering face and wild accusations flashed before her, and with a shudder she started the car.

As she backed out of the garage into the pelting rain the steering wheel felt icy and hard under her bare hands. She had forgotten to bring driving gloves. Looking back from the street she saw the garage door yawning open as if calling her back. Angrily she punched the button that signaled it shut.

She felt an immense, irrational gratitude for the snug little compact car as it nosed along the streets through torrents of water. The pavements were flooded, especially at intersections, where she had to slow and proceed at a snail's pace, peering through steamed-over windows between sluggish and almost ineffectual wipers. But the car was warm and watertight and dependable. After a few minutes, she was able to reflect on Arthur's incredibly explosive reaction. What hurt most was the feeling that Arthur had been storing up that kind of feeling about her, especially the kind of suspicions he had expressed about Charles Banning. To think that a short time ago Arthur had talked so easily about being her friend! A feeling of bleak desolation swept through her, intensified by the isolation she felt in the small car with the world around her churning with the fury of the storm. She felt alone, truly alone for the first time in her life.

A blur of flashing red lights penetrated the thick mists that engulfed the car, and she slowed as the traffic in front of her came to a stop. She had reached the Coast Highway just north of Santa Monica, and as so often occurred with heavy rains, a huge section of the palisades had fallen to the road. Workers in bright yellow rain slickers worked among emergency vehicles with warning lights flashing, erecting barricades, diverting traffic around the massive mud slide to one lane of the highway that still remained open. As the car in front moved Helen quickly wiped her eyes to hide her tears as she became aware of a young man who stood beside the cars, waving them onward. As she passed him she saw sheets of water coursing over his face. She relaxed at once and felt an instant kinship with him and all storm battered souls like him, all the lonely, battle-weary adventurers, like herself.

Jimmy was one of them too, she thought. He too was alone with his struggle. Like a courageous little soldier Jimmy had faced onslaught after onslaught from an unfriendly world, and had stood his ground. Here she was, feeling sorry for herself and alone in the world because of a ridiculous scene with Arthur that would no doubt be resolved as soon as the two of them had time to get their egos back in place. But Jimmy, her brave little traveler in the realms of death, her sweet little friend, her heroic little son, was truly alone. She began feeling better about herself as she drove on through the rain.

She had fought for the right to stand by the side of the wonderful child who had chosen her to be his mother, and by God in spite of everything her decision made her feel proud.

CHAPTER TWENTY-NINE

Helen stopped the car as near to the beach house as she could. She sat for a moment dreading another confrontation with the freezing rain that continued to assault the roof of her car as if trying to batter its way through. After a minute of listening to its undiminishing fury, she opened the door and the wind blew it back on its hinges. She struggled out, head down against the elements, managed to get the door closed again and hurried to the trunk of the car to remove her suitcases and carry them to the house.

She banged on the door once and it opened, with Jessica standing inside, backing away from the rain.

"Lordy! Look at you! Get in here!" Jessica cried, and reached out to help her with her luggage.

"Thank you, Jessica. Whew, what a night!" Jessica pressed the door closed behind her as Helen set the suitcase she held down next to the one Jessica had taken from her and looked up. Jessica's eyes were wide and filled with loving concern.

"You've done it, haven't you," Jessica said.

"Yes. I guess I have. I've really done it. I'm afraid we had quite a scene. But how's Jimmy?"

"I'll tell you in a minute. You'd better get those wet things off or you'll catch your death." Jessica turned quickly to a cupboard and took out a hand towel.

Helen took the towel and answered the question she

saw in Jessica's look. "It isn't that bad, Jessica. He'll get over it. And so will I. Now, how is Jimmy?" She dried her hair and face as well as she could as she listened.

"Now he won't eat anything at all," the nurse explained. "I took him his dinner and I thought for a minute he was going to throw it at me." She concluded with a shake of her head that expressed both irritation and sympathy. "He's a sight tonight."

"I'm going in. And I'm taking these." Helen picked up both her suitcases and Jessica sensed immediately what she had in mind. The nurse led the way to the closed door of Jimmy's room, whispering, "He made me shut it, said he didn't want to listen to me eating."

Jessica opened the door and stepped aside. Helen waited as she saw Jimmy lying flat on his back with both hands cupped behind his head staring straight up at the ceiling. After a moment of silence, he glanced toward the door with a scowl. "Jessica, what are you . . ." He saw Helen.

Without a word Helen stepped into the room and set the suitcases down beside her on the floor. He sat up.

"Mom? What are you doing here?"

"What does it look like?"

"Are those your suitcases?" His eyes were fixed on her face, a look of hope dawning in them. She didn't have the heart to prolong it any further. She hurried to the bed and took him in her arms.

"Yes they're my suitcases, and I've come to stay!"

He threw his arms around her, crying, "Oh, Mom! Wow! You did come! You did come! I was praying you would! And you came!"

She hugged him close and suddenly realized that she must be getting him soaked. She pulled away quickly. "Oh my goodness, you'll get a chill! I'd better change."

He grinned from ear to ear, showing that dazzling charm of his for the first time in what seemed like months. "Wow, Mom! And you brought your clothes and everything!"

"Yes," she laughed. "I came to stay. Now you just settle there for a minute until I get into something dry. Have you got a room for me? You've been asking me to come all this time and I'll bet I have to sleep on the couch."

"Show her, Jessica! Show her what you did!" He was beaming with delight. Helen turned questioningly to Jessica.

Jessica shrugged and led her across the hall to the spare room. "He saw me freshening things up in here. I told him I was expecting company and he thought I meant a boyfriend. I didn't tell him any different, not knowing."

Helen entered the small spare bedroom. As she turned to close the door behind her she heard Jimmy saying, "Jessica, is there any food left, or did you eat it all up?" She closed the door, suddenly flooded with feelings of assurance that she had made the right choice. Helen silently thanked Professor Mays and breathed a prayer for Arthur, that somehow she would be able to make him understand. Then she began to undress.

A half-hour later Jimmy had finished his dinner amid a happy three-way conversation that included Jessica telling a wild experience about taking care of an elderly man and wife who did nothing but scream and yell at each other all day long. She merrily described a fight between them in which the two of them tried to upset each other's wheelchairs. She concluded, "Then the old lady took real sick and had to be taken to a nursing home. And you know, that old man who never did anything but fight with the woman almost died without her there. He wouldn't eat or sleep or nothing until he'd convinced everybody he had to have her back. And she was the same way, worried about him all the time. So her doctors let her come home, and the minute she got in the door they started to fight. And you know what they fought about? About which one missed the other one the most!"

They all had a good laugh over it. Then Jimmy quietly said, "I'm not going to fight with you, Mom. You'll see. I'll really be good."

When the time came for Jimmy to go to sleep, he asked Helen to read to him. Jessica had gone to the kitchen to finish cleaning up, and the two were alone together for the first time. Helen scanned the double shelf of volumes looking for a suitable book and was amazed at the choices. Some of them seemed right for a boy, but others appeared to be far too adult. "Have you read all these?" she asked.

"Most of them," he replied casually.

"The Divine Comedy?"

"Well, not all of it. I saw it in a bookstore and I thought it would be funny. Dad bought it."

"The Happy Hooker?"

"I didn't read much of that one. Dad bought it, too."

She chuckled. "How about this one, *The Life of Lou Gehrig*?

"I read that one. He died of something like cancer."

"Oh. I didn't know that."

"Dad bought that one, too. Hey, I know! *Treasure Island!* Dad just sent it to me. It's up on top!"

Helen straightened and picked up a beautiful new edition of the classic children's story. She opened the cover as she moved toward the bed. An inscription on the flyleaf said, "To the Champ, love from Dad."

"The Champ, is that what he calls you?"

"Yeah. Hey, sit beside me on the bed." Jimmy patted the covers next to him and moved aside. He moved with effort, using his hands to help slide his helpless limb a few inches. He looked up as he found her staring.

"Well, go on. Read." He snuggled down beside her. "We'll do a chapter every night."

As she neared the end of the opening chapter Helen glanced down and found Jimmy's eyes closed. He was smiling in his sleep. She lowered her voice and read another paragraph as his breathing became more regular and she was sure he would not waken. Then she slipped off the bed, adjusted his pillow, pulled the covers up under his chin and quietly turned off the light.

She found Jessica sitting in the living room watching a TV movie. Seeing her, the nurse quickly rose and turned it off.

"It's okay, Jessica. I'll watch it with you."

"I thought you might want to talk a bit."

Helen leaned back in the deep, comfortable lounge chair in which Charles had been sitting on Thanksgiving Day. The memory flashed before her and was gone. It was a snug house, warm and quiet in spite of the storm that still raged outside. She felt deeply happy.

"Did you want to talk?" Jessica asked quietly.

"I don't know. I am just so sure this is right. I know Jimmy's going to get better now, and that's what really counts."

Jessica leaned back on the couch and put her feet up on the coffee table, smiling. "You're sure the best medicine right now. I have to tell you, though, I think his father's neglecting him more than he should. You shouldn't have to be doing this, is all I'm saying."

Jessica folded her arms and pursed her lips and kept staring at the blank TV screen.

The remark puzzled Helen. "What do you mean, Jessica? He does have his work. And I'm sure all he's doing for Jimmy costs money. This house, the medical bills, it must take nearly everything he can make."

"I'm not criticizing. I just think he could be here more instead of . . . well." Jessica stirred herself out of it. "You want a cup of coffee?"

Helen followed her to the kitchen as Jessica put the water on to boil. Helen did not want negative feelings brought up right at the start of her stay here, and not resolved.

"Jessica, I don't know much about Charles. But he does care about Jimmy. I know that much."

"I'm sorry. I'm just rattling on. I've been needing company too, I guess." Jessica opened a cupboard, took down a coffee filter and began measuring in the grains. "You know where he stays when he's in town, don't you?"

Helen said, "No, I have no idea."

Jessica grinned. "With one of his girlfriends. It's no secret. He tells me all about them. This one's a Japanese gal from the hospital."

Helen couldn't suppress a grin of her own. "From the hospital? I'm sure he doesn't spend many lonely nights. But you're saying when he's in town he could be here with Jimmy."

"At least once in a while, couldn't he?" Jessica replied.

Helen thought about it as they drank their coffee in the living room. Some of the speculation at Katie's party was proving true. Charles Banning did seem to be shacking up with a woman, or women. But what did that prove?

She opened the subject again, trying to get Charles in some kind of focus. "Jessica, when he works, where does he have to go?"

"Oh, all over this part of the state. He's a district manager of some kind, I think."

"So how often is he in town, do you know?"

"Most every weekend. And he's not spending all that much of his own money, if you don't mind me saying so. There's a trust fund of some kind that takes care of Jimmy."

"There is?"

"Charles told me about it once. He gets a little to drink and he gets talkative, you know. The money for this house and for my services comes from the trust fund, and so does the money for Jimmy's medical care."

That took some swallowing. Helen found herself sharing some of Jessica's doubts about Charles Banning, but not all of them. After a moment she said, "Jessica, you told me once that I'd have a hard time figuring him out."

"I know," Jessica replied. "And I don't mean to set you against him, either. In some ways he's very good with Jimmy. Well, you know that. You've seen them together. I guess it just puzzles me, why he wouldn't be here every chance he gets."

It puzzled Helen too, so much so she found she couldn't sleep. Seen in one light the fact of Charles's neglect, if that's what it was, had brought Helen into the difficult involvement she had undertaken in coming here. If Charles paid more attention, would Jimmy need her so much? She found herself wishing Jessica hadn't brought it up on her first night at the beach house. It cast a shadow over her decision to come there. In the midst of these dark thoughts she heard Jimmy cry out.

Helen had left her door open so she would be able to hear him in the night. She entered his room and stood listening. Jimmy was whimpering in his sleep as if troubled by a bad dream. She crossed the room and stood in the darkness. Gradually her eyes became adjusted to the dim light that entered the room from a small night-light in the corridor. She saw Jimmy lying on his back with his hands under the covers, pulling them tightly up under his chin. He moaned and turned his head toward her, but his eyes remained closed. Not wanting to waken him, she sat quietly on the foot of the bed. He whimpered softly, pathetically, and was finally still. He began breathing deeply again.

She sat there for several minutes, thinking. This dear boy had come into her life because he had found something in her that he needed. Did it really matter why, or what his father might or might not be doing? Did it matter what anyone else thought or did, or was it something just between the two of them? Was it destiny? She had never given much thought to questions of that sort, how things happen or why, or how two people happen to meet. But here, now, sitting in the darkness of Jimmy's room, she was sure that it was meant to be. For some reason unknown to herself she had been selected and prepared to walk with this child toward whatever lay in store for both of them. Her decision to come and live with him was never really hers to make, any more than the choice of responding or not responding to him that first day on the beach. Much as she might dread the dark fate that almost certainly lay before him, she knew now that she would go with Jimmy even down to the doors of death itself. Not even that could frighten her now. They were together as they were meant to be.

CHAPTER THIRTY

At six-thirty the next morning Helen was wakened by the sound of Jimmy's voice yelling, "Hey, Mom! Wake up! The rain's stopped!" She opened her eyes to find sunlight streaming in through her window and faced a moment of disorientation before she realized she wasn't in her own bed at home. Promising herself to call Arthur as soon as she possibly could, she rallied her forces and called back.

"Good morning, Jimmy! I'll be right there."

She found him cheerful, talkative, and hungry. He already had her day planned for her. "We'll eat breakfast in here together, then you can bring the TV in and we'll watch a couple of cartoon shows, then we'll get that electronic TV game out I got for Christmas. Jessica hasn't been able to figure out how to hook it up, but you can. And we'll play that for a while . . ."

Jessica entered then and reminded him that he had forgotten a couple of details like his morning medication and his bath. He stormed at her, "Get out of here, Jessica. This is between Mom and me!" Then he glanced toward Helen and became meek as a lamb, "I'm sorry, Jessica. I didn't mean it."

After breakfast, as Helen sat on the living room floor over the instructions for connecting the TV game, she saw Jessica enter Jimmy's room with his morning pill. It was almost the only visible sign in the house of Jimmy's illness, and for some reason it immediately reminded Helen to call Arthur.

It was just a few minutes after eight o'clock as she dialed and listened to the ringing phone. Arthur usually left for work at around eight-thirty so Helen expected him to be there. What they had to say to each other would be better discussed from home than from the office. She waited, letting the phone ring seven or eight times, then just as she was beginning to despair over having missed him, and after a moment of speculation about where he could possibly be at this hour, Arthur answered.

His manner was reserved from the start as if he had known it would be Helen. He tersely explained that he had been shaving, then asked, "So how is it down there?"

"It's fine, Arthur. He was very happy to see me. I wish I could help you understand just how much this means to him."

"Good." He waited for her to speak and Helen could feel the tension in his silence.

"Arthur, I'm sorry about what happened, for my part, but you must know how you hurt me with—your wild accusations."

There was a very long pause and she wondered if he intended to respond at all. His silence made her feel manipulated. "Do you want to talk to me at all, Arthur?"

"I was awake all night, Helen. And I have a splitting headache. Do I have your phone number down there? I could call you later if it's convenient." There was something in the way he said "convenient," but she fought down the urge to argue about it.

She repeated the phone number and Arthur made appropriate noises of writing it down. Without deviating once from the cool, distant, injured-party tone he seemed to have decided on, Arthur said he'd phone later and hung up. Two months earlier such treatment would have sent Helen scurrying to call back and try to repair the breach between them, but now it only made her angry.

Helen put Arthur out of her mind with a determined effort not to let him spoil her relationship with Jimmy. She entered the room to find Jessica preparing to give him his morning bath.

"May I do that, Jessica?"

The nurse had just set a basin of warm water, soap and towels next to the bed. Jimmy looked at Helen with alarm. "No, you'll see me!"

"What?"

"Tell her, Jessica! She can't! Just get out of here, Mom!"

Jessica calmed him and took Helen by the arm to lead her out to the kitchen. "I think it's because he feels ugly."

Helen was determined. "I don't think we should give in to that sort of thing. I would like to do everything a good mother would do around here, and a bath seems like . . ."

Jessica nodded, understanding. "It's because of Virginia. He tells me she left him because he got ugly. That's what Jimmy thinks."

"All right, then this is a good time to show him I'm not Virginia."

As she returned to the room, backed up by Jessica, Jimmy was sitting rigidly upright in the bed with his arms locked across his chest. He glared at her.

Helen walked to the basin and put her finger into the water. "Why don't you want me to give you a bath?"

"You'll see me, and I don't want you to."

"And what would that do, if I saw you?"

"You'll think I'm awful."

"Awful, how?"

"Awful, like ugly."

"Jimmy, I love you. I'm your mom and nothing about you is ugly to me." She deliberately picked up the wash cloth and began soaking it in the warm water. "So off with the shirt, Champ."

Her use of his father's pet name jarred him into something of a smile. It lasted an instant and was replaced by his usual look of defiance. "No."

Helen dried her hands on the towel and reached for the top button on Jimmy's pajama shirt. "Jimmy, you chose me to be your mom, right?"

Grudgingly he nodded. "Right."

"But I also chose you, didn't I? You didn't make me come here. I came because I wanted to."

Jimmy said not a word, but she could see a flicker of assent in his eyes. Slowly his arms relaxed and fell away from his chest, permitting her to open the rest of the buttons. Just as she finished the last button his hand grasped hers and she glanced into his troubled eyes. He was warily scanning her face for any sign of aversion she might show, as he let her remove his shirt.

The pajamas came away from his thin body revealing a jutting collar bone and knobby little shoulders. He let her work the sleeves down his wasted arms and over his hands. She could feel his warm breath on her cheek as she leaned over him.

There were three or four prominent skin bruises on his upper body, those angry purple splotches Helen had read about and had only glimpsed once. As the snap came undone on his pants he grabbed her hand again.

"Okay, you can give me a bath, but I won't take off my underwear."

"I don't care about your underwear or anything else." She couldn't help grinning, and as she glanced toward Jessica she saw the nurse holding back a laugh. There were several more bruises on Jimmy's legs and one large spot on his right buttock. He squirmed aside to help her work the pajamas over his useless right leg.

As she lifted it, she was aware that she bore its full weight in her hands. Touching him so intimately on the limb over which they had shared so much grief, Helen felt he was her son as never before. He continued staring silently, his eyes big and watchful as she picked up the washcloth and soap and began washing his back. Only then did he relax completely. He looked past her toward Jessica.

"Hey, Jessica," he called. "She's a lot better at it than you are!"

By eleven o'clock Helen and Jimmy were into their tenth game of electronic ping pong when the phone rang. Helen stopped playing, suddenly remembering Arthur.

"Why did you stop, Mom?" Jimmy complained. "I was winning!"

She explained that she was waiting for a call from her husband, and as Jimmy's face fell, she added, "It doesn't mean I'm leaving. I just have to talk with him once in a while."

Jessica had answered it and soon came to the door carrying the phone on its extralong extension cord. She entered the room holding it out toward Jimmy. "It's your father."

Jimmy eagerly took the phone and said, "Hey, Dad, Mom's living with us now!" He chattered away for a few minutes, bubbling with the news about Helen fixing the TV game, which seemed to have impressed Jimmy greatly, then handed the phone toward Helen. "He wants to talk to you."

"Hello, Mr. Banning."

His voice came through as if from some distance away, but buoyant and charming as ever. "Well, I thought we were on a first-name basis, Helen. Anyway, thanks for doing this. I know it means a lot to Jimmy. I'm surprised he hasn't hopped out of that bed and onto his crutches by now. With a lovely lady like you around there, he sure doesn't act like any son of mine!"

"We'll have to see about that. But he's doing fine today."

"I sure appreciate this, Helen. I have to run to a meeting right now, but tell Jimmy I'll be in to see him over the weekend. And you just dig in there and make yourself at home. Anything you need, you just tell Jessica. She has carte blanche where you're concerned, I've already told her that. So good luck, dear, and tell that skinny kid of mine I expect him to be up and about when I get there. Enough of this already."

It was all rather breathless, but it was pure Charles. Helen hung up with a smile and handed the phone back to Jessica.

Jimmy poked her and held out the controls for the TV game as he asked, "What'd he say?"

"That he's coming on the weekend and you're supposed to be on your crutches when he gets here."

Jimmy scowled and laid the control device in her lap. "Let's play. And remember I'm three games ahead of you."

By the twentieth game and Jessica's announcement that Arthur was on the phone Helen was seeing spots from the effect of staring at the bounding balls on the tube as she made her way out to the phone stand in the corridor. She tried to keep her voice low as she leaned against the wall and braced herself for an encounter.

"Arthur?"

"I had a few things come up this morning. Sorry for the delay. Before you say anything I want to tell you I've had a chance to think a bit. I feel like a heel."

Well, that was something, Helen felt. He seemed ready for sane conversation, anyway. "It really didn't make a lot of sense, Arthur. I knew you would feel differently about it in time."

"I get carried away. The same old thing, like you always say. Trying to hold you in a pattern, you know. But hey—how about lunch tomorrow? Is that impossible? Let me know if it would interfere in any way."

Arthur. He could be so dear and suddenly turn so

abruptly into something else. And here he was back on track again. It made her wonder which one was the real Arthur. "I'll try, Arthur. Suppose you call me about ten or so in the morning, and I'll try to make it."

He agreed most cheerfully, told her he loved her, and wished her a good day. Upon hanging up she had a lingering feeling of frustration, as if there were things she had wished she had been given the chance to say. There were real problems between them that needed to be talked out, but by giving in so easily Arthur had effectively disarmed her. She vowed to bring it up again and again if necessary. It was time for them to take a long look at their relationship, whether he thought so or not.

The day continued to be sunny and warm throughout the afternoon and when Jimmy awoke from a short nap at five-thirty the sun was touching everything with tones of gold. Helen entered and was pleased to find him responding to the beauty of it with something like his old enthusiasm.

"Push the shade up and pull the curtains back more, Mom. Look how beautiful that is."

Helen did his bidding and stood looking at the clouds high above the horizon and out of Jimmy's range of vision. "You should see the clouds up there, Jimmy. They're just starting to turn all rosy, and there are two jet trails crossing right through them. The jet trails look like gold bracelets on the clouds."

She heard him stir in the bed and turned back to find he had squirmed down flat on the bed and was leaning out toward the window to look up at them. "Are there any seagulls?" he asked.

"Yes, they're feeding now over by the rocks. The tide's out."

He had straightened up in the bed and was sitting, looking around the room. "I wonder where Jessica put my crutches," he said and went on without looking at her. "I'll bet they're in the closet."

Hardly breathing, fearing to break the spell of the

moment, Helen slipped across the room and opened the closet door. Jimmy had turned to look out the window again and he said, "Better hurry, Mom. You know how sunsets are, they're gone in about two minutes."

She found them leaning against the back corner of the closet, partially hidden by clothing. They were very light, made of aluminum tubing with tan-colored pads to protect his armpits. She had a passing thought that they might not be strong enough to hold his weight.

As she brought them to the bed on his side, Jimmy rattled on as if nothing whatever was happening. "Tomorrow maybe we can check out the tidepools, you know?"

"Yes, that would be fun. We haven't done that for a while." She tried to keep her voice as nonchalant as his own, as if the step he was about to take was not a breakthrough and a triumph and a cause for jubilation. She reached forward to support his back as he edged his legs down over the sides of the bed. He took the crutches from her other hand, adjusted them under his arms and slid another inch forward, testing his weight.

"I feel a little dizzy. Why's that?"

"Well, you haven't been up this way for a long time. I think it's normal."

He leaned his head and shoulders forward and planted his good left foot solidly on the floor. As he lifted his head he tottered briefly and her hand shot out in support. Jimmy glanced up at her with a frown.

"Walking on crutches is no big deal, Mom. I can handle it." He swung his good foot forward and took two steps to the window to look out. "Thanks for telling me about this," he said. "And don't worry about me with these crutches. I got up this afternoon while you thought I was sleeping and Jessica helped me practice."

He knew he had done something sensational. His grin put the sunset to shame.

CHAPTER THIRTY-ONE

Charles Banning sat on the porch of the beach house watching Helen and Jimmy. The two of them were working their way from tidepool to tidepool collecting shells or whatever else they found of interest. Charles marvelled at the changes Helen had wrought in a few short days. She had transformed his son from a bedridden, defeated loser into a valiant little fighter who was not only up and about on his crutches but was now looking forward to a trip to Marineland on Sunday. Over the sound of the surf Charles could hear Jimmy's shouts of pleasure and Helen's laughter as they added another sea prize to the canvas bag she toted along with them.

The woman had something special. On her own she seemed a rather placid sort, not the kind you would expect miracles from. Sometimes she could seem downright dull. Her sense of humor was quick enough and her smile was easy and even quite lovely at times, but compared to other women he had known she certainly wouldn't register as a ten. But with Helen and Jimmy it was another story. Between the two of them there was some kind of chemistry working that defied analysis.

Unfortunately, Charles thought, he was going to have to tell her about the phone call from Virginia. Thinking about it brought a bitter taste of revulsion. He hauled himself up out of the deck chair.

In the kitchen he took his time putting together a Bloody Mary, heavy on the worcestershire sauce and tabasco to wipe out the taste of Virginia and all the other females. Including Miss Tsusumita.

"A permanent relationship, Charles, that or nothing," she'd said. Miss Tsusumita's velvet eyes had become craftier and craftier as things had moved along. "I lived with Dr. Barnstable for four years, Charles," she had sighed. "If I'd been smart there would have been a contract."

Now she wanted either a contract or a marriage license, and preferably both. Charles carried his concoction back to the porch and flopped into the redwood lounger thinking angry thoughts over his drink. Helen and Jimmy were slowly making their way toward the house. From his point of view the two of them were framed as if in a picture, the top rail of the porch banister above, two vertical slats to either side of the frame and the porch floor below. Within that rectangle the boy and the woman worked their way slowly through the resisting sand. Once Jimmy lost his balance and nearly toppled forward, and as Helen caught him the sound of their laughter came to Charles like a song, a hymn to the miracle of what transpired between them. Virginia cannot be allowed to destroy this, he vowed, not even if it cost him every cent he had.

From where he was sitting Charles could see down the full length of the narrow porch stairway that led to the sand. As Jimmy approached the bottom step on the crutches, Charles wanted to hurry down to the boy and pick him up in his arms. Jimmy started up the stairs and Charles could see the strain of each thrust forward of his trunk and shoulders, each awkward pullup of his stretched neck muscles, each uncertain moment as Jimmy teetered on one step gained and gathered his strength for the next. Behind the boy Helen held her hands ready to aid if he should fall, but did nothing to make his ascent any easier.

From her position behind Jimmy Helen glanced upward toward Charles. She saw the man's neck and facial muscles moving in empathy with his son's. As Jimmy paused to catch his breath Charles Banning caught his own breath, his expression showing concentration on the boy's struggle, sympathy also, but something else: admiration. Though the father was obviously concerned, she could see he was battling the overprotective instinct that was so deeply part of him, and was letting Jimmy win his own small victory with the crutches and the stairs. She felt a sudden surge of warm affection for Charles; at that moment she could have taken him in her arms.

Up Jimmy came toward his father, the boy's face red with strain but lined with dogged determination Charles felt he had never seen before in his son. The boy paused a moment and nearly lost his balance backward. Helen steadied him, but Charles's hand shot out reflexively.

"Don't help me, Dad. I can make it. Mom's been reading up on exercise. This is called overload," Jimmy beamed. He swung himself up the last step to the porch and stood upright, panting for breath. "We've decided I have to build myself up."

Charles leaned back in his chair. "Whatever you say, Helen's the boss," he assured him. He watched as Helen smilingly laid her hand on Jimmy's golden hair and bent to kiss his cheek. Her own breathing was heavy and her fair skin flushed. Charles caught his breath in surprise as he saw their two faces together. It was uncanny how closely they resembled each other.

"I'm gonna get some lunch," Jimmy announced. "I'm starved!" And with that he swung his way to the door, balanced himself to open it and disappeared inside.

Helen sank into a deck chair beside Charles, still breathing heavily, and feeling a numbness in her knees that did not come from climbing the stairs but rather from the impact of that moment of studying Charles's face and being suddenly overwhelmed with affection for him.

Hearing her heavy breathing, Charles laughed, "Who's getting overloaded here?"

"Both of us! According to the experts the only way

to develop a muscle is to push it beyond where it is now. That's overload." She did not trust herself to turn her head to the side and look at him, not until she could sort out her feelings a bit. She lay back and closed her eyes.

"Are you shooting for the Senior Olympics? Just kidding, Helen. You're fantastic. And I'm beginning to be a believer."

His tone was suddenly so grave she forced herself to turn to him. "What do you mean?"

"I'm beginning to think he might make it," Charles said. "That's the first sign I've seen in Jimmy of a real will to live. You are working something of a miracle." Now it was Charles who looked away. He had seen something new and warm and very penetrating in Helen's eyes. He leaned back beside her, their heads no more than two feet apart, and looked at the sky.

Helen also sensed something in the movement of Charles's face to avoid looking at her, and a thin but very tangible tension grew between them. She tried to toss it off with, "Do you think Jimmy'll soon be chasing girls and trying out for football?"

Charles caught the clever reminder of what he had said just a few months ago. What had ever made him think this woman was dull? "Touché," he acknowledged her rejoinder and kept looking toward the sky. "I just think he has a chance now. I really do."

"Oh, Charles, I'm so glad." Her voice radiated such pleasure and warmth that Charles was forced to look at her. Her hand rested for a moment on his forearm that lay on the redwood armrest of the lounger between them. "I'm glad for you and for Jimmy." Those wondrous blue eyes of hers rested on his eyes for a fleeting second, then she looked away toward the sea, adding, "He's doing very well on the new drug. No more nausea, his hair's coming back so beautifully. I can't wait for his next tests. I just know he's in good remission this time."

Charles entertained an urge to lay his own hand on

top of hers, a gesture of companionship and a recognition of the bond Jimmy had formed between them. Her hand fluttered away at the moment he thought of it, and came to rest palm upward on the armrest of her lounger. He shook himself, aware that he was suddenly becoming conscious of a lot of her gestures and movements, reading a lot into very little evidence. Keenly aware of a new, undeniable attraction to Helen as a woman, he was immediately reminded of the phone call from Virginia. With a determined effort he shoved it aside and concentrated instead on appreciating this new feeling. He glanced at Helen as she closed her eyes and basked silently in the warm sunlight. Her lips were parted in a lingering half-smile of contentment that was relaxed and, suddenly, quite sensuous. The realization struck him with a jolt that Helen was a woman with a very passionate nature beneath her calm, almost ethereal exterior. He almost bolted from the chair.

"Did you say something?" she asked. "I was daydreaming."

"No, no I didn't," he stammered. "I—uh—I was just going in to have some lunch." For the moment Charles felt he had to put distance between them, and lunch was as good an excuse as any. He lurched through the front door, closed it behind him and turned to look back at her through the glass. Helen had relaxed back into her chair again, and the sunlight danced on her yellow hair. He jerked himself away from the sight.

"Jimmy! Hey, Champ, where are you?" he called out as cheerily as he could as he made his way toward the kitchen, thinking, slow down, old man, she's not for you. This is no playmate, she's Jimmy's mom. Just cool it.

Jimmy's mom, meanwhile, was feeling somewhat less than cool herself. Though she had no idea why Charles had shot out of his chair, apparently suffering from a sudden onslaught of starvation, she was relieved to be left alone for a moment. She needed time to consider a host of new sensations and notions that seemed to swarm about her. The fact that she had seriously misjudged Charles was one of them. How had she ever thought of him as flashy and shallow? "Transparent," she had told Arthur. Well, he wasn't at all. He wasn't any of those things. Now that she knew him well, especially after the sides of his nature she had seen during the kite flying episode, and at Thanksgiving, and in the hospital, she realized that he was far from shallow. There was both a liveliness and a maturity in Charles that she liked, among the many other positive things she had seen.

Throughout the afternoon Helen found herself wishing she could spend more time with Charles, time to become better acquainted, perhaps to know him well enough to confirm some of her new notions about him. Certainly the man wasn't perfect! He did have some faults, and being able to pinpoint one or two might help shake her out of what seemed, the more she considered it, a developing schoolgirlish kind of infatuation. Charles, however, seemed to find it necessary to run several never-clearly-defined errands during the afternoon that kept him busy until quite late in the evening.

By ten o'clock, she was already in her dressing gown and reading in bed when she heard him enter the beach house. The suspicion suddenly presented itself that he had been with one of his girlfriends, the contemplation of which enabled Helen finally to begin thinking about going to sleep.

Charles stretched out on the couch, drink in hand, and stared down the short corridor at the door to Helen's room and the pencil-thin strip of light that underlined it. Ten minutes after he had settled into position the light went out, signifying that Helen was not going to come out and join him for a nightcap and perhaps a romantic walk on the beach in the moonlight, and he was a fool for thinking he had to keep making up silly trips to stay away from her all day, and that he was exaggerating all those subtle signals he thought he'd detected, and, finally, that it was a pretty silly thing for him to be staying awake with such thoughts when she was obviously not sharing the same vibes.

The Sunday trip to Marineland brought Helen a curious sense of displacement and disorientation. She sensed for the first time how a woman might feel who had left one marriage and family to become part of another. They were very much like a family, Charles, Jimmy, and herself, as they watched the amusements and ate their lunches and shared the excitements of the day. Jimmy's need for their mutual aid now and then as he propelled himself through the crowds on his crutches only served to bring them closer together and to deepen Helen's feelings of oneness with Charles. She became aware that her confusion was showing when, as they lunched on hot dogs and Cokes under the colorful metal umbrellas with the crowds of children and parents milling about them, Helen twice addressed Charles as "Arthur."

Upon wakening that morning to prepare for the trip to Marineland Charles had determined to stop nagging himself about how he should or shouldn't feel about Helen and just hang loose and enjoy the day. And he did; he enjoyed it thoroughly. To Charles it seemed for a while that the three of them comprised a happy family. Jimmy was in such fine shape and Helen was such a relaxed, easy-to-take companion, he was sure people who saw them at the amusement park must have taken them to be a couple happily spending the day with their son.

Sunday night presented the problem again of where Charles would stay. Jessica had been given the day off and the two of them were alone at the beach house. Miss Tsusumita's hospitality could no longer be relied on. She had turned out to be too young and too mod; she was all name brands. Her stereo, complete with Dolby and quadrophonics, played nothing but the top ten, at full power. Her labels were all Gucci, Pucci, Yves St. Laurent and Levi Strauss. Her Porsche had everything, including a burglar alarm. She read nothing but fashion magazines. "The Price Is Right" was her favorite TV show. And she seemed to get most of her political opinions from old war movies. In bed she was like too many of the young women he had known, trying much too hard, which made her only trying. After a sickeningly contemporary parting scene, replete with such things as "You must understand my need for my own space," and "The relationship must be mutually supportive," Charles had come to the beach house seeking a refuge from the world of youth. Why, he wondered, do the young agonize so much over loving? And how did he ever let himself get sucked into such jargon?

No wonder the calm, mature, serene Helen was beginning to look good to him. And after the day's trip to Marineland, where he had seen the light in Jimmy's eyes every time the boy looked at her, how could Charles not feel some spark of warmth for the lady?

Now it was Sunday night. Jimmy had been tucked in with his clothes on after falling asleep in the car during the return from the amusement park. Charles was walking alone on the beach wondering where to spend the night. His suitcase was packed and stowed in the car. With Jessica gone Charles had pretty well decided the safest bet was to drive to a nearby motel for the night and get out of temptation's way. Monday afternoon he was scheduled to be at a sales meeting sixty miles away in San Bernardino, so maybe he would cover some of the distance tonight and be close to his appointment the next day. It annoyed him to feel so uncomfortable about Helen, but he was determined not to make any moves that might disturb what she was doing with Jimmy.

As he toyed with various scenarios for the night he spotted Helen standing on the porch of the beach house. She waved and came down the steps to join him. She had put on a blue sweat jersey, zipped up the front. The hood was up, covering her hair, and her hands were jammed into the pouch pocket sewn to the front of the sweater. The moonlight was playing tricks; Helen looked like a tall, slim teenager, and the hood that framed her face gave her the sweet, innocent look of a young girl, alluring yet untouchable.

"Mind if I join you?" she smiled.

"No. I've got to hit the road soon." It came out a bit more abruptly than he'd intended. "In a little while. Want to walk, or would you rather go skinny-dipping?"

She laughed. "I got into that surf yesterday with Jimmy, by accident. It's freezing. A walk will be fine." She fell in beside him, her long strides matching his. They trod the beach in silence for a while, walking north toward what Jimmy called "Helen's rock." As if by mutual consent they stopped as they reached it.

"I want to thank you for this weekend," she said quietly. "And for the change in your attitude about Jimmy's chances."

"Terrific. I'm a hero."

"Don't put yourself down. I think you're a lot better father than you pretend to be." Helen watched him shift his feet about in the sand, toeing the rock as he pondered his reply.

"I haven't been. To tell the truth Virginia's leaving was a hell of a blow to me." Suddenly Charles found himself wanting to explain himself to her. She listened silently, shoulder to shoulder with him and looking away toward the sea as he went on. "I think what hurt most was the feeling that as far as Virginia was concerned I didn't count at all. It was like Jimmy was everything. I think I took it out on him in a way, like he was my rival. Sick?"

"I don't know. Maybe it was." Helen felt that an honest reaction was called for, not much else. The fact that he was opening up to her this way was touching, somehow.

"I think—well, I gave up on the boy, because I was so down. Does that make sense?"

Helen quickly tried to reassure him. "Maybe you were giving up more on yourself. It would be hard to face being rejected by a lovely woman like that, I suppose."

She was not trying to pull anything out of him, Charles knew, yet he felt he wanted to unburden himself, to clear something up. A nagging voice reminded him that he had not yet mentioned Virginia's phone call, but he put it behind him. Not yet.

"After Jimmy was born everything changed between his mother and me. To say she doted on him is the understatement of the century. She guarded him like a lioness. If he cried she would call the doctor. She fired three nurses for carelessness, she claimed, because he would fall down when he was learning to walk, or bump into a chair, or worst of all, for letting him play with a stranger's kid in the park and get dirty!"

"You make her sound horrible."

Charles sensed there was always doubt in Helen's tone when she talked of Virginia, as if she was willing to listen to whatever he might say about his ex-wife, but would hold all judgment of her own in abeyance.

"I know, you've never met her, and you're a kind soul, Helen. But give me the benefit of the doubt. Really, she overprotected him something incredible."

"When she found out that Jimmy had leukemia, it must have been a terrible shock. If she was that kind of mother, don't you think she must have felt responsible? Almost as if she had caused it to happen? Doesn't that explain why she left, that she just couldn't bring herself to face it?"

Charles, who had lived with the reality of Virginia, and had tried to explain her at least a thousand times to everyone from prospective girlfriends to court-appointed psychiatrists to his fellow salesmen, always felt he had to battle that same disbelief he sensed in Helen, an unwillingness to accept Virginia for what she was. The effort to explain her had consumed so much of his time and energy that he always felt he was boring his audience, because he was repeating himself. However, he felt Helen did deserve something of an explanation. He tried again.

"I feel that Virginia—well, she might be a little crazy. That sounds harsh, I know, but she's unbalanced, I'm sure of it. I don't think she is really capable of love as you or I might think of it."

Helen shivered and crossed her arms, hiding her hands under her armpits to warm them, wanting Charles to continue talking. "You said once that she is a genuinely selfish person. I guess I'm naive but I can't imagine someone intentionally setting out to put herself first over everything, including her own child."

"Of course you couldn't imagine it. Good people see goodness in others, evil people see evil. Goethe or someone said that."

Charles found Helen studying him closely, then quietly saying, "There are times when you just don't sound like a pantyhose salesman. And I'm not all that good, either."

He could not keep from laughing, though it was said in all seriousness. "I think you are guilty of prejudice, lovely lady. Why shouldn't a pantyhose salesman know about Goethe? And you *are* good. You are something pretty special, Helen Long. If you're naive about anything, I'd say it's about just how good you are." It came out all at once, and he was glad he said it, though she suddenly turned away.

"I'm getting a chill, Charles. Could we walk a bit?"

"Oh sure! Do you want to go in?"

"Not yet. Let's just keep moving," she said quietly. Her shoulder brushed against his arm as he stepped in beside her and without conscious thought about it, Charles put his arm around her. She snuggled closer and he could feel her shivering beneath the light sweatshirt.

"Here, let me give you my jacket," he said, starting to pull away.

She put her own arm about his waist and held on tightly. "No, this is fine."

They walked together for a few steps in silence. Helen felt a sudden rush of that disarming affection for Charles that had struck her so forcibly Saturday. She wanted to talk about it, but was not sure how to bring it up. Charles brought it up first.

"Helen, I'm getting to be very fond of you. That sounds very oldfashioned and formal, doesn't it?" His quiet chuckle was self-conscious and touchingly shy. "I think you're a hell of a woman."

Charles was pleased to find that she didn't pull away, but rather looked up at him and smiled.

"I have had to change my mind about you," she said rather abruptly. "I had the feeling you were selling all the time. You're not just selling now, are you?" There was a look that was almost pleading in her face as she stopped and looked up at him.

He couldn't resist stooping to kiss her upturned cheek, feeling her soft skin very cool against his lips. "Hey, let's get inside and get a fire going. I'll get you warmed up a bit before I hit the road, all right? It wouldn't do for you to catch a cold and infect our patient, now would it?"

Charles set off at a rapid pace toward the house, towing Helen by the hand. They ran together, laughing, up the steps and into the house.

He surprised her by letting go of her hand and walking directly into the guest room, her room, saying, "Just a second. I've got an old wool bathrobe in here that should just do the trick."

She sat down on the couch in front of the small stone fireplace and listened as he rummaged about in her closet, apparently shoving her things aside to search among the hooks on the back wall. The prospect of a fire and a snug robe cheered her and inspired an idea of her own. As he returned with the robe she slipped it over her clothes, after taking off the sweatshirt. Then she announced she was going to brew two large mugs of hot chocolate.

"On one condition," Charles corrected. "That I get a shot of brandy in mine."

"Ummm, sounds delicious," she agreed. "Mine too."

While Helen worked in the kitchen, Charles set to work preparing the fire. "What am I getting us into?" he asked himself. "Am I creating a little seduction scene here? Well—whatever," he concluded. "Que sera, sera." He made his way to the liquor supply.

Helen set two large mugs of steaming hot chocolate on a small silver tray she had found stored in a cupboard, and prepared to carry them into the living room, where she could already hear the crackling of the burning wood in the fireplace. She sensed the intimacy of the moment they were structuring and brushed aside an insistent, though distant, sense of guilt. What were they doing that was wrong? Part of her problem throughout her life had been the picky, hesitant, frightened way she had entered every new experience. Well, she had to get over that. Her decision to act in a spontaneous way regarding Jimmy had taught her that there are times in life for following your feelings. Besides, she was not going to bed with Charles. He would be leaving soon, as he'd said, but meanwhile they would have some time to get to know each other better, apart from Jimmy and Jessica and everyone else, just two adult human beings who felt something for each other and needed to talk about it. That was certainly not something to be feeling guilty about!

"Ah, there we are," Charles smiled as she entered. He advanced a brandy bottle toward the cups as she held them out and poured a small amount into each. "Just a touch to take the chill from the bones," he grinned, and returned the bottle to the small side table.

Helen made her way to the couch and for an awkward moment Charles paused, cup in hand, then moved to the large easy chair an arm's length away where he sat and grinned again as he toasted her, "For your heart a memory, for your lips a song, just one drink and I'll move along."

"The fire's beautiful, Charles, and the drink too." She was aware of being very warm. He had taken off his jacket as they came in and was wearing the attractive beige sportshirt he had worn during the afternoon. Helen set the drink down and squirmed out of the wool bathrobe. "I don't think I'll need this any more," she said, folding it and laying it aside. She was very conscious of his eyes admiring her bare arms and the rest of her beneath the close-fitting blouse she was wearing. She resisted an immediate impulse to cross her arms over her breasts, thinking, what a prude I am, conscious at the same time that her comfortable idea that this was to be a casual, impersonal conversation was being dashed against the reality of the fact that she was alone with a very attractive man in a very romantic setting. And Charles wasn't helping.

"Helen, what I said on the beach, it wasn't a salestalk. What are we going to do if we suddenly start liking each other a whole lot?"

It rattled her completely. She stammered, "I—I don't know. We will just have to deal with it when we come to it, won't we?"

He stared at her, smiling, as if to say, We have come to it. She quickly added, "Charles, I think we can be friends—can't we?"

"I certainly hope so."

"You know what I mean. Two people can be very fond of each other, and enjoy each other's company, and work together on something, as we have with Jimmy, and not—well . . ."

"Not become involved? I agree. Shall we drink to not becoming involved?" He lifted an eyebrow quizzically.

"I'm afraid I'm a pretty oldfashioned sort of woman for you," Helen heard herself saying. Her thoughts were running in circles and her heart was hammering out such confusion that she was barely aware of what she was saying. She hastened to add, "I didn't mean that the way it sounded. What I meant was that you—

you're used to meeting a lot of different people, going all kinds of places, while I'm—I haven't even been alone with another man besides Arthur for more than twenty years. Not like this."

Charles fought down an impulse to take her in his arms and get all of this confusion over with. At the same time he was painfully aware of the message he had received from Virginia, and knew that before the night was over, whatever happened, he was going to have to tell Helen about it. As the silence stretched between them he leaned back in the chair and stared into the fire. He was aware of Helen moving about on the couch, kicking off her shoes and curling her feet under her. It was as if she was waiting for him to make a move, to take charge and break through the indecision of the moment. He knew that he wanted her, had been wanting her and fantasizing about her for two days, and yes, even before that, since their week together with the hang gliders. Physically he felt a deep, gnawing hunger for her, troubling in a way because it was mixed somehow with treasured memories of his first wife, who, if she had lived would have been precisely Helen's age. He wanted her as he had not wanted any of the young chicks he had pursued and caught so easily. He ached to hold a grown woman again.

Helen was beginning to wonder if what she said had angered Charles. She was about to try to collect her thoughts and explain it all again when he suddenly stood up. He walked to the fireplace and prodded a log into place to make it burn more brightly. Then he strode back toward the couch, unbuttoning his shirt wider at the front, his eyes glowing with a kind of merriment.

"That chair is too close to the fire," he said. He sat down so close to her that his thigh pressed against her knee. He laid his hand palm up on her leg, opened as if he wanted her to take his hand. She laid her hand into his, aware of the breadth of his palm and the solid strength of him. Her own hand that she had so often felt to be too large seemed lost in his. He squeezed it very firmly.

"Helen," he said matter-of-factly, "I want you very much. You and I are two adults and we're going about this like a couple of kids."

With that he leaned toward her and kissed the bare flesh of her shoulder. "If you're going to yell stop, Ma'am, I'd say this is the time," he murmured into her ear.

Helen took his face into her two hands. Dear Charles, she thought, how boyish and yet how sure of himself. Loving him, she felt, would be the most natural thing in the world.

Helen had always thought that loving another man would have to be a sordid, guilt-ridden experience for her, but from their first breathless, passionate kiss to the final quiet moments as they lay snuggled together in her bed, it was a beautiful, joyful, incredibly playful and pleasurable time. She found herself pleasantly free of what she had always imagined would be troubling comparisons of any other man to Arthur, and she took Charles to her heart and her bed for what he was, not for a moment thinking, or being permitted to think, of anything or anyone else. She cried a little when it was over, not from disappointment, but because of the pure beauty of it, of him and of herself, and because Charles touched and released in her a great sense of aching, starving loneliness she had not known she possessed.

Lying there enfolded in his arms, her face inches from his, she tried to put it into words. "I have been so lonely all my life. I didn't know how lonely." Again the tears came, and Charles kissed them from her cheeks, silently, letting her cry.

"I think I never felt really wanted. Do you know what I mean? I have always thought of myself as too tall and too plain, and boring—that's the worst, I guess. Just so ordinary and sort of humorless, and sort of just going along, and all the time wondering what was wrong with me!"

He kissed more tears and didn't seem frightened by her crying, or defensive. He was just there, his attention and devotion fully concentrated on her, a strong, loving man comforting his lover.

"It doesn't matter what happens between us now, Charles. I mean, I don't want you to feel obligated to me in any way. Maybe it's silly to bring it up, but I just want you to know that you and I—what am I trying to say?"

"That we can be friends even though this has happened?"

It was wise and it was kind of him to be so understanding. She basked in his wisdom and maturity, fully content to let the more experienced Charles define what their relationship might be or become in all the days to follow. She suddenly recalled what Professor Mays had said about her needing a sexual kind of liberation and she lifted her head to share it with Charles. She found him staring at the ceiling with a troubled, distant look on his face.

"What is it, Charles? Is something wrong?"

Without answering he slipped off the bed and began putting on his clothes. She sat up, watching his face and wondering what could possibly have changed him so quickly.

"I have something to tell you, Helen. It's—unpleasant. I'll stir up the fire."

Helen rose quickly, pulling his heavy wool robe over her bare skin and feeling the harsh, masculine scratchiness of its material where only moments before she had felt the caresses of its owner. She clutched it around her and followed him to the living room, where she perched expectantly on the edge of the couch and watched as he added a log to the fire.

She moved aside on the couch to make room for him but he settled into the easy chair, for a long moment staring into the flames as if afraid to look at her.

"Charles?"

He stood then and took a step toward the bar.

"Please, don't make me wait, Charles," she pleaded. "You can tell me, whatever it is."

He paused with a stricken look on his face, a kind of pleading of his own, his eyes begging for understanding, as he said, "I had a call from Virginia three days ago." He moved to her then and sat close beside her, taking her hand for a moment, then releasing it quickly as he said, "She wants Jimmy back."

Helen felt her heart sink within her breast as a flash of horrified realization surged through her. "Wants Jimmy back? But that's impossible. It's unthinkable! I—Charles, why didn't you tell me this sooner? How could you keep it from me when . . ."

He threw his arms around her and Helen suddenly felt like a trapped animal. She twisted in his grasp and tried to stand, to breathe, to move somehow and throw him and this ugly new fact aside. But his arms held her like steel bands and his voice became leaden and very commanding.

"Stop it. Just hold still, just stop and listen to me, Helen. Please, just wait now and let me explain. I couldn't tell you before. I just couldn't. I knew it would hurt you, can't you see that?"

"You knew it would keep me from going to bed with you!" she whispered hoarsely, trying to keep her voice low, trying to keep Jimmy from waking. "You knew it would change things between us!"

"Why? Why does it change anything?" he demanded, suddenly releasing her and getting up to move to the bar and begin fixing his drink. "You're behaving like a child," he scolded. Then he turned and let out his breath in a long sigh, adding, "Helen, I'm sorry for all this. I want you to believe me, though. I think I'm in love with you. And I didn't want Virginia to spoil that, the way she's spoiled so much."

She wasn't sure she believed him, or that his apology made any sense at all. But she couldn't bring herself to pursue the argument any further, sensing that there were things to be discussed that concerned Jimmy, and he had to take precedence.

"What does it mean, Charles? Is she sincere? Does she really want to come back and be a mother to Jimmy, because if she does . . ."

He laughed harshly as he tipped his glass and drained it. "Sincere? Virginia? She wants my father's money. Unfortunately Jimmy is part of the deal."

Helen remembered what Jessica had told her, something about a family trust. Charles returned to the easy chair and sat down, shaking his head grimly, a sarcastic smile on his face. "I'll give it to you in a nutshell, Helen. It goes like this. There's a trust fund, some money from my father's estate. My dad never liked Virginia. He particularly didn't like the way she handled Jimmy. He was a worrier, and a planner. So he had set up a trust to take care of Jimmy in the event anything disastrous would ever happen to him."

"He foresaw it?"

"He was a remarkable man. And shrewd. He set it up in such a way that Jimmy would inherit a considerable sum when he reached maturity. He also put in a clause that would make the trust funds available in the event of emergency. Those funds paid for this beach house, for Jessica, and for a lot of Jimmy's medical care."

"Jessica said something about that."

"Okay. But the hooker is this. If Jimmy should die, the funds revert to the parent who has custody. Dad never believed the marriage would last."

"She just wants the money, that's what you're saying."

"I'm afraid that's it—well, most of it." She had to know the rest. He could sense the stiffening of Helen's spine as she tensed for more.

"I want to hear it all, Charles."

He tried to soften it as much as he could, controlling his own anger to say, "The hellish part of it is, Virginia and her Beverly Hills lawyers have come up with a real beauty. She's accusing you of alienating the affection of her child."

Helen moved numbly through the hour following that revelation, listening to Charles and replying somehow, automatically, half consciously, as her senses whirled. She could not focus clearly on what Charles was saying or summon the strength to question him more closely as he described Virginia's lawsuit implicating her and all it might mean. There was something about a trial or a hearing date and something about Charles finding a lawyer, and how they would try to keep it from Jimmy for a while, and a great deal more, all of which she heard with one part of her mind while somewhere else another part of her eavesdropped and hinted that none of this was that important and that what had happened between her and Charles was not what it seemed, and she had been a fool. Her thoughts went on whirling in that fashion until she found herself exhausted and longing to be alone and in bed.

Charles made no attempt to resume their earlier intimacy, seeming to have shrunken within himself in embarrassment, or despair, about Virginia and his failure to tell Helen. As a result Helen simply told him she wanted to go to sleep, and he kissed her on the cheek, and that was that.

In her room Helen removed the woolen robe, found the hook in the back of the closet and returned it to its place. The act filled her with a kind of dull anguish, as if she were laying to rest a set of feelings and dreams that had never quite been born and had existed for a brief moment only as possibilities. She closed the closet door, making sure the catch held it shut, and putting on her own familiar nightgown she forced her thoughts away from Charles and what had occurred between them in this very room. Her mind leaped to Jimmy, her anchor to sanity and meaning, but all she could feel amid the tidal wave of emotions that coursed over her as she lay down upon the bed was that her life with Jimmy was now threatened by Virginia.

She found herself weeping, silently and controllably at first, dabbing her eyes with a tissue. Then as the floodgates opened the dark, looming sense of loneliness that Charles had made her aware of lurched at her out of the swirling darkness of her fears and doubts like the gaping jaws of some nightmare terror from the deep. Her body was wracked with sobs as the loneliness grew and grew within her; a void had opened within her, a vortex into which she plunged, feeling like an abandoned child. She buried her face in the pillow so Charles could not hear.

It was the sea that ultimately rescued her. After what seemed hours of weeping Helen gradually became aware of a kind of counterpoint to her own sobs. It was a sound that was always there at the beach house, so constant it had become part of her consciousness. The high tide had come in and with the regularity of an immense heartbeat the ocean sent its rumbling vibrations through the sand and up along the support beams of the house to the floor and upward into Helen's own body. The eternal moaning, the never-ending surge and retreat of the restless deep, seemed to Helen like the weeping heart of the world. Her own sobs gradually ceased, and she let the image of that sad, pounding, lonely heart of Mother Earth gather her to itself and sing her finally into sleep.

CHAPTER THIRTY-TWO

"Well, Artie, you can't say I didn't warn you. Cheers."

Jim O'Donnell had gotten pretty chummy since Helen had left. Now he was calling Arthur "Artie."

"It still may not be what you think, Jim, but thanks anyway."

Jim leaned back on the outdoor bar stool and his eyes rested for a moment on Katie's substantial rear end as his wife tested the water in the redwood tub with a tentative toe. Katie was wearing the lastest bikini, cut very high at the thighs and revealing more of her than was flattering. The look on Jim's face turned sour.

"Here's to girls," he said. "Women are something else."

Arthur had somehow become part of Jim O'Donnell's personal conspiracy against women. It irked him, but he was so unsure of his feelings in that department he let the comment ride. With Helen gone he had suddenly found the O'Donnells inviting him over again and offering him loyal, though questionable, support. Both of them seemed to agree that Helen was having an affair. Arthur stared at his drink, feeling depressed.

"So how's Helen?" Katie called from the redwood tub. "Come on over and fill me in. And you can fix me my usual, James."

Jim looked put-upon, but he obediently reached for the gin bottle. Arthur moved over beside the redwood tub and lowered himself into a chair.

"You should have worn your bathing suit," Katie purred. "It's very nice in here."

She lay back, letting the water lift her as she pedaled her legs and her breasts broke the surface. There was little left to imagination up there either, Arthur observed.

"Helen's fine, I guess. She calls me every day or so." He was determined not to give Jim and Katie too much to go on. What he felt was his own business.

"And do you call her?"

Jim squatted next to her, handed her the drink and sat with his legs dangling in the water.

"It's not whether he calls her, but what he calls her. Come on, Artie, open up. We think you're getting screwed."

What am I doing here? Arthur wondered. He had other friends. Not many, though. Most of their friendships over the years had come through Helen. In the past few weeks he'd had a chance to kick himself several times for not having more people in his life.

"I don't think so. I really don't," he told them. They both looked skeptical.

"So what are you doing with yourself these days?" Katie asked.

"Working. Eating a lot of TV dinners. Watching a lot of television."

"Terrific," Jim said.

"Even if she's not involved with that Charles Banning, I think you're getting a raw deal. How long has it been now?"

"Two and a half weeks—about."

"Look at him, how he's keeping track," Katie sighed. "I'll bet you know exactly, and to the hour. You're so loyal, Arthur. Not like some people I know."

Jim prodded her in the side with his toe and grinned. Somehow, Arthur thought, these two people had something going between them. They would probably be the last to admit it, but in a way they were a couple. They sure didn't keep anything back from each other.

"Have you asked her about this Banning guy?" Jim asked.

"Are you kidding? I mention his name and she blows up." Arthur was feeling the effect of the drink and loosening up. Hell, he was getting tired of defending Helen. Maybe he should listen to these two a little more. "How about a refill?"

Katie snapped, "Jim, your guest is out. Get off your ass and get him a drink."

"Hell, help yourself, Artie." Jim put out one large hand to the top of Katie's head and shoved her under water. As Arthur got up to fix his drink, Katie grabbed Jim's leg and dragged him into the tub, drink and all. He went down with a roar and pulled her under with him. Arthur could hear them sputtering and floundering about in a battle royal.

As Arthur returned with his glass refilled, Katie came up with a scream of rage. "You son of a bitch! You almost drowned me!" She smacked Jim's face with the palm of her hand and he put her under again, looking up at Arthur with an expression borrowed from Boris Karloff.

"Turn your back, Arthur my boy. I don't want any witnesses while I drown this bitch."

Katie's legs flailed the water and she finally managed to get one of them under her just when Arthur was beginning to get worried. She shot herself straight up and she rose with Jim's drink glass in her hand, giggling crazily. "Take that, Dumbo!" She threw water in Jim's face and as he sputtered she pushed him under, wrapped her legs around his neck and sat on his shoulders. Jim playfully stayed under for an incredible length of time, until Katie stopped giggling and began to look a little worried. She pulled on his hair and he still failed to come up. With a look of sheer terror she opened her legs and slid off, crying, "Jim!"

He came up with a roar, bringing Katie's legs and bottom up in his arms. He straightened and with one lunge sent her flying out of the tub and sliding on her wet backside across the concrete surface beside the pool. They looked at each other and burst out laughing.

Arthur watched the whole performance in total amazement. These two played like young pups together. Now they were collapsing with laughter as Katie crawled back to the tub on her hands and knees and threw her arms around Jim. She got back into the water. Jim immediately clambered out.

"I'll fix a couple of fresh ones. And if you spill my next drink I'll drown you, so help me God."

"Isn't he a slob?" Katie said. "Why couldn't I have married a nice civil, earnest soul like you?"

She was panting after her exertions, and her attempts

to disguise her pleasure failed. As Jim walked toward them with the drinks the look in Katie's eyes made Arthur envy the man.

"So where were we before this freak tried to drown me?" Katie asked. "How long now? Three weeks? No, two and a half."

"Artie was saying every time he mentions this guy Helen blows up."

"She walked out on me once when we were having lunch together," Arthur informed them. So why shouldn't he share some of his problem with them?

Jim quietly asked, "How is the kid? Does she say?"

"I think he's doing better. She told me he's up and walking around now, with the crutches. You know he had an operation and can't use one leg."

"You told us," Katie said. "I'm sorry about the blowup Helen and I had before Christmas. I'll bet she could use a good friend right now."

"Aw, come on, Kate," Jim drawled. "Helen's so wrapped up in that thing, she doesn't even know Arthur's alive."

"Maybe she has something to talk about she can't tell Arthur. Maybe I should call her some time."

"After that scene you had?" Arthur winked at Katie. "She's changed. Helen is a different woman now." He knew it sounded bleak and forlorn, but what the hell.

"What's so bad about that?" Katie shot back. "People do change, Arthur. If you ask me, Helen could use some guts. When she jumped on me that way when we were shopping, sure I blew up at her, but later I got to thinking, Hey, that's okay. Helen's getting her act together."

Jim looked at Arthur and shook his head. "Now comes the bullshit. Getting her act together at whose expense?"

This was the real sore point between Katie and Jim, Arthur could tell. The playfulness was gone now from both of them. Katie lifted herself out of the redwood tub and began drying off with a large orange and white beach towel bearing a female circle and cross symbol, with the words "I am a Woman" in bold orange letters.

"Helen is growing up," Katie announced. "This little boy of hers came along just in time. And I think you should know that, Arthur. She's never going to be the same." Katie wrapped the towel around her shoulders and slid her feet into rubber thong sandals. As she walked away, the sandals slapping the concrete, she said, "I'm going to toss the salad now. I'll tell you the only thing I don't like about this, and I mean the only thing, Arthur. She should be more honest with you."

Jim O'Donnell was quiet for a while after Katie made her departure. He sipped his drink and stared after her long after the door of the house had slid shut behind Katie.

"I think she's right, Artie. I hate to admit Katie's ever right about anything. But she knows what she's talking about."

Arthur let it soak in for a while. He wasn't sure that Helen wasn't being honest. He had such a damn hard time talking to her at all.

Jim said, "You and I are part of an old scene, Artie. We'd like to think nothing's ever going to rock the boat, right?" He pulled himself out of the tub and dried the upper half of his body while he sat with his feet dangling in the hot water.

"What do you mean, an old scene? What's wrong with not rocking the boat, when things are going smooth?"

"Yeah. But smooth for who? Let's face it, the women don't know where the hell they're at these days. And maybe the fault's our own."

"Am I hearing right?" Arthur tried to joke.

Jim was serious. He looked at Arthur very soberly, meaning every word of it. "I love that silly broad, you know? And what I can't figure out is how to be her friend. That's the sticker, how to be friends with someone you love. Funny, isn't it? Sometimes I think the friendliest thing I could do for Katie is to cut her loose. Just let her go, for her own good."

"Hey, Jim, come on. You're kidding. Katie'd die of boredom without you to pick on."

"Would she?" Jim asked doubtfully.

"Well, wouldn't she?"

"That's what I don't know. These games Kate and I play, they're getting old, Artie. The real friendly thing might be to find her something like what Helen's got."

"Helen? What's she got?"

"A reason for living."

It set Arthur back for a moment. He wasn't sure just exactly what Jim meant by that. "Do you mean the boy, Jimmy, or his father?"

Jim replied quietly, "What difference does it make?"

"It makes a hell of a difference. And I think you're pulling my leg."

"I was never more serious in my life. Your problem is you're a moralist, Artie. You see everything in terms of right and wrong. But the question is Helen's happiness, and Katie's. Or is it?"

Arthur had always thought of Jim O'Donnell as pretty much of a slob, as Katie said. The man had never given the slightest indication of any concern in life deeper than his bank account or who would win the Superbowl. Suddenly here he was, trying to get Arthur to ponder the meaning of his own love for Helen.

He thought about it for so long that Jim finally said, "You don't get what I'm talking about?"

"I get it. I just don't know what to make of it. Or of you."

"Like Katie says, people change. Katie's like a caged bird. I clipped her wings once. Now I think maybe I'd like to see her fly."

"So she'll fall on her face and have to come winging home again?"

Jim looked up quickly and laughed. "Maybe that's it! What the hell, let's go in and get ready for dinner."

Jim threw his towel over the back of a chair and led

the way toward the house. Inside they could see Katie setting the dining room table. Under the crystal chandelier, her slight figure framed in the light that shone through the glass doors, she did look like a lovely little caged bird.

CHAPTER THIRTY-THREE

The court hearing on Virginia Banning's plea for a change in custody was set for February twentieth. Arthur called Helen on the nineteenth and asked her to lunch. She accepted readily.

They met at a steak house on Wilshire Boulevard, a place unfamiliar to either of them, but very suited to the occasion and to the mood Helen was in. The restaurant was dimly lit and not too crowded. The booths were padded in rich black leather while stained glass windows in tones of deep red and gold added a soft, sober background to the quiet conversations of the diners.

Arthur had arrived first and when Helen joined him he quickly embraced her with a warm smile and kissed her cheek. Then as she slid into the booth he presented a small bouquet of roses. It was a touching gesture, very much in keeping with the feeling she had that they were almost like two lovers sneaking off from work for a noontime rendezvous. Almost.

Arthur placed himself next to her and took her hand. "How are you holding up?" he asked.

"This court business scares me," Helen confessed. She and Arthur had discussed it on the phone several times, but the nearer the court date came the more uncertain she felt of her own role.

"Courts are always tricky. You can never tell how things will come out."

"I'm glad you called, Arthur. It's good for me to get away from there once in a while."

They ordered their drinks and as they waited, Arthur toyed with a salt shaker on the table, moving it from square to square on the checkered table cloth like a chess piece. He had released her hand when the waiter came. Now he looked worried.

"How's Jimmy?" he asked.

"That's another thing. His tests aren't good. This drug isn't working."

"What does that mean?"

"Now, all of a sudden he's started losing weight, losing energy, and talking a lot about dying again."

Arthur looked up at her with real pity in his eyes. "I'm sorry. It must be hell watching him go along well for a while, then back down again."

"I really needed to see you today, Arthur. Thank you for this, and for the flowers."

The drinks arrived. Arthur sipped his in silence and then said, "I had an unusual experience the other day, in the park. The one that's on top of the hill in town looking over the beach?"

She knew the place, a small strip of green grass and trees that ran along the top of one of the palisades in Santa Monica. A little oasis close to the business section, frequented by a few senior citizens and occasional tourists.

"I was just taking a walk there one day last week, and I saw a young woman with a handicapped child. It was a girl, oh, about eight or nine."

Helen held back an urge to ask Arthur what he was doing there. The picture of her husband, lonely, hanging about in a public park, depressed her.

"There are swings there now," Arthur continued. "Anyway this woman was pushing the wheelchair along and all of a sudden the little girl wanted to swing. I was sitting there on a bench, not far away. And the woman said no. Then the girl started begging for a chance to swing and when the woman told her no again, she really started to cry. I guess the woman, her mother or whoever she was, gave in and decided to try, but I could see she was having trouble getting the child out of the chair. The thing is—I watched them. I paid attention to this."

"I'm not sure what you mean."

"Well, it came to me there on the bench. There was a time when I would have looked away, you know? I might have even got up and left. But I stayed and I listened, and I looked. And when the woman couldn't lift the child, I went over and put my arms under the little girl's and lifted her up. She gave me such a smile. I stayed around until the little girl had enough and then I helped her back into the chair. I know it wasn't much, but I think this thing with you and Jimmy—maybe I'm getting more aware of things like that."

Their food was brought to the table, and Helen stared at Arthur's face as he began to eat. She found it hard to shake off a feeling of old familiar guilt about neglecting him.

"How are you managing, Arthur?"

"Oh, fine. I miss you, but you know that."

As they continued talking, small talk about the weather and Arthur's work and the house and Sharon, Helen was aware of holding back many far more significant things she should be sharing with him. Yet she was no longer sure about her feelings for Arthur. The shattering impact of their parting a month ago still lingered. What troubled her most deeply was her knowledge that Arthur could be two men, one loving and thoughtful and steady, the other suspicious, accusing, possessive. His story about seeing the child in the park was touching, but Helen was not convinced that the basic Arthur had changed. Neither was she sure he was trying to convince her of that. He really seemed to be just sharing it with her and not demanding much of anything. She began to wonder what else he might be holding back on his side, and finally concluded that she really had no right to pry.

As they neared the end of their lunch, Arthur brought up the court hearing again. He approached it carefully.

"Do you need any help tomorrow, with getting to court or anything?"

"I have my car."

"You'll see this woman, Virginia, right?"

"Brr," Helen shivered. "That's going to be the hard part. But I am curious."

"No doubt. Do you think she's got a case?"

"I told you about the money. Beyond that, I just don't know. Charles says she has a very smart, slick lawyer."

"What about your lawyer?"

"Ours? I don't know. He wouldn't be my choice, but Charles says he's a diamond in the rough, and in court he'll shine."

"It's going to be a tough day for you."

"Thanks for caring, Arthur. I do appreciate it."

Suddenly Arthur looked into her eyes and reached for her hand. "Helen, we're not doing too well, are we?"

"How do you mean?"

"You and me. We talk along here, and we just can't say any of the things that ought to be said. Like I love you. And I miss you like hell. And I wish to God you were home. And I know things aren't right between us." He let go of her hand and rolled his napkin into a knot between his fists.

She held her breath, fighting an urge to give in. She managed to say, "Things are not right, Arthur. And it isn't just because I'm with Jimmy."

He stared at his hands. "I know. So, okay. I would like to ask one thing. I want to be in the courtroom tomorrow."

"Arthur, I don't know . . ."

"It's my place to be there, Helen. You don't know

what you're going to face before this is over. I would just like to be there."

There was the side of Arthur she could always count on. She had tested that durable dependability of his over the years, and in a crisis his strength had always helped. It was what she loved most about him and yet it was what in some ways made her most dependent.

"I'm going to be there anyway," he said. "So I just wanted you to know."

When the day of the hearing finally arrived, Helen set out for the long drive to downtown Los Angeles, starting at seven in the morning. Even though Jimmy had suffered some pain during the night and had been able to sleep for only two or three hours, he insisted on seeing her off. Helen had gone into his room when she had finished dressing.

"You look terrific, Mom," Jimmy had said. Then after assuring her that he would be fine in Jessica's care, Jimmy made it a point to cheer her up. "Tell them I said you're my mom now. And I'm not going back to Virginia no matter what. I'm going to be with you until I die, and that's it."

"I'll tell them, Jimmy."

In a moment of sudden fear his face had changed and he had held his arms out to her, begging, "Don't let Virginia take me away from you, Mom. Please."

She had hugged him, patting his thin shoulder blades that jutted sharply against her hand from inside his thin pajamas, and had promised that she and Charles would "fight like hell."

He cheered up with that, always ready to smile any time Helen used profanity of even the mildest variety. His parting shot was, "Tell them the trouble is Virginia doesn't have a happiness button, and you have!"

They had told Jimmy about Virginia's attempts to regain custody, after they had waited through the unnerving suspense of early negotiations to the final setting of the court date. When he heard it, Jimmy snapped, "I don't care what she does, I'm not going back to her.

You're my mother now." And though she probed a little just to make sure it was Jimmy's true opinion and not just what he might think she wanted to hear, the boy would not alter his reaction one inch. He finally said, "I don't think she ever wanted to be my mother in the first place."

Helen drove the thirty miles or so to the Los Angeles County courthouse in a state of near panic. In a final precourt conference with Charles's attorney the man had cautiously approached the subject of Helen's relationship with Charles. Very apologetically the lawyer said, "It might come up. You can never tell. Hell hath no fury, and all that. She might try to make a case for wild orgies going on around her dear boy's sickbed. You know how those things go."

In one glance Helen and Charles settled what their story would be, and that they would not even tell the attorney. Helen managed a shy smile and Charles reacted with a self-conscious laugh that they both felt was quite convincing. The lawyer never raised the question again. But for Helen the prospect of taking the witness stand and being asked, while under oath, and with her husband sitting in the courtroom, "Have you and Charles Banning ever been lovers?" had kept her awake many a night. She steered her little car through the maze of what Jim O'Donnell called "the world's fastest moving traffic jam, the LA freeways at rush hour" bathed in cold sweat and wondering how she could compose herself for the task of lying under oath.

Arthur would be there, and he could read the expressions on her face easily. However she might fool the judge and Virginia Banning, she knew she would not convince Arthur. If she took the stand and was asked that question, Arthur would know.

As the traffic ground to a dead halt for the tenth or twentieth time, Helen turned on the car radio for the morning freeway report. The helpful announcer also made breathless reports on the time about every thirty seconds. Her panic grew as she realized the hearing was due to start in ten minutes. What happens if you're late to court? She had no idea, but imagined some dire punishment that would jeopardize their case.

The hearing was set for eight-thirty. At eight twenty-five she was at the off-ramp and trying to remember Charles's instructions about where to find the parking lot. When she did find it and emerge from her car she had two blocks to run to reach the immense tan marble building she had been told she couldn't miss. As she neared the door she thought it the most imposing structure she had ever seen. Inside she peered down a corridor a full city block in length and paused as she collected her wits to search for the elevator.

Fortunately Charles had given explicit directions on what door to use, how to find the elevator and what floor button to punch. As she came to the second floor and made the right turn he had instructed her to take she saw Charles hurrying toward her. In contrast to her state of anxiety and near exhaustion Charles appeared cool and relaxed.

"Am I too late?" she cried.

"Just in time. It's this way." He led her along past benches of people who sat staring stonily at the floor. Their attorney, Cal Watkins, came idling out of a door ahead of them and greeted Helen with a broad grin that showed his large, wide-spaced front teeth. Cal was from Oklahoma and always looked as if he had just taken off his cowboy hat and boots and felt hemmed-in by his vested suit.

"Well, good morning there, Helen. My, don't you look nice! Come on right in and just make yourself comfortable. We'll get to you in a while."

The room was not as large as Helen had imagined it. There were only twenty or so seats for witnesses and spectators. It was a panelled room, and it looked cold.

Virginia Banning and her attorney had not yet arrived, and neither had Arthur. Helen, Charles, and Cal Watkins, were the only people present with the exception of a uniformed officer who stood near a rear door

Helen supposed was the entrance to the judge's chambers and a court stenographer who sat at a small table in front of the judge's bench. A large clock on the wall indicated the time to be eight-thirty-four.

"Nervous?" Charles asked.

"Are you kidding?" Helen replied, then wondered, "Do you think they might not show up?"

"They're here. I saw them getting coffee in the cafeteria a while back," Cal grinned. Then, seeing her evident state of mind, he patted her arm and directed her to a seat in the front row. "You just sit down and relax now. You've got nothing to worry about."

He nodded toward one of the two benches that faced the judge's area and he and Charles moved toward it. Charles stood whispering with him as the attorney lifted some papers from his briefcase. There was a stir at the back of the room and Helen saw Charles look up, then quickly look away. She turned and saw Virginia Banning entering alone.

For a moment the woman's attention was toward the door through which she had just come. It was open slightly. Helen could see the attorney holding the door. Her first impression of Virginia, even from that distance and from behind her, was one of elegance. Virginia turned at that moment and the attorney entered with her. She came down the aisle toward them with leggy strides, a confident, beautiful woman chatting back over her shoulder with the lawyer and taking them in with her wide-set brown eyes at the same time. Her dress was stylish but tastefully conservative. Her hair was done up and back, enhancing her appearance by making her look just a touch dramatic, and possibly a tiny bit tragic. She was the beautiful woman and the brave victim in one masterful stroke.

She passed Helen without a glance in her direction. Her attorney guided her past Charles and the two of them inclined their heads coolly without a word. Charles quickly looked back past Cal and toward Helen. He winked.

The judge entered at that moment and the proceedings began. Since it was Virginia who was asking for a change in the original court order granting custody to Charles, as the lawyer had explained to Helen, the role of plaintiff was Virginia's. Charles was the respondent, there to answer satisfactorily to the court why he should be permitted to retain custody of Jimmy.

The lawyers were standing behind their respective benches talking to the judge. The judge was a small pale man who looked almost lost in the wide-shouldered formal gown of his office. He flipped through pages of material on his desk. Now and then he asked for clarification of some item of information and one of the attorneys would supply it. In sharp contrast to Cal Watkins's easy manner and country boy drawl the attorney for Virginia Banning seemed like the most urbane and civilized man in the world. His expensive suit was perfectly tailored. He looked very much like a movie star or a well-established senator from some eastern state. A tall, broad-shouldered man, he exuded a sense of power tempered by reason and compassion.

We're sunk Helen thought. The judge's eyes seemed to gravitate back to Virginia Banning whenever someone else was not directly speaking to him, and even then he would glance at her, all the while saying, "Um-hum, I see. Yes, I see." What he was seeing, Helen thought, was that gorgeous woman deprived of her child.

Just as Virginia herself was about to take the stand Helen became aware of someone else entering the room. She glanced around quickly and saw Arthur sliding into the back row of seats. He caught her eye and gave her a nod. With a sense of impending doom Helen made herself concentrate on the proceedings.

Virginia's voice was low-pitched and controlled. She seemed at home in the witness chair and took the oath and answered the opening questions from her attorney with an assurance and poise that were bound to impress the judge.

"Now tell us, Mrs. Banning," said her attorney, "in your own words, what were the circumstances that led up to the tragic separation of you and your son, Jimmy."

"My husband and I had not been getting along well for some time before Jimmy was taken ill. When I found out that my son had leukemia," she paused and swallowed as if choking back tears, "I just went to pieces. He was all I had. The doctors said he was going to die. Oh, yes there was hope, they said, but in the state of shock that came over me, I was unable to hear anything or believe anything other than that Jimmy was going to die."

She paused again and the judge very sympathetically urged her to take her time. She thanked him very sweetly and continued, "I left him in such a state that I just couldn't bring myself to call him or write to him for quite a while."

"And where did you go?" her attorney asked quietly.

"I consulted with a psychiatrist, and he recommended that I spend some time in a convalescent hospital in Switzerland."

"Was this a mental hospital?"

"No, definitely not. It was more like a resort than anything else. It gave me the opportunity to rest and recover, but it was not a mental hospital, no." For the first time it seemed to Helen that Virginia was uneasy. The judge did not seem to take notice of the way she stiffened and the lines of tension that appeared on her forehead. Maybe the judge couldn't see from where he was, Helen thought.

"Go on, Mrs. Banning," her lawyer said.

"I was there for some time, for three months to be exact. I returned home and accepted a position in the buying office for a local department store chain."

"So you are well able to provide for yourself and your child," the lawyer added.

"Yes."

"And now, Mrs. Banning, will you tell the court why

you feel the custody of your child should be returned to you?"

"I am his mother."

It was said as if no further argument were necessary. That simple declaration, it seemed to Helen, carried more weight than anything else she could possibly say. This time the judge seemed hardly to be listening.

Virginia's attorney shifted his weight and paused to let the remark sink in. "Go on."

"I gave my son up only because I was in a state of complete shock. I think it's fair to say that I didn't know what I was doing. It is probably also fair to say that, in such a state of mind, it is good that my husband, I'm sorry, my former husband, took over with the care of my son. But a boy in that condition should be with his own mother."

"Do you believe that your former husband is neglectful in any way, Mrs. Banning?"

"Yes, I believe he is neglecting the child. Oh, I'm sure the medical aspect is being taken care of. But Charles is a salesman and travels almost constantly. My son is in the care of a nurse and another woman."

"And how did the other woman, Mrs. Long, get involved, according to your information?"

"I have heard that Jimmy saw her on the beach and asked her to be his mother, which I think is a lie. My son would not do that."

Helen sat in frozen amazement. The woman was simply denying the facts. Virginia's eyes swept over to Helen's and it was as if she looked through her, seeing only the woman her imagination had created. Helen began to doubt her sanity at that moment. In shocked disbelief she listened to the testimony, dreading the inevitable questions about herself and Charles, and feeling suddenly very sorry for Arthur.

"I believe that Charles brought the woman to the beach for Jimmy to see and made the whole thing happen. And if he didn't do that he made Jimmy hungry for human companionship by being gone all the time!

So anyone that came along, even a stranger sitting on the beach, looked good to the child. And no matter what she has said about me, or what the two of them have going for each other, that woman should not be allowed to replace Jimmy's natural mother!"

The impact of what the woman was saying was somehow diffused by her distraught manner. It was a sudden outburst that Helen thought destroyed the whole facade of beautiful-mother-as-victim, and made Virginia suddenly seem capable of very irrational behavior. The judge apparently saw it too. He straightened in his chair and cleared his throat, with a warning look over his glasses toward Virginia's attorney.

"That will be all," the slick lawyer smiled, and acting as if nothing at all had gone amiss, he strode to his chair.

Cal Watkins rose up behind his table, pushing his chair back with his legs so it squeaked loudly on the bare wood floor. Virginia Banning recovered her composure quickly and regarded him with a slightly deprecating smile. Cal leaned his weight on one foot and took his time about starting. He toyed with the papers on the table in front of him and then spoke suddenly and softly.

"Well, Ma'am, I would like to ask you just a question or two by the way of clearing up a couple of details. You wouldn't mind if I kept you up there for just a little while longer, would you?"

It seemed an innocent enough question, but it implied that Virginia was under stress and might crack at any minute.

"No, I don't mind at all." Her smile was just a little too broad.

"Thank you. I'll be brief. The one thing that you didn't mention was what happened, ma'am, after you came back from Switzerland, from that hospital?"

"Convalescent home."

"You said you were there for three months. Does that mean you've been back here at your home in Encino for, well, let's see now, about seven months. Am I figurin' that right?"

"I returned in early August."

"And did you write to your son, or call him or try to communicate with him in any way during that time?"

"I tried, yes." Helen saw a quick look pass from Virginia to her attorney. "By phone, several times. There was never any answer."

"I see. Well, that happens. People just aren't home a lot of times. In Jimmy's case, though, he's home most of the time when he isn't in the hospital. Did you ever try to reach him at the hospital, by any chance?"

"I was never sure where he was, or when he might be there."

"Do you know the name of Jimmy's doctor?"

"Yes. Dr. Jacoby."

"That's right, ma'am. Jimmy's still got the same doctor. And Jimmy's not doing too well again. I'm sure you'll be sorry to hear he may have to return to the hospital again. I was a little surprised you didn't stop and ask your former husband about Jimmy when you came in today, seeing as how you don't know how he's been, and since you're his mother."

Virginia Banning's attorney stirred in his chair and the judge said, "Go on with the questioning, counselor."

"The point is, ma'am, you could have called the doctor at any time for seven months. Did you, ever?"

"Well, I—I do have my work. I've been trying to get my own life going again."

"Oh, I can understand that. Would you intend to continue working if you have the full care of your son, ma'am? You know how important it is for someone to be with him, with all he's going through."

Again Virginia looked to her lawyer for aid. The attorney looked at her steadily for a moment and merely smiled.

"I would want to devote all my time to Jimmy. I've missed him terribly. No, I wouldn't continue working."

"How would you manage, ma'am? With the medical payments and all. Could you handle all that?"

"I believe I could. Money is not the question here."

"I think you're right, ma'am. Love is the question here, isn't it? And I suppose you know about the trust fund, the money from Jimmy's grandfather?"

"I believe there is some money available for Jimmy's care, yes."

"Wouldn't that money be some help to you? I mean, it's there for you to use if you've got the custody of the boy. Did you know that?"

"I—I know there is money . . . I didn't understand the question."

"Wouldn't you use that money if you had to give up your job to take care of Jimmy?"

"I suppose I would, for Jimmy's care."

"And do you know that the parent who has custody of the boy in the event of his death stands to inherit a considerable sum?"

"No. I didn't know that."

"Now, I wouldn't want to dispute your word, ma'am, but according to records you were present at the reading of the will of Gregory Banning. Maybe it slipped your mind that there are three-quarters of a million dollars in that trust. You never heard of that?"

Virginia looked trapped. She glanced from her lawyer to the judge and quickly back toward Cal Watkins. Suddenly she jumped to her feet.

"I know what you're trying to say! You think I'm after the money, don't you! You're taking a mother's love for her son and making something else out of it!" She gripped the rail in front of the witness chair with both hands.

Cal did not answer. He allowed her to stand there, staring wildly, all her cool composure shattered. Very quietly Cal said there were no more questions and sat down.

Virginia Banning remained standing as if transfixed, her eyes wide and staring. Then she began talking rapidly in a jerking staccato fashion, her words tumbling together, her face twisted into a horrible raging mask.

"He did it! Yes, Charles, you! It was your blood that made Jimmy sick, and your influence! Hah—all the subtle ways you pretended to love him and protect him and all the while you were infecting him, and making him die! They told me! In the hospital in Switzerland! Doctor Pretzger—he'll tell you! All my doctors say the same thing! I did not make Jimmy sick. No. No, I didn't! My mistake was in marrying a man with bad blood, my only mistake! The psychiatrists don't agree with me on that, but I know! And I don't have to feel guilty for that. I was young. I was young and very beautiful and very, very desirable, oh yes! And with all the men, the clean men I could have had."

She began to cry. She was a pathetic sight that wrung Helen's heart. She wanted someone to stop her. But Virginia went on, sobbing and screaming her rage.

"But I married you, Charles, and you gave my son the evil infection that was in you! Not in me! I swear it wasn't my fault. I didn't make Jimmy ugly! I didn't make him die! And now we're going to take him away from you, and as far as I care you can keep your filthy family's money. Everything about you is dirty! Dirty and cruel and cold!"

Her attorney was at her side in three long strides, calming her, taking her arm, leading her back to her place at the plaintiff's table.

Virginia Banning no longer looked beautiful as she made her way silently from the witness stand to the chair beside her attorney. The judge's eyes followed her and rested for a moment on the two of them before he said, "We'll take a few minutes' recess. And I would like to see you two gentlemen in chambers."

With that the judge swept through the door at the rear of the room and the two attorneys followed. Helen saw Charles turn to look at Virginia as she stonily stared at the closed door to the judge's private quarters. Then Charles turned to her.

"Is that Arthur back there? I'd like to meet him."

Helen turned to wave Arthur toward them. At the same time she noticed that another man was just rising from a seat near the back of the room and was making his way toward Virginia. The man was tall, well dressed, wearing a short, pointed beard and glasses.

"Virginia's psychiatrist," Charles whispered. "We've called him as a witness. But I don't think we'll need him. I think it's all over." Charles stood and put out his hand to Arthur. "Hello, I'm Charles Banning."

Arthur smiled his gentle smile and shook Charles's hand. "Good to meet you. That poor woman," Arthur whispered, with a glance toward Virginia. "I was right, wasn't I?"

"About what?" Helen asked.

"At that party that time at Katie's. I said she was in a mental hospital."

"The psychiatrist is still treating her. She's been an out-patient for seven months." Charles informed them. "That's what's been happening, and why she hasn't tried to reach Jimmy. She had a complete breakdown."

Helen saw a look of compassion come over Charles's face as he stared at his former wife. There was pity there, and love, or something very much like it. Charles said, "Cal Watkins called all over Switzerland and finally came up with the place. She's been sick all right, very badly off."

"So what's going to happen now?" Arthur asked.

"The judge will decide it in there. Cal thinks Virginia forced the lawyer into it, even against the psychiatrist's advice, because she's now totally convinced I'm to blame for Jimmy's sickness. Now it's just a matter of her competence. The fact that she stayed out of touch for all that time is really against her. Don't worry. We've won. I had no idea she was so far gone."

Charles turned away as the door opened and the three men walked in. None of their faces betrayed anything. Arthur slipped into the seat next to Helen, saying, "Thank God, you won't have to get up there."

Then he saw the relief that swept through her and added, "You were really scared, weren't you?"

Cal Watkins walked to the table and sat down, his attention fixed on the judge, who arranged his robe under him and cleared his throat.

The judgment came out in coldly legal terms that, thankfully, disguised its impact. "The court finds in favor of the respondent. Custody remains with Mr. Charles Banning. The court recommends that visitation rights for the plaintiff be suspended until such time as a duly appointed court psychiatrist ascertains the advisability of such visits under the guidance of the court." With a sharp rap of his gavel the judge signaled the end of the proceedings.

As Helen and Arthur walked together down the corridor behind Charles and Cal Watkins, Cal said ruefully, "We got stuck with half the court costs, doggone it."

Charles laughed it off, but Helen thought she detected a look of profound sadness in his eyes. Whether he still loved Virginia or not, he had been deeply affected by the sight of that once lovely woman in the grip of the horrible thing that possessed her.

As he left them at the second floor elevator Cal Watkins shook Charles's hand. "I'm sorry, Charles. I didn't think she'd break down that way on the stand. We could have won it without that. Darn it, you'd think those tranquilizers they have now would have helped her. I'm sorry."

Charles seemed unable to reply. He merely nodded his head to Cal and led the way into the elevator.

CHAPTER THIRTY-FOUR

Jimmy was readmitted to the hospital on the twenty-sixth of February. His red cell count had dropped so low that he was nearly unconscious by the time he entered the hospital, and for days he lay nearly in a coma.

The usual routine of blood transfusions began again.

On the first day of March Helen moved out of the beach house and Charles Banning moved in. A truce of some sort seemed to take place in the Long household as Helen returned home and concentrated her last ounce of energy on being with Jimmy at the hospital during a time that began to take on the characteristics of a final assault on the disease. Using a bed provided by the hospital, Helen stayed with Jimmy day and night, returning home only for changes of clothing and an occasional shower.

After a week of building Jimmy's resistance and strength with transfusions of red cells, white cells, and platelets, the doctors began to administer what they called a program of "consolidation." There seemed to be dozens of doctors surrounding the boy, and as Helen questioned Jessica about it the nurse explained.

"Consolidation means they're using a combination of drugs now. They're mixing things, trying different combinations to see if they can hit on the right one."

"It sounds so experimental!"

"Well, every patient's different." Jessica paused and shifted her position on the waiting room couch. "Could you stand to walk around a bit?"

Helen welcomed the exercise and the two of them strolled down the corridor to an exit that led out to a rooftop solarium that they had discovered to be unoccupied for most of the day. It was part of the general patient wing, a recreation and rest area where nurses often brought patients needing light exercise and sunlight. They walked between gaily colored lounge chairs of green and white toward a low wall topped by a chainlink fence that overlooked part of the UCLA campus.

"How are you holding up?" Jessica asked.

"The bed they've given me is comfortable enough, when I get a chance to use it."

"He still won't let anyone else feed him but you?"

"No. But they tell me it's normal, that even adult patients sometimes do that. Why does it take so many doctors now, Jessica?"

"I guess you know that these drugs they use—they're really poisons. They have the power to kill tissue. Even when they're used right they kill a lot of healthy cells while they're getting at the cancerous cells."

"I've heard that."

"When they start combining it takes a whole team of doctors to supervise the dosage. They also give a patient what they call 'rescue factors,' to try and protect the normal cells. It's very complicated."

Helen shuddered. "Jimmy has had so many needles in him they couldn't find places to put them any more, so they put one of those built in receivers on his back."

"He's still vomiting all the time?"

"It's gone on constantly since they started trying to find a new drug."

"It's D-Day, Helen." Jessica said it quietly, looking away toward the campus where scores of healthy college students were milling about on their way to classes.

"I know." Helen turned her back on the sight of all those bright, normal young people and stared back toward the hospital, her back against the chainlink fence. "How long can it go on, Jessica?"

"If he doesn't get a good remission this time, I'm afraid it's all over."

"In a way it would be a relief to Jimmy. I never thought I would come to that, but to see him suffering so—it's too much to expect of any human being."

"The problem is, Helen, that Jimmy has never really had a good solid remission. When you first met him he was the best, but it wasn't good enough. Sometimes a good remission can last a year or two right at the start, but the best Jimmy's had was the four or five months just before you came along."

"Why is that? I don't understand."

"Who knows? But it's usually a matter of finding just exactly the right drug and the right dosage."

"That black boy, Marty Taylor, he seems to be making it. Why not Jimmy?" Helen did not intend it as a prejudiced remark. "It's not that Marty's black," she hastened to add.

Jessica smiled. "I know that, Helen. It's that Jimmy's yours and Marty's not."

"I hate the mouth sores. I think they bother him more than anything else."

"They'll go away in time. It's another side effect of the drugs. Just changing the amount or the combination a little can change that."

"Thank God they know what they're doing," Helen sighed.

Jessica moved away from the fence and sat on one of the outdoor chairs. She gestured toward another chair nearby and said, "Let's just sit and chat for a bit." Helen felt there was something behind the invitation, as if Jessica had something on her mind. She slid into the proffered chair and waited as Jessica's almond eyes slid over her face and grew troubled.

"What is it, Jessica, is something wrong?"

"I just don't know quite how to talk about this, Helen. I like you. I think you know that. I think you're a fine woman—too fine for some people."

"I don't know what you're trying to tell me, Jessica." Helen felt herself tensing, dreading something that she felt vaguely might have to do with Charles. Other than

Jimmy what link was there between her and Jessica? Finally, as the nurse sat quietly smoothing a wrinkle from her skirt, looking remote and pensive, Helen said, "It's Charles, isn't it."

Jessica nodded, saying with sudden bitterness, "He's somethin' else, that man."

Helen felt a tingle of resentment at that, a sharp stab of defensiveness. "I have always felt you don't like Charles much, Jessica. The first night I came to the beach house, remember? You seemed to have to say something against him."

"I was trying to warn you." Jessica smiled, her eyes warm, her lips tight. "I know that man."

It had been one month since the night at the beach house when Charles and Helen had been lovers. During the intervening weeks Helen had gone through several changes in her feelings about him. It had taken time for her to get over the feeling of betrayal, that Charles should have told her about Virginia earlier, and not waited until after they made love. Then as time passed Helen had grown more tolerant and forgiving, and had come to see the experience from what she hoped was Charles's point of view, that of a man attracted to a woman who could give him a mature kind of affection and companionship when he was down and needed support. The sting of it had lessened somewhat and had been replaced by an eagerness to see him again and at least talk about what had transpired between them. Charles, however, seemed to be dodging her. He managed to come to the hospital when she was at home changing her clothes or running a household errand, and they hadn't really talked since the days of the court hearing.

"I haven't really seen Charles to talk to him in weeks," Helen finally replied.

"Helen," Jessica said, seeming to choose her words very carefully, "what Charles and you may or may not think about each other, that's none of my business. But

I have to tell you we had a fight last night, Charles and I, and it was over you."

"A fight?"

"I told you once how he comes down there to the beach and gets a little too much to drink once in a while? Well, he did that last night. And when he drinks too much he gets talkative, 'philosophical' he calls it. I call it depressed. He thinks the whole world stinks and everybody in it, then he drinks some more. Then, it's what a rotten deal Jimmy's had."

Helen recalled the time in the restaurant. It was the same pattern. She felt Jessica was telling the truth.

"And after a few more drinks it's what a rotten deal Charles had with Virginia. I listened to about all that I could take, then we got it on."

"What is it about Virginia? What does he say?"

"He talks to me different than he probably talks to you. That's one of the things that gets me about him. Around me, because I'm black, he thinks he can be vulgar. He talks to me like dirt."

Helen could not believe her ears. A gasp of shock escaped her and Jessica looked up at Helen with a sad smile.

"It's okay, honey. I'm used to things like that. Some men see a black woman and they think just one thing. That's some of what I've kept trying to warn you about. I wouldn't be doing this, believe me, if he hadn't spouted off some things about you and him. I feel like I owe it to you."

Helen's breath caught in her throat. "He—told you about—about, what? What did he say, Jessica?"

"He was drunk. Maybe you should make allowances for that. But he told me—things he shouldn't. Now, I'll shut up if you want, but I think you should get your eyes open about that man."

Helen stood to her feet, her head swimming, her vision of the fence and the campus blurring, her stomach flip-flopping convulsively. She leaned against the hard metal of the chain-link, pressing her face against it. After a moment she felt Jessica beside her.

"I'm sorry, Helen. I thought you should know. He's not a fit man for you. It's not that he's all bad, but there's a side to him I just felt you ought to know about."

Helen turned away, nearly retching, leaning her back against the fence, looking upward, trying to breath against a taste of gall in her throat. "It's all right, Jessica," she gasped. "I know you meant well. It's just such a shock, such a horrible, ugly shock."

Jessica's own eyes were tearful as she touched Helen's cheek, saying, "I'm sorry, sister. My dear old mama used to say, 'Us women's got the hard part, and we got to stick together.' "

Helen gained enough control to ask, "How long will Charles live at the beach house?"

"For a while, I guess."

Helen's efforts at self-control melted away against a sudden assault of angry tears. She dabbed at her eyes and collapsed into the chair again. Visions of Charles drunkenly babbling to Jessica flooded her thoughts, vague, distorted images heightened by the fact that they were only products of her distraught imagination.

"Tell me what he said, Jessica. Did he brag about having me, or give you lurid details, or what? It would help if I knew!"

"It was later, after I got on him about the way he talks to me. After he said how tight-assed and cold Virginia always was. He wasn't so vulgar about you, if it's any help. He was gettin' to the sentimental stage by then."

"But he did tell you that we . . ."

"Helen—don't let yourself fall in love with this man, okay? I think that's what I really mean to say. I know you pretty well now, and I know him too well. You got to him, you really did. He got knocked off his pins pretty good there for a while. That's why he's been avoiding you. Some of his old girlfriends here at the hospital have been letting him know when you go out, and that's how he always manages to come see Jimmy when you're gone."

"I was wondering about that." It cheered her somehow to think she might be giving Charles a little problem. "Why do you think he's avoiding me. Did he say?"

Jessica chuckled, "He's afraid, that's why. He doesn't know how he would handle it if you got serious, or he got serious. So that's why he's got this other girlfriend now."

"What? What other girl?"

"Oh, didn't I mention that?"

"No!" The small particle of good feeling about Charles Helen had begun to recover vanished in a surge of jealous anger. "You didn't mention that, Jessica. But that's enough. I think I've heard quite enough. Oooh, what I've been putting myself through over that man! Well, thank you, Jessica. Thank you very much!"

Jessica laid her hand on Helen's shoulder and patted it. "You don't know how I suffered over whether to tell you all this or not. You sure it's okay?"

Helen assured her that she appreciated Jessica's concern for her. They walked arm in arm back to the hospital a few minutes later, and Helen resumed her vigil by Jimmy's bedside.

Late that night when the hospital corridors were silent and empty, Helen made her way to the first floor coffee machine. Sipping the lukewarm, bitter-tasting brew she returned to the waiting room near Jimmy's room and sat for a while, feeling more exhausted and emotionally drained than at any time in the five months of knowing Jimmy and his father.

One thought was troubling her. Why had she let Charles Banning make love to her? Was she so dumb about men in general, or was it because she had been vulnerable that night, reacting to her situation with Arthur? Or was it something else? Jimmy's face kept floating before her mind's eye, alternating with the older, fuller, yet very similar features of Charles Banning.

Perhaps, she thought, it was because of her love for Jimmy, because she sensed so much of the boy in the man. Jimmy, thirty years older, with the same flashing, disarming smile, but without the innocence. If he lived, would he grow up to become like his father? She dismissed that disturbing thought. Charles was the flawed image of his son, and what he had seemed that night was not all he was, obviously.

Sipping her coffee, she realized she was no longer angry. The jealousy, the rage, the feelings of rejection had all been growing dim during the afternoon. She could think rationally now. Charles was less than she had thought; all right, she could accept that. Jessica's revelations, though hard to take, had settled something for Helen, the nagging question of what to do with her feeling for Charles. She could put it all in perspective now, bury it for good, with regret and a lingering taste of having learned a lesson about her own vulnerability. But she could live with it, and now focus her mind fully on helping Jimmy fight his seemingly neverending battle.

She returned to Jimmy's room and stood silently looking down at his thin, pale face, listening to his slow, deep breathing. A tiny speck of light from the corridor caught a drop of intravenous fluid as it slid downward in its plastic tube like a slowly falling star descending to her beloved child. Jimmy, an innocent in a world of confused and sometimes cruel adults.

Jimmy's innocence had built a shield of childish fantasy between him and the reality of what he suffered. Helen had often stood in awe and sometimes in envy of him, but now she wondered if a person had to be purged of innocence in order to grow. She was beginning to sense that she had always seen life as a kind of chessboard of black and white, "good" and "bad" squares, a contest to see who would stay innocent and who would not. Her upbringing by deeply religious parents had inclined her to see her life as a kind of moral proving ground. She had been protected by fantasies of her own, of good guys and bad guys, romantic heroes and stainfree heroines, of herself as above temptation, and not without a degree of judgmental aloofness about the failings of others. Now she questioned that vision. The world seemed to her now more like a fog-shrouded field of gray upon which faulty human beings groped their way toward each other, sharing, aiding when they could each other's struggle to survive.

Stretching out on the bed, she thought of Katie O'Donnell, for some reason. She smiled, remembering Katie talking about Arthur's "morality fixation." She felt she was beginning to understand what Katie had been talking about.

She went to sleep feeling a little sorry for Charles Banning.

CHAPTER THIRTY-FIVE

Throughout the months of March and April they were engaged in a desperate battle for Jimmy's life.

Helen, fifteen pounds lighter, pale, her eyes circled by telltale patches of blue no eye shadow could disguise, was finally ordered home for a brief rest. Jessica assumed what she could of Helen's role, a temporary arrangement only acceptable to Jimmy because the boy was unable to tell most of the time who was beside him and who was not.

During the second week of April Helen watched in benumbed horror as little Marty Taylor was readmitted to the ward. For a time the two rooms were directly across the hall from each other. Helen and Marty's gentle, optimistic father would nod and wave occasionally as the days passed and both boys battled to survive.

Helen awoke one morning to find Marty's bed empty. The local high school had lost its courageous swimming star. Her last memory of the boy's father was of seeing him in the corridor the night before, wiping his gold-rimmed glasses with a spotless handkerchief, saying wearily, "He's going to beat it. He's still going to beat it."

The disease struck Jimmy like a tide which had been held by a dam until it could no longer be contained. It ravaged his frail body, resisting all human efforts to quell its power. Dr. Jacoby and the team of physicians were methodically ransacking the arsenal of chemical poisons available to them.

As the month of May drew near and Helen lay in tranquilized half-sleep at home, Jimmy's life was being maintained by constant infusions of blood, food and drugs. It seemed to Helen that everyone she had ever known was now donating blood for Jimmy.

Professor Mays had appeared one day. She saw him from the doorway of Jimmy's room, striding off the elevator from the laboratory on the first floor, his red beard longer and fuller than ever, and followed by five of Helen's former classmates. They were the same giggly sophomores who used to surround the professor's desk after every lecture, a group she had always thought of as little more than children themselves. They had all come to donate blood for Jimmy.

With a quick perusal of her face the teacher had said, "You'd better take care of yourself, Helen. You've still got a lot to go through." Whereupon he had handed her a note from Dr. Miller.

In her note the kindly exponent of humane death apologized for being unable to donate blood. "For it is vitally necessary to prolong human life to give every chance in the world to a patient like your dear boy. However, Mrs. Long, let me encourage you to follow your warm-hearted instincts in these closing days, and at the appropriate time take the child home. The dying should be surrounded by familiar scenes and by those they love at the end. If I may be of any assistance at all, please call. Someday we must discuss a possible career for you in Hospice. Irene Miller."

Hospice, Helen had learned, was the organization of volunteers who devote themselves to making the final hours of the dying as dignified and painless as possible. A career of this? Helen had shivered and put the thought aside.

Though all the signs pointed to Jimmy's death, Helen still found in the back of her mind an insistent voice that said, keep hoping, don't give up. Arthur had become the strongest ally. Her husband had been one of the first volunteer blood donors in her own circle, shortly before Helen's arrival at home. Given the full details of the peril Jimmy faced, and after an outburst of concern over Helen's own condition, Arthur had swung into action.

The first person Arthur called was Jim O'Donnell, telling him, "It doesn't matter what type you are. He needs platelets, white cells, red cells, everything. Even plasma will help. Just get in there and tell them it's for Jimmy Banning." Arthur then started down a list of men and women he knew at the electronics firm.

And now, on her third day at home, Helen had a phone call from Katie, who wasted no time with useless chatter. "Helen," Katie said, "if you're going to be home for a while, I'm coming over. It's time we talked."

Thirty minutes later Katie breezed in. Helen was stretched out on the living room couch, and Katie's reaction made it plain there was no need for apologies or recriminations as she took one look at Helen's face and said, "My God, Helen, what you've been through. What can I do?"

Helen managed to fix them both a good stiff drink and they sat down for a chat. Helen explained the full extent of Jimmy's condition and his need for blood. Katie leaped to her feet, picked up the phone and made three calls, all to presidents of organizations of which she was a member. She presented the situation, reminded each of them of the financial contributions she had wrung out of her husband on their behalf, and arm-twisted them into action.

"Katie, I've missed you," Helen said.

"Let's not shed any tears over the past, kiddo. Just tell me how things are with you."

"I'm not sure. But I could sure use somebody to talk to," and with that Helen gradually began to unload, starting with her feelings about Jimmy. "He's going to die, Katie," she heard herself saying. "I never thought I would hear myself admit it, but he's going to die."

Katie snorted. "Have the doctors given him up?"

"No, not yet. They won't, I suppose. They'll fight right down to the end. But my God, Katie, the suffering! He's so thin, his face—you should see how thin he is. I just can't stand it."

As Helen dissolved in tears, weeping on her friend's shoulder, Katie stroked her back and held her tightly, whispering, "Let it all go, kid. I'm good at this. If encounter and consciousness-raising and all that crap doesn't do anything else, at least it gets you used to hearing people cry."

The tears dried up quickly and Helen settled back, chuckling and drying her eyes. "Katie, you are one of a kind. I've been doing a lot of this lately. Can't say I recommend it for the nerves."

"Want to stop talking?"

"No. About Jimmy, yes. I think I'm starting to accept whatever's coming there. But I need some advice, or a chance to sound off, or something."

Katie nodded knowingly. "It's Arthur, right?" She went on to tell Helen about some of Arthur's visits to their place, and their attempts to support him. "Really, Helen," Katie said, "Jim and I do care about both of you. We felt Arthur ought to grow up a bit and we tried to help. I know, subtle we aren't, but we have been trying to help him see that you really are a separate person, and that you just might change some time."

"There was a time when I wouldn't have understood that Arthur needs help. But I do now."

"And now you've got some choices to make. You've put a little distance between you and Arthur. Has it helped?"

"I don't know. I'm very confused."

"Aren't we all? You've got one thing, though."

"What's that?"

"A reason for living. I envy you that, Helen. I really do. What have I got? I know what you're going to say, or think and not say, that old Katie's too flighty to worry about such things, and that I'm really just trying to get Jim's attention again, right?"

"I'm sorry for saying those things in the past, Katie."

"I'm not looking for an apology. I mean it. I would just give my eye teeth to have something that meant as much to me as Jimmy means to you. So what do I do, buy a dog? I'm too smart for that."

It was impossible not to like Katie. There was honesty in her, and Helen loved her for it. "There is plenty of Jimmy to go around," Helen said. "You're welcome to anything you can do. There are other children there, too, at the hospital. It's another world, Katie."

"Can I make a suggestion about you and Arthur?"

"What?"

"Let him see the boy. He's giving blood, rallying people to help. Can't you let him see Jimmy?"

With a start Helen realized that it was the obvious thing to do. After Katie left she wondered how she could have failed to see the importance of it for Arthur. She could only conclude that her keeping Jimmy and Arthur apart was an ingrained habit that had outlived its meaning.

In the afternoon of the following day Helen took Arthur to Jimmy's room at the hospital. When she had mentioned it the night before Arthur had seemed hesitant at first, then admitted finally that he hadn't wanted her to feel he was interfering between her and Jimmy in any way. He was actually very anxious to visit the boy.

They arrived to find that Jimmy had been transferred once again to the "clean room." The nurse informed them that he was conscious but that the doctors were with him supervising more drug dosages. Helen led Arthur to the room and into the antechamber where guests could stand and look through the plastic curtains without the use of sterilized gowns. Inside the small enclosed sterile space that surrounded Jimmy's bed they could see three doctors in gowns and masks hovering over what remained of Jimmy's wasted body. Two nurses similarly gowned were working with the doctors, attaching the needle of yet another IV bottle to the child's body, using the permanent needle that had been attached to his back some time before.

The group around the bed moved aside for a moment and Arthur was able to glimpse the thin, frail form lying there. To Helen Jimmy's head had seemed to enlarge as his body had lost weight. His eyes were dark sockets in his pale skin and his cheekbones protruded. His hair had fallen out again and he lay on his back with his eyes listlessly following but not seeing the forms moving about his bed. If Helen had any lingering hopes for his recovery she lost them now, seeing how far gone he appeared, how much he seemed to have lost just in the few days since she had returned home.

She heard a gasp from Arthur and then his voice, low and trembling. "The poor kid. Oh God, that poor kid." He turned quickly away and his face when he glanced at Helen was stricken with anguish. He walked rapidly away toward the elevator and Helen hurried to join him. Once they were inside the elevator going down, alone for a moment, Arthur reached for her, gave the gentlest of hugs as if Helen was too precious or too remote somehow to be touched, and pulled away as the doors opened again.

He almost ran to the car in the parking lot, and was inside with the engine running as Helen joined him. "I wish I could have seen him before, Helen," he said. And after they had driven for some distance he added,

"It would have been good if I'd seen him. I didn't know. I really didn't know."

That night, for the first time in many weeks, Arthur came to her and held her in bed. What he had to say seemed beyond him and Arthur did not attempt to cross the barriers with words. He merely held her close for a long time without saying anything at all. Then he muttered into her pillow, "I've been a fool" and began to move away. Helen quickly tightened her arms, letting him know that he was forgiven, and in her own wordless way that she needed his closeness. For perhaps a full five minutes they lay with their faces cheek to cheek in complete silence as if they both knew that speech could not make them one but could only reinforce their separateness. Helen discovered, to her surprise, that her body ached for him even though she felt that the distance between them had grown and that there were many things to be resolved. He stirred against her and she realized he was eager too, that somehow Arthur also needed this silence, this communication that was entirely physical. Helen responded by moving closer and sliding under him. They spoke to each other with caresses that were possessed of a new, gentle fire. Their love was not a surrender on her part and not a capitulation on his; it was a union of two troubled, hungry, confused and somehow separate people.

When it was over they continued holding each other side by side until Helen heard Arthur softly snoring. Neither had broken the silence of that strange experience even to say "I love you," the conventional phrase they had often repeated when they made love in the past. I have always been so conventional, Helen thought, always doing the expected things, feeling the expected feelings, working at the accepted tasks. Jimmy had taken her out of that charmed circle of other people's expectations, she realized gratefully. It was Jimmy who had forced her into new paths. She thought of the first time he had spoken to her, standing behind her draped in seaweed like a creature who had risen from some distant kingdom under the sea. It was as if he had been sent from his world to invade hers, to break through the shell in which she lived and to lead her back with him into the dark terror and adventure of the depths.

Arthur stirred in his sleep and turned toward her on his side. She turned and touched his face, feeling the warmth of his cheek with the flat of her hand. When they were making love she had been tempted to tell Arthur about Charles, to make confession and relieve the nagging guilts that troubled her. But something had held her back, had said to be patient and give both of them time. She knew she would share it with Arthur sometime, not just to ease her own conscience, but to deepen and enrich their relationship when life's own rhythm demanded it. She felt herself a much stronger person since she had walked with Jimmy. She could endure quiet pain, could bear with a private grief or even a secret guilt for the sake of nurturing the adventure of life.

Helen quietly whispered, "Yes." It was yes to death as well as yes to life, and it filled her with a profoundly restful peace.

CHAPTER THIRTY-SIX

As May approached Helen felt ready to resume her place at the hospital. Then, on the last day of April, they received a phone call from Sharon, in tears, asking if she could come home. The affair with Michael was over.

Arthur hung up the phone and did not say he had

told her so. "She'll be some help around here, while you're with Jimmy," was all he said as he prepared to pick Sharon up at the airport.

Two hours later Sharon burst through the door and threw herself into Helen's arms, sobbing, "I loved him, Mom. I wanted to marry him!"

The three of them sat around the kitchen table and talked the afternoon away. Much to her surprise Helen found Sharon turning to her rather than to Arthur. She had always been daddy's girl, but now it was as if she sensed that her mother had some resources out of which to bring understanding and help. Arthur, too, seemed content to sit back and let the two women talk.

Finally, Sharon dried her tears and said, "It's hard to lose someone you love. But I thought about you, Mom, and Jimmy. I know it's not the same, but it helped me. If you can be so strong, I thought, then maybe I've got some of that in me."

The next day Helen resumed her daily vigils at the hospital, fully prepared now to accept Jimmy's death. Throughout the first week in May, while gray skies hung over the hospital, Jimmy remained in a semiconscious state with no perceptible change in his condition. The doctors continued their consultations and seemed intent upon ignoring the evidence that their valiant young patient was not responding.

Arthur and Sharon visited frequently, sometimes making use of the special sterile clothing and entering the room to stand beside Helen near the bed. Doctor Jacoby, with his quick, darting eyes and brusque manner, assured them that the battle was not over. Helen remembered what Irene Miller had said about the doctors not ever wanting to admit defeat, and felt only a kind of helpless sadness for him.

On the eighth of May she was alone in his room when Jimmy suddenly opened his eyes and said, "Hi, Mom. Is it dinner time yet?"

She stammered, "Jimmy—hello. No—it's three in the afternoon. But I'll see if I can get you something."

He managed a weak smile and she hurried to the nurses' station.

On duty was the young nurse Helen had once felt like scolding for her rough treatment of Jimmy. The nurse, she now knew, was a loving and enduring soldier of the cancer ward known to the staff and all of the veteran parents as Goldie.

"Goldie, he's awake. And he's hungry!"

The nurse seemed to take it all in stride. She turned aside to consult Jimmy's chart and said she would get him something.

"He's awake, Goldie, and talking. All of a sudden!"

"They do that sometimes," the nurse smiled. "You think they're gone and they bounce back. I'll notify Dr. Jacoby."

Another two weeks passed in which Jimmy steadily improved. Helen almost held her breath as she sat beside his bed. By the end of that week he was sitting up and chatting with his visitors and friends as if nothing whatever unusual had transpired.

A few days later, on May twenty-fifth, Charles Banning, Helen, Arthur and Jessica sat in Dr. Jacoby's office at the hospital as the doctor leaned one pudgy shoulder against the edge of a bookcase packed with medical texts and explained:

"We are all very proud. This team has worked on Jimmy's case in a way I've never seen. I think you had something to do with that, Mrs. Long. They know about you and the boy. In any case we worked, and that means we consulted with all the major cancer centers here and in Europe. Now we have the combination. I've just seen the results of his last tests. For the very first time in the boy's case, I think Jimmy is going to have good remission. I don't know what you're going to do, but the team is going to have a little celebration."

"What does it mean," Helen quickly asked, "for the future?"

"If it keeps going the way it is, you might think of putting him back in school, letting him resume a normal life. We'll keep him for about a month longer and then you can take him home."

That night Charles took the entire group to Chasen's, one of the finest restaurants in Los Angeles. Helen was so off-balance and glad and confused that she forgot to count the glasses of champagne that began arriving when the meal was over.

She sat, feeling buzzy and glassy-eyed, and stared at the two men sitting side by side across the table from her. Charles Banning was at his very best, full of tales that kept Arthur and Jessica laughing. Occasionally Helen would find both men looking into her eyes at once, both faces wreathed with smiles and warmed with love. Under the giddying influence of the champagne she found the two faces swimming together into one glowing image of masculine attention and affection. And over all the celebrating and good cheer she felt the presence of Jimmy, who upon hearing that they were going to have a party replied, "Fantastic! Bring me a piece of cake. They don't give me enough to eat in here."

On the twentieth of June, sooner than Dr. Jacoby had predicted, Jimmy was driven home from the hospital. Arthur was driving and Helen sat beside him in the front seat while Jimmy bounced around excitedly in the back. He seemed not to mind Arthur's presence at all, as if, along with everything else connected to his bad days, his shyness also had departed.

When they reached the beach house, Jimmy hurled himself out the rear door of the car on his crutches, yelling, "What a day! Look at that sun! And smell the ocean! I'm gonna get my bathing suit on!" He waved one of his crutches wildly in the air.

He dashed into the house and Arthur said, "You know, this is the first time I've seen this place. Mind if I look around?"

"He doesn't seem to mind you being here at all. What a change," Helen said. "Everything at once, boom. I'm not sure I can take all this."

Arthur grinned, "Welcome to the club."

Charles Banning had been unable to drive Jimmy home that day because of a business appointment in San Diego. When Helen arrived at the beach house the following morning she found Charles there. Jimmy and Charles, with their heads together, were seated at the dining room table going over some books.

"I stopped at the Board of Education offices and explained the situation," Charles said. "They sent over some books so Jimmy can start catching up."

"Boy, this math is tough! Dad can't even do some of these, Mom. Take a look."

Helen sat down with them, confessing her weakness in math, and soon throwing up her hands in resignation. "What grade is this?" she asked.

"Fifth," Jimmy replied promptly. "Dad says if I study real hard this summer, I can get right back in with my own class this fall."

For the first time in many months Helen thought about her own brief academic career. She had dropped her classes after Professor Mays's shock treatment in the faculty lounge and just before Jimmy had taken such a dramatic turn for the worse, and now here he was looking forward to school again. It depressed her, and her conscience made her feel a bit guilty for that depression, since it only meant Jimmy was feeling better.

At noon, Charles glanced at his watch, and with a sly look told Jimmy and Helen to step out on the porch of the beach house. Jimmy, expecting a surprise, ran ahead of them and glanced around on the porch, his eyes full of expectation.

"What is it, Dad? Where did you hide it?"

Charles grinned and lifted a thumb toward the sky. Helen glanced up as Jimmy did and hovering overhead they saw the three hang gliders. Jimmy hurried down the steps and out on the sand as Charles explained, "I called them and told them the good news and we set it up. Ready for another party?"

Helen stood alone for a moment as Charles went

down the stairs and across the sand toward his son. Bobbie and Frank and Jack had all landed their gliders and Jimmy was swinging himself through the sand from one to another on his crutches. As the yells of delight rose and the group signaled for her to join them, Helen felt a stab of sudden realization. Jimmy was alive and well, surrounded by friends, and she was losing him. As she moved through the sand toward the group she felt for the first time like an outsider.

On each succeeding day the beach house seemed to bustle with more and more activity. After a week had passed Helen entered one morning to find Jimmy looking forward to the arrival of a tutor. "She's going to help me with my math, Mom," Jimmy explained.

Mrs. Gilbert, the tutor, had a son of her own, a boy of Jimmy's own age. Tad Gilbert was a freckled eleven-year-old who packed enough energy in his short, compact little frame to soon turn Jimmy's room into a shambles. Jimmy had greeted the boy's first arrival with considerable hesitation, but Tad was the kind who could not be long ignored. As bright as Jimmy and interested in everything, Tad soon became his constant companion.

By the beginning of July, Helen began to feel irrelevant. She arrived one day to find that Jimmy and Tad had gone off to play with some new children who had moved into one of the beach houses for the summer. From the porch Helen watched Jimmy playing a game of kickball in the sand far down the beach. He had become so adept on his crutches that he now made use of only one during the day, but in the game he had both under his arms. He would balance himself on them, swing his good leg back and drive the ball as hard and as far as the best of them. She heard a step behind her on the porch and turned to find Charles standing there regarding her with a fond smile.

"Hello, Mom," he said. "Life is full of surprises, isn't it?"

He knew what she was feeling. No doubt it showed

on her face. With a shrug Charles lowered his body casually into one of the chairs. "He's making it, Helen. You were right all along."

At that moment Helen knew for sure that her place in Jimmy's life had changed, that the experience was ending. Unable to stop the feeling of near-bereavement that swept through her she said huskily, "I don't think I'm going to be needed here much longer."

Charles looked up at her and suddenly stood to his feet. "Let's take a walk." He held out his hand and she took it with a feeling of relief.

"I've been wanting to tell you," Charles said as they took the familiar path toward the rock, "that Jimmy and I have been talking about selling the beach house. We think it would be best for him to return to his same school, and the old neighborhood. I've been looking at a place in Encino, not far from the old house, in fact."

So it was going. Helen stood looking down at the large, dark gray rock in the sand, the exact spot where Jimmy had first come to her draped in seaweed. It was ending. She leaned against Charles, fighting off silly tears. This was what she had always wanted, wasn't it? Jimmy well and able to take up a normal life?

Charles's voice brought her out of it with something of a start as he said quietly, "Are you back with Arthur now?"

"In a way. We're trying. And how have you been?"

Charles looked away, his profile presented to her much as it had been that first day on the beach when he had told her about Jimmy. With the same kind of catch in his voice he said, "It wouldn't have worked, you and me."

So now this was being laid to rest also, along with everything else on this dreadful day. Helen heard herself saying, "No, I don't think it would have."

"I just had to stay away from you for a while, Helen. I just wasn't ready for any kind of commitment. I needed space."

She was aware of his weaknesses. They were showing

now beneath the brisk smile he turned on her, in lines of tightness about his lips that reminded her of Jimmy's first tentative smiles of uncertainty. "I understand, Charles," she told him. "I really do understand."

His hand squeezed hers and dropped away. He told her she was a lovely woman and added quickly, "Arthur is a very lucky man."

That was final. This day was bringing everything to an end, burying it all beneath the spreading, inexorable progress of Jimmy's new-won health. There remained for Helen only one more question and she raised it with the feeling of getting all the pain over with at once.

"When will you be leaving the beach house?"

"The house goes on the market tomorrow. We want to move before summer's over. If Jimmy's remission holds, he'll need to get settled in before school starts."

She could think of nothing more to say and Charles seemed embarrassed by her silence. He shifted his feet about in the sand and looked away toward the horizon. "You and Jimmy will always be friends," he said.

They met Jimmy running toward them on his crutches, his blue eyes dancing and his cheeks flaming with health.

"Dad, Helen!" he yelled. "Did you see me kick that ball?"

That was the parting stroke, keenly severing the one link that still bound them together. Jimmy was no longer calling her Mom.

After a full night of weeping in Arthur's arms, clinging to him like a sailor to a wave-washed vessel while breaker after breaker of anguish swept through her, Helen awoke the next morning to begin planning a sensible and orderly separation from Jimmy.

In the days that followed she had only the satisfaction of knowing that she was controlling her involvement, setting her own limits, deciding how much time to spend at the beach house and what part to play in the preparations for moving day.

Jimmy remained preoccupied and exhaustingly active

with his young companions at the beach. By early August the tests on bone marrow were showing that Dr. Jacoby's prognosis was entirely correct. Jimmy, for a time, perhaps for a very long time, had beaten the leukemia. He had a good chance now to join the ranks of the blessed fifty percent of children who have life expectancies of from five to ten years, or possibly, with new discoveries, a lifetime of remission.

The distance between them lengthened as the long days of summer drew on, and finally on August fifteenth the long-hoped-for, long-dreaded day arrived.

The moment came when Jimmy, acting on his own, walked away from saying goodbye to his beach friends, including Bobbie, Frank, and Jack, and put out his hand to her.

"Let's go look in the tidepools," he said, and she walked beside him as he swung along on the crutches. He chatted about the new house and his hopes for school and how he knew she would be glad that he wasn't afraid any more for people to see him with his bad leg. Then he suddenly stopped talking as they reached a small silvery pool that lay like a mirror in a bowl of rock.

"This is where I saw the starfish on the first day I talked to you."

She stared down, looking at the reflection of his face. How healthy he looked, how rosy and glowing. How beautiful. His eyes shifted to hers, and in the mirror of the water he spoke to her. Her creature from the depths looked up at her from his element and said, "I don't want to say goodbye. I want you to know that you will be my friend, my most special friend, for as long as I live."

"I love you, Jimmy."

"Hey, don't cry, Helen. I'll call you a lot, and we'll get together all kinds of times. Okay?"

She gathered her last ounce of strength and dropped to her knees in the sand and hugged him tight. Then she made herself laugh when he lost his balance and fell against her, and she straightened him up and stood and dusted the sand from her knees. It was all she could do to smile and choke back the tears and say, "Thank you, Jimmy."

"For what? I should be thanking you, for everything."

"Thank you, for choosing me."

The orange and black Allied Van Lines truck whined and wheezed and lumbered onto the Coast Highway. Charles and Jimmy followed in the red Mercedes, both of them waving from the windows until the car was out of sight.

Jessica, who was accompanying them to the new house, carried a small suitcase to her little blue Volkswagen and tossed it inside. Arthur and Helen stood by their car, which was parked beside it.

Jessica walked back to her with her hands outstretched and hugged both of them. "My dear old mama used to say the best friends in the world are the ones who've gone through hell together and come out alive."

For an hour after they had all gone Arthur and Helen walked together on the beach, listening to the roar of the surf and the far-off cries of the circling gulls.